Fall

Cop ... ... T. L. Payne

All rights reserved.

Cover design by Deranged Doctor Design
Edited by Melanie Underwood

No part of this book may be reproduced in any form or by any electronic or mechanical means, including information storage and retrieval systems, without written permission from the author, except for the use of brief quotations in a book review.

Don't forget to sign up for my spam-free newsletter at www.tlpayne.com to be among the first to know of new releases, giveaways, and special offers.

Check out other books by T. L. Payne

The Gateway to Chaos Series
Seeking Safety
Seeking Refuge
Seeking Justice
Seeking Hope

The Days of Want Series
Turbulent
Hunted
Turmoil
Uprising
Upheaval
Mayhem
Defiance (Coming Summer 2021)

Although much of this story takes place in and around Houston, Texas, some aspects and locations have been altered to enhance the story. Most of locations within Calcasieu Parish, Louisiana are fictional. Thank you for understanding an author's creative license.

"Texas is a blend of valor and swagger." — Carl Sandburg

❀ Created with Vellum

For Nathan,
Aim High
&
Dream Big

FALL OF HOUSTON SERIES BOOK THREE

NO TURNING BACK

T.L. PAYNE

Contents

Prologue

It was windy. It was noisy. And analyst Rachel Stephens could smell the fuel as the vintage, propeller-driven, two-seater T-6 Texan airplane climbed to twenty thousand feet and headed toward Killeen, Texas. The pilot, seventy-five-year-old Ernest Elliot of Crosby, Texas, had over seven thousand hours of experience flying the thing—or so he kept saying every time she asked if it were safe.

She'd thought she hated flying in a 747, but this was like being strapped to the outside of the space shuttle and launched into space. If the nation's fate had not been at stake, she would have walked to Fort Hood before getting in the ancient machine.

Stephens wanted to kiss the ground when they landed safely at Fort Hood. Armed escorts met her, and she was whisked away to meet with the base commander, Major General Brian Waltrip. The central Texas army base was a buzz of activity, with Joint Light Tactical Vehicle trucks lined up heading somewhere.

From what Stephens had learned, the Greywolf brigade and 1st Cavalry Division had been undergoing huge modernization efforts in recent years. They looked to be mobilizing, ready to take the fight to the enemy. It was an encouraging sign after what she'd witnessed first-hand down in Houston.

They escorted Stephens through a maze of hallways to a secure room at the end of a long corridor. The sensitive compartmented information facility looked much like the one at Ellington. She waited in the SCIF for at least an hour before the base commander appeared. He asked for his aide to wait outside.

"I'm sorry to keep you waiting, Analyst Stephens. As you can imagine, we've been quite busy." Waltrip took a seat across from her, leaned forward, and interlaced his fingers. "Tell me what you've got there."

Stephens gave him a brief background on the investigation her team had been conducting into Chinese illegally crossing the border with the Mexican drug cartels' aid. Only a minute into her briefing, Waltrip began tapping his index finger on the table. He was getting impatient, so she skipped the rest and opened the laptop. She typed in her login and password, pulled up the encrypted file, typed the password, and turned the computer around to face him.

He leaned in and studied the screen. His eyes met hers. "What am I looking at?"

"Names, dates, locations."

"How did you get this?"

"A Chinese double agent. It's legit. We've confirmed it. The commander at Ellington sent troopers to twelve of the locations indicated here, and all had already been targeted. Pipelines, roads, refineries—"

Waltrip held up one hand. He stood and walked to the door, opened it, and spoke to the soldier on the other side. "Your counterparts will be here in five minutes. I need to inform SOUTHCOM we finally have something actionable."

"You're in contact with Southern Command?"

He hesitated. "Through the 4th Fleet," he said as he exited the SCIF and shut the door behind him.

Minutes later, the door opened. Stephens stood.

"I heard you were down in Honduras," Brad Smith said as he closed the door and approached her.

It shocked Stephens to see Smith in Texas as the last she knew, he'd been in London. He held his arms open as if to give her a hug. She took a step back and held out her hand. She'd called off their relationship, and they hadn't spoken for over nine months. He was going to act like nothing had happened. She wasn't.

"I was, for a while. I've been in Houston for the last three months following the money."

"Waltrip's aide said you've got something there," he said, pointing to the computer.

This was it. He was going to move right in and take over. He'd take the credit, of course.

"At first, I thought it was a decoy, something to throw us off, but it checked out. They've already hit several of the targets on this list. Ellington was hit—overrun with insurgents."

Smith reached up and lightly touched her forehead. "Was that where you got that?"

Stephens ran a finger across her forehead just above the brow. It was sticky. "I had a building blow up around me."

He smiled. "I'm glad you made it out."

She sensed she was giving in to his charms but pulled back. She wouldn't let him get to her—not again. She reminded herself why she'd called it off. "How's Victoria?" she asked.

His smile faded. "Fine, as far as I know. She's in London."

She pitied him, momentarily. She would be a wreck if she had a significant other and a newborn child that far away at a time like this.

"Show me," Smith said, pointing to the laptop. "Let's see if we can put a stop to their little plan."

~

They spent an hour going over every piece of information contained on the flash drive that Kim Yang had stolen from her Chinese handler. It was like old times. They bounced ideas off one another and even laughed occasionally. Soon they were joined by Chinese interpreters and several other analysts in the tiny SCIF. Stephens grew increasingly claustrophobic. As they discussed what they'd learned, her face flushed and her pulse rate increased. She was feeling lightheaded and wondered when she last time ate. It had been a crazy day. There hadn't been time to take care of her body.

"We cut off communications between General Dempsey and Colonel Edwards. Ellington has Edwards in custody. Now Dempsey has no way of coordinating with the Chinese through him," Stephens said.

"We need to make sure that he cannot contact anyone else from the People's Liberation Army," Smith said.

"What if the PLA's Navy has already landed their expeditionary force somewhere along the gulf coast?" Stephens asked.

"We've already intercepted several amphibious assault ships. They'll utilize hovercraft and helicopters to land troops. They'll use something similar to our San Antonio Class to do it from much further offshore than traditional landing craft," a man in a naval uniform said. She'd forgotten his name already and looked for a name tape. "Shaffer." She raised an eyebrow when she noticed the green beret on the table next to his right hand.

"But we have ships in the gulf to stop them, right?" she asked him.

"Most of our ships were in the South Atlantic and got here as quick as they could. But we don't know what or where they got through before we formed the blockade," Shaffer said.

"What about the Chinese troop buildup in the Bahamas? I know officially that was denied, but we have intel that says otherwise. What about those two hundred thousand illegal "workers" they brought into the Caribbean?" Analyst Brown asked. He looked up from the laptop, adjusted his eyeglasses on his face, and shifted toward Smith.

"They're not going anywhere. We've had submarines there since the beginning. If they move a muscle, it'll all be over for them. The initial assault will most likely be from the PLA's army amphibious assault brigades. China's Marine Corps may play a role at some point, but the main amphibious force will be their army. They're equipped with amphibious tanks and troop carriers. That's where we'll get them," Shaffer said.

Stephens' head was spinning. They sounded confident that the invasion would be put down quickly, but she'd been on the ground in Houston. She'd seen what fighting with limited technology looked like.

"How are we going to be effective without all our modern technology?" she asked.

Shaffer turned to her and smiled. "Most of our technology works fine. We've had hiccups with our coms because of cyber-hacks of our satellites, but we're quickly working around that issue. Don't worry, sweetheart. We've got this. You'll see."

Stephens cringed and gritted her teeth. She was accustomed to the misogynistic terms and usually called them out on it, but she let it go this time. She needed to stay in the loop, not be frozen out.

"Just wait until you see all our new toys," Shaffer said.

"Can they stop tanks and helicopters?" she asked.

"Sure can. We've got anti-tank missiles that'll stop them in their tracks."

"And you're able to move sufficient troops that way to prevent them from successfully invading?"

"They're on their way. Everything's being planned from a room just on the other side of that wall," Shaffer pointed.

"What's the plan for all the citizens down there caught in the middle of a war zone?"

Shaffer gave her a blank stare.

"Houston alone is a city of over two million people. Is there no plan to evacuate them?"

Shaffer shrugged. "That's above my pay grade."

"I heard that FEMA was setting up a shelter in Texarkana. A cable went out to Shreveport to send troops there to help receive refugees. I heard nothing about a plan to help them get there or anything. That is supposed to be our rear operating base. Major General Waltrip will be moving his headquarters there in the coming days," Smith said.

"Retreating?" Stephens didn't receive an answer.

The door opened, and Waltrip appeared. Everyone stood. The officers in the room saluted. "Clear the room. I need to speak with the analysts," he said.

When the officers had exited, Waltrip took a seat at the head of the conference table. "Now tell me how General Walter Dempsey got involved with this plot."

ONE

Will

Will Fontenot watched from the window overlooking the parking lot as two figures moved between the buildings across the way. They remained hidden among the shadows so he was unable to recognize them. He doubted that it would be Gus or any of Kevin's bandmates. His brutal murder still had residents there unnerved, even though the killer had been brought to justice.

Isabella and Cayden were sleeping. The sun would be coming up soon and the three of them would be leaving to begin their journey to his sister's homestead in Louisiana. He should have been relieved—it was all he'd wanted since the lights went out— but he wasn't. Now, fear of the unknown had set in. He had no idea what to expect out there on the road. People were his greatest fear. He'd seen what they were capable of now that law enforcement wasn't there to protect the citizens.

A scream sounded from across the way. It was a female voice. Will had thought the only females still in the apartment complex were located in Isabella's building. Will raised his rifle and moved to get a better look, but all he saw was darkness. He waited and listened. A moment later, the shadowy figures of two men ran from a ground-floor apartment and headed toward the street. Will debated with himself. Should he go see if the woman was all right? He glanced toward the bedrooms. He couldn't leave Isabella and Cayden sleeping and defenseless. Going out there alone wasn't smart either.

The incident only went to show him how difficult it was going to be out there. They would have to have one person awake and guarding their location at all times. He and Isabella would need to sleep in shifts, which would mean none of them would be getting enough rest. There were moments when he considered whether staying put was a better plan. At least they had a defendable position. That's fear talking, he reminded himself.

It wasn't sustainable. Eventually, they'd need to leave to find food. They'd already been competing with all the other hungry and desperate people for the scant resources still available in the city. For that reason alone, going was their only option.

"I thought I heard someone scream," Isabella said. She pulled a thin purple robe over her slim frame and joined Will by the window.

"From there." Will pointed. "I saw two people running from that downstairs apartment."

"That's supposed to be vacant. You checked it when—" She stopped herself.

He and Gus had checked that apartment and all the others in that building when they'd searched for Kevin's killer. But that didn't mean that someone hadn't taken up residence there since then. There would be thousands, maybe hundreds of thousands of displaced residents seeking shelter around Houston. The security gate that once separated and somewhat protected the apartment complex from outsiders no longer worked. Anyone could just walk up and move on in.

"It was empty. That whole building was unoccupied. People could have moved in while we were gone, though."

She stretched her arms above her head and yawned. Will could barely make out her face in the moonlight coming through the open window. "What time is it?" she asked.

"No idea. Has to be close to sunrise. See the hint of light on the horizon?"

She leaned in close to the window. He could smell the fragrance of her shampoo and recalled their kiss the day before. He'd just pulled her from the rubble of the flight museum. They'd been in a fierce battle with Chinese insurgents, and Isabella had just learned that Agent Betley had been killed in the fight. She'd been distraught. He was trying his best to comfort her. She may not even remember the kiss. She may not remember, but he couldn't forget it. He had qualms of conscience about it now. It was too soon—for both of them. He was still grieving the death of his wife —and Isabella had just lost her boyfriend. The timing was awful. It would never work between them. Guilt resurfaced. He was sick of the feeling.

"I think I'm going to get dressed and then make some coffee." She touched his shoulder. His heart rate sped up. "We're still heading out at first light?" she asked.

"Yeah. If you think you're up to it. I don't think we should wait. I'm hoping we can come across some form of transportation. I think bicycles are still our best bet until we can find something better. Even though you can't pedal, I could push you, and we could put our supplies on another for Cayden to push."

"I don't want you to have to push me on a bike. I'll be okay. I can walk. We could put supplies on both bikes and carry twice the stuff," Isabella suggested.

After seeing the gash in her leg the day before, he knew she was lying, but they could start out, and she'd soon realize she was slowing them down by not getting on the bike. He'd make sure to load them in a way that she could still ride when she chose to.

∿

By the time Isabella and Cayden were up and ready, Will had all their supplies loaded into backpacks or trash bags and sitting by the door. Lieutenant Sharp had instructed the soldiers to return the gear they'd taken from him, but all he'd received was his empty rifle. He'd carry it, in hopes that he might come across ammunition for it somewhere. Going out there without a weapon was crazy, but he didn't have any other option.

Isabella's hair was pulled back and stuffed inside a ball cap. She wore an oversized T-shirt, baggy jeans, and Timberland style boots. Will did a double-take. She looked like a dude.

"Is that a five o'clock shadow on your cheeks?" Will leaned in to get a closer look. Her previously feminine eyebrows now appeared bushy and unkempt.

"It's amazing what you can do with an eyebrow pencil."

"Why?"

"Women were targets for all sorts of perverts before all this lawlessness. I don't want to stand out as weak. From a distance, someone will think we're just three dudes. It might deter trouble. At least, that's the hope."

The corners of Will's mouth tilted up in a weak smile. "It could work, I guess." He doubted it would fool anyone up close, though he hoped to avoid people in general as much as possible.

"I think you look good as a guy," Cayden said.

Isabella laughed. "Thanks. I think."

Cayden pointed at her legs. "You still walk like a girl."

"Oh, yeah. Should I walk like this?" Isabella stood with her legs squared with her shoulders and moved like a bowlegged cowboy from a spaghetti western.

Cayden chuckled. "No. Definitely do not walk like that."

"I'm with Cayden. You walk like that and you'll attract attention for sure," Will said, throwing a backpack over his shoulder. He pulled open the door and came face to face with Gus.

"Well, hello," Gus said. "We came to see if you guys were heading out anytime soon?"

Jaz stood beside him. She was not disguised as a man. In fact, there'd be no mistaking her for a dude in her tight shorts and a tank top. A small baby bump was barely visible. If he hadn't known she was pregnant, he might not have even noticed. At least she was wearing running shoes. No doubt, within five minutes outside, she'd regret not covering up every inch of her skin. The mosquitoes after a hurricane were relentless.

"We're heading out now. I was going to go see if I could locate that bike you told me about and we'll see if we can find a couple more on our way," Will said.

Jaz's face lit up. "How about a ride in a car?"

"You found a running car?" Isabella asked.

"We did. Well, a crew cab pickup truck. It's old and beat up, but it will fit all our stuff and still have room for the three of you."

Isabella turned to Will. Her eyes were brighter than he'd ever seen them. "Did you hear that? I don't have to walk around like a dude and worry about getting attacked by perverts."

"Where did you say you were going?" Will said. He didn't want to burst her bubble, but if they weren't heading in the same direction, it wouldn't work.

"My mom lives in Liberty," Jaz said.

"See, Will. That's sort of on the way to Louisiana," Isabella said.

It was forty miles north of Interstate 10. They'd have to take US 90 into Louisiana. It wasn't a deal-breaker since they'd be traveling by vehicle, at least to Liberty, but he wasn't sure.

"We thought the Crosby Freeway would be the best road to take. It likely had less traffic on it when the event happened," Gus said.

The more Will thought about it, the more he agreed. He just wasn't as familiar with that route. He'd selected places along I-10 that they could stop and rest and maybe find supplies. He'd be blindly taking another way.

"You can have the truck after we reach my mom's," Jaz said.

Gus's head whipped around, a look of surprise filling his face. She smiled, and his features softened.

"Yeah. You can take the truck. It'll be safer," he said, casting a glance at Cayden.

A smile crossed Will's face. Things were looking up. In a few hours, they'd be rolling into Vincent, Louisiana. He hoped Savanah had something hot and spicy cooking. He was dying for gumbo and boudin.

TWO

Isabella

Isabella found it challenging to do anything with her left hand in a splint and her right forearm sore from second-degree burns. Getting dressed had taken far longer than normal, and applying the makeup to disguise herself was painful. She hadn't been at all looking forward to walking all the way to Louisiana, so when Jaz and Gus showed up offering them a ride, she'd been beyond thrilled.

Isabella made one last sweep of her apartment while Will and Cayden carried their supplies down to the truck. She stared at the framed photos of her family lined up on top of her chest of drawers, running a finger across a black-and-white photo of her mother when she was Isabella's age. She'd been beautiful and lively. Tears welled in Isabella's eyes and spilled down her cheeks. Would she ever see her parents again? Were they safe?

Her mother kept a small garden and a few hens. They should have food for a little while. But knowing her mother, she'd share with the neighbors so it wouldn't last that long. If her sister were smart, she'd take her family to their parents' place. Oklahoma City was no Houston, but by now, people there would be desperate enough to be dangerous.

The small town of Chickasha, Oklahoma, where Isabella was raised, was filled with friendly and generous people. They always knew their neighbors and often ate with them following church on Sundays. It had been such a shock to her when she'd moved to Houston and people were so standoffish. It had taken her a while to adjust and not have her feelings hurt when people didn't respond to her friendly greetings. Soon she learned that people who lived in cities the size of Houston just weren't as trusting of strangers as she was.

She picked up her nephew's baby picture. He was five years old now. Old enough to understand that things were different. Her heart hurt thinking of him living through this nightmare. What type of childhood would he have if the lights didn't come back on soon? What about Cayden? He had turned thirteen on the day of the EMP. How different would life be for him than when she was a teen? There'd be no Friday night football games, no homecoming dances, and no graduation. Will had said that his sister home-schooled her children so at least Cayden could continue his education. She was sure that Will would do everything he could to give him as normal a life as possible. She just wasn't sure what their new normal would look like.

"Isabella, we're ready," Cayden called from the living room.

In a few hours, they would be in Louisiana, and she'd be meeting Will's family. She almost felt guilty that she had somewhere like that to go, not knowing if her own family was going hungry. How long could someone go without food? She couldn't stop thinking about them. Maybe after we get to Savanah's, I can take the truck and go get them. Would it be too rude to ask her to take on several more people?

"Okay, I'm coming," Isabella called back.

She scooped up her family photos and shoved them into the backpack with all the socks and panties from her drawers. Since they wouldn't be walking now, she could bring more than two pairs. Isabella glanced in the mirror as she turned to exit her bedroom, surprised by how effective her disguise was and how much she looked like a guy. She patted her chest and considered loosening the ace bandages binding her breasts. She raised her shirt, found the end of the bandage, then stopped. Will's Jeep had been carjacked, leaving them on foot. If that happened again, she'd still need the disguise. Out of habit, she flicked the light switch off before closing the bedroom door.

"Otis! Here kitty, kitty!" she called. Isabella stopped at the door to the guest room and waited for the black-and-white cat to emerge. "Otis, come on, buddy." There was no sign of him. He always came when she called him.

"Cayden, is Otis in his spot in the kitchen?" she asked as she walked down the short hall leading to the living room.

"I haven't seen him today."

Isabella stopped still. She hadn't either. Her head pivoted toward the open window where a hole had appeared in the screen. Isabella ran over and touched the spot. "Otis must have clawed his way out sometime in the night."

"Oh no," Cayden said. "I'll help you look for him."

"He might be in the woods behind the apartments. He goes there when he escapes. If he's up a tree again, I'm going to…"

Isabella and Cayden raced past Will and Gus as they were loading the truck to search under cars and around piles of debris. After searching the grounds around Isabella's apartment and the woods behind the complex, Cayden finally found Otis stalking birds near the playground.

"You scared me to death, you bad boy," Isabella scolded the cat. Once Otis was tucked inside his carrier, Isabella joined Cayden near the truck.

"Let's get the heck out of here," she said, placing a hand on his shoulder.

"I'm so glad we're not walking or taking bikes," Cayden said.

"You and me both, buddy."

"We could actually be there by lunch. I bet Aunt Savanah has bread baking right now. I can almost smell it."

"Stop! You're making my stomach growl," Isabella said.

Will and Gus spread a tarp over the bed of the truck, concealing all their belongings. It looked like Jaz had packed their whole apartment. Isabella wondered if the sight would make them a bigger target like a running vehicle wasn't enough to attract attention.

Isabella awkwardly grabbed a handhold with her right hand to pull herself up into the back passenger seat of the old pickup. Cayden placed the cat carrier on the floorboard at her feet. There wasn't much room to stretch her injured leg. She'd just have to grin and bear it until they reached their destination.

"What's with the disguise?" Jaz asked as she climbed into the front passenger seat.

"I'm hoping to not become a victim out there."

"Well, that will probably do it. Sorry to say, but you make a cute dude."

Isabella chuckled. "Thanks."

Cayden walked around and climbed into the middle seat next to Isabella. He placed his book in his lap and looked for a seat belt. "How old is this thing? Does it even have seat belts?"

"Old, I think. Maybe from the seventies. My mom said they didn't have seat belts when she was a kid. It's a wonder they survived, the way my grandpa drove," Jaz said.

"My great grandpa's Jeep had seat belts and that was from the seventies."

Isabella twisted and dug inside in the crack between the seats, finally finding the strap for the middle belt.

"Here," she said. "Buckle up for safety."

"My mom used to say that," Cayden said, his voice low.

16

"I bet you miss her," Jaz said. "How'd she die?"

Isabella winced. That wasn't something she thought people should ask a kid. The boy had lost his mother. It was likely too painful to talk about.

"Car accident," Cayden said, picking up his book and turning to a dog-eared page.

"Sorry. That sucks," Jaz said.

Something loud banged in the back of the truck. Isabella jumped and spun in her seat to see Gus dropping a long, thick chain into the bed. Her heart was still racing when he climbed in the pickup's cab. "What is that for?"

"In case we need it. It came with the truck," Gus said. "Is everyone ready?"

"Freaking more than ready," Jaz said.

"Absolutely," Will said, climbing into the seat next to Cayden.

His smile warmed her heart. She couldn't recall ever seeing his teeth. He had a nice face. A flush grew behind her cheeks as she recalled their kiss, and she turned away.

"Let's get the heck out of here," Jaz said as Gus put the truck into gear and pulled from the parking space in front of their building.

Kevin's bandmates stood at the second-floor landing. Isabella raised her hand and waved. They waved back, but none of them were smiling. She regretted leaving them there like that. They might have been able to make room for them in the pickup's bed, but it wasn't her truck, and where would they take them anyway. She couldn't be responsible for every person she knew. Hell, she couldn't even take care of herself at the moment. They'd have to find their own way home or stay and fight it out with the rest of the desperate residents of Houston.

As the truck turned out of the parking lot onto the main road, a pit formed in Isabella's stomach. Dread crept up on her—the dread of the devastation they would see and the unknown dangers they faced. A couple of hours' drive pre-apocalypse would have been no big deal, but now that same trip could be filled with danger around every turn.

THREE

Will

DAY SEVEN

There were some tense moments as the truck rolled through Isabella's neighborhood, heading toward the freeway. Some residents were camping in tents on their front lawns due to their homes' conditions following the hurricane. Now that the floodwater had receded, large groups had made camp in the parking lot of the grocery store where Will and Gus had been the day before. Will wondered how long they would wait around for help to arrive before leaving to find better resources. He doubted much was left inside the store and with that many people to feed, it wouldn't be long before they ran out completely.

The on-ramp for the Gulf Freeway was filled with abandoned vehicles. Beyond them, the interchange had been blown up. They wouldn't be taking that route. After backtracking a few blocks, they headed east to hop onto Interstate 610. When Gus suddenly stomped on the brakes, Will's head whipped around to see why.

"Military vehicles up ahead," Gus said.

"Are they ours?" Isabella asked.

Gus glanced back over his shoulder at her. "Who else's would they be?"

"Um... I don't know."

Will leaned forward to get a look for himself just as they entered the cross street. They were American. He felt the tension ease and sat back as they disappeared from view. A moment later, a loud explosion rumbled through the area and black smoke rose above a row of businesses ahead. Gus floored it and sped through the intersection. Isabella's eyes were wide, and her hand covered her mouth. Cayden was stiff in his seat. The event had freaked them all out.

Will craned his neck to see what had caused the explosion. One of the Humvees in the middle of the convoy was on fire. The two behind it stopped in the middle of the street. He didn't have time to see if there were enemy fighters in the area. His head swiveled back and forth, searching for any insurgents as Gus sped down the street, swerving in and out of cars and debris left in the road by the hurricane.

"That was freaking close," Isabella said, her hand still covering her mouth.

"Too close," Will said, leaning back in his seat. He placed his hand on Cayden's knee, feeling him trembling. He couldn't wait to say good riddance to Houston and the chaos it had devolved into.

"What was that?" Jaz asked. "Did the military just blow something up?"

Will thought about telling her the truth, but if he did, he'd need to tell her all of it. He didn't want to scare them any more than they already were. They needed clear heads for whatever they faced ahead.

"Maybe," he said finally.

They were quiet for the next few blocks as everyone took in the damage from the storm. The destruction was massive. Shingles had been blown off and windows were broken. Trash and debris were everywhere. How would the people of Houston ever recover?

Could she? Would "Texas tough" be enough this time? Maybe, if they survived the insurgency.

Gus turned the corner at the next traffic signal and again slammed on the brakes.

"What now?" Isabella asked as they were thrown forward by the inertia.

Gus pointed to two small children standing in the middle of the road. The baby, likely no more than a year old, was completely naked. The older child, a girl around six or seven, was dressed in shorts and barefoot. The girl's eyes were as big as saucers as she eyed the truck in front of her. The dark-haired baby cried when she sat him down on the ground. The door to the truck opened, and Jaz slid out. She slowly approached them, speaking softly in Spanish. They responded, and Jaz held out her hand.

"Gus, get me that box of crackers and some tuna," she said.

"This is going to be a very long trip," Gus mumbled as he exited the vehicle and went around to the truck's bed. A moment later, Jaz was serving the children tuna on crackers and some bottled water.

"She's going to want to take them with us. Just watch," Gus said as he got back in.

Isabella leaned forward. "Where are their parents?"

"They said they went looking for food and didn't come back."

"That's awful. Poor things."

"Jaz, we can't just sit here in the middle of the road like this. We're a freaking target for a carjacking," Gus called out of the window.

Will had a flashback of his own carjacking. Having the Jeep stolen was bad, but the terror he'd felt with his son being taken with it was beyond terrifying. He'd replayed the moment over and over in his mind trying to figure out what he could have done differently to save both Cayden and the Jeep. It had taken him by such surprise. When the police officers grabbed the guy, he'd backed off, thinking they would get things under control. They hadn't.

Jaz waved a dismissive hand in the air and continued feeding the children.

"This isn't good, Gus. If she's bringing the kids, she needs to get with it," Will said.

Gus opened his door and was about to get out when Will spotted two men approaching. A bearded man dressed in camouflage print pants and a T-shirt with no sleeves waved his arms above his head.

"Gus. We have to go. We're attracting attention," Will said, pointing at the men.

"Jaz, let's go!" Gus yelled as he slid down from his seat. "We're going now. If you're bringing the kids, grab them up, and let's get the hell out of here."

Jaz's gaze went from Gus to the two men. The second man, short and rounder than the first, held his hand out in front of him with his palm out. "Stop. We just want to talk. We're with the Cajun navy."

Will was very familiar with the Cajun navy. He'd seen them helping evacuate people from flooding many times. The Cajun navy were volunteers who helped rescue people after major disasters. They'd likely come to south Texas to help people following the hurricane. Many would have found themselves stranded after the EMP and in need of assistance themselves.

Jaz grabbed up the children with both arms and yelled at the men. "Stop right there."

The two men froze in place.

"I'm sorry to scare the kids. We saw you have a working truck and were wondering…"

"No!" Jaz said.

"We came over from Lake Charles before the hurricane to help rescue people. We got stranded. We just wanted to see if we could catch a ride out of town. It's getting pretty dicey around here," the first man said.

"We don't have room," Jaz said.

"We could ride in the back. We'll be no trouble," the bearded man said.

"She said no," Gus said as he approached Jaz. He took the older child from Jaz, placed her on the ground, and then stepped in front of her.

Will slowly exited, wanting to steer any potential trouble away from his son and Isabella. He studied the men as he did, looking for weapons of any type. None were visible from the front, but that didn't mean they didn't have pistols stuffed behind their backs.

"Gus, Jaz, just get in the truck," Will said, pulling his empty rifle from the pickup's footwell.

He didn't point it at the men, but he didn't have to. As soon as they saw him approach with it, they immediately started backing away.

"Just drop that rifle on the ground and back away," Will heard someone call out behind him.

Jaz spun. Her mouth dropped open and her eyes widened. Will knew he likely had a weapon pointed at his back and had better comply, so he slowly lowered the AR-15 to the ground. Before he could straighten, the man in camo pants whipped a pistol from his waistband and fired. Will dove toward the front of the truck as Gus and Jaz scrambled to find cover behind a nearby sedan.

The firing continued for only a few more seconds before whoever had approached Will from behind had fled. The two men ran over and helped Jaz and Gus to their feet. The little girl had scraped her knee on the pavement as they fell and was crying. The baby was wailing loudly. The man scooped the girl up while the second man pulled a medical kit from a backpack.

He held the spray can over her knee. "It's okay. It's just a little cold, but it will stop the pain," the man said as he sprayed antiseptic onto her scrape.

"Thanks," Jaz said, taking a Band-Aid from the man.

"They would've taken your truck. You can't stop around here," the shorter man said.

"We found these kids in the middle of the road," Jaz said.

"Been lots of orphans running around the last few days," the man said.

"I'm not sure how we'd go about finding their parents," Isabella said.

"Doubt you can. The Catholic church is taking in orphans. You can drop them off there. People know to look for missing family members there," Camo pants guy said.

Jaz glanced up at Gus. "It's the best thing for them, Jaz. It's the only hope there is for them to be reunited with their parents."

Her gaze bounced from Gus to the children. Will couldn't imagine why their parents had abandoned them, but Gus was right. It was their only hope of being reunited with family.

"All right, I guess." She shifted the baby to her other hip and stared down the street. "Where's the church?"

Will wasn't all that comfortable with the two men riding in the truck's bed. They had saved his life and likely saved them from having the truck stolen, but could they really trust them? The whole incident only made Will more determined to find either ammunition for his AR-15 or some other weapon. It was just too dangerous without one.

Camo guy tapped on the truck's back glass. "There. Turn here. We should go the rest of the way on foot."

Gus pulled the truck into a high school parking lot and shut off the engine.

"We'll be back in five minutes," Gus said. He glared at the two men in the back as he pocketed the keys.

"Be safe," Isabella called after them.

Will stepped out of the truck and scanned the surrounding area. It was devoid of the cars that on a normal school day would have filled the parking lot. He thought of all the young lives that had suddenly been thrust into life and death situations like the ones they'd faced over the last week. Will was ready to put all that behind him and settle into life at Savanah's. He wasn't naïve. He knew it wouldn't be easy there either, but at least they wouldn't have people putting guns in their faces every day.

"Cayden, stay in the truck. I'm going to step over there and check out the side of the building and make sure no one is lurking about," Will said, pointing to the front of the school.

"We'll check out the other side," the camo guy said. "Tanner, you keep an eye on the road."

"You sure you want to split up, Monte?" Tanner asked.

Monte laughed. "You scared?"

There was a familiarity about the men. They reminded Will of his uncles and cousins. He still wasn't ready to let his guard down with them, but they seemed like they knew what they were doing.

"I'm not scared. I thought you might be," Tanner said as he turned his back on them to eye the road.

Will glanced back and forth between the truck and the east side of the block building. He wasn't sure what he could do if he found anyone loitering about, but he didn't want any more surprises.

Debris was piled two feet high around the building. The flood-water had shoved a car up against the air-conditioning units. Will's boots stuck in the six-inches of muck covering the parking lot. He wasn't sure he'd ever get used to the stagnant water smell. Would breathing the air cause them long-term health issues? If so, what would life be like without quality healthcare? Short, he decided.

A thought dawned on him. Did school libraries have physical books these days? Would they have any medical books? He doubted it but if they found any, they'd be valuable to have as they might be able to tell them what pills were in the prescription bottles they'd taken from the pharmacy.

The east side of the building was clear. No one lurked in the shadows or around the entrance, so Will slowly and carefully made his way back across the muddy parking lot toward the truck. Tanner stood near the road, scanning right and then left. Monte was nowhere to be seen.

"I hope Gus and Jaz aren't gone long. This place looks sketchy."

Will wasn't sure what Isabella was referring to; with all the destruction and debris, everywhere looked sketchy to him.

"This area wasn't the greatest before the storm," she said.

"They shouldn't be very long. I'm sure Gus wants to get on the road to his mother-in-law's."

Suddenly, Will heard yelling, and a moment later, Monte came running across the parking lot. He slid twice and righted himself, looking over his shoulder as he did. Will stepped away from the truck to see what had him spooked. Monte reached the truck just as a group of teenage girls ran from the side of the building, each with a baseball bat in their hands. They were yelling something at him in Spanish.

"We've got to go," Monte said, running around to the driver's side of the pickup.

"No. We're not leaving Gus and Jaz," Will said. "What the hell are they so mad about."

"I don't know. I don't speak Spanish," Monte said.

"They're calling him a pervert," Isabella said.

The girls all appeared to be under the age of fourteen. Why were they out on the streets all alone? Didn't they understand how dangerous it was now?

"They got tent city set up in the quad," Monte said. They got a shit ton of canned food stacked up back there. I bet they took it from the cafeteria or something," Monte said.

The girls kept coming, shouting, and waving the bats.

"Isabella, can you tell them we aren't here to take anything from them? We're just waiting for friends?" Will asked.

Isabella opened the truck door and poked her head out. She spoke to the girls, calmly at first, and then she stepped out of the vehicle flailing her arms and speaking fast. Will wished he understood what she was saying. He wasn't sure what he should do. He didn't want to have to defend himself against teenage girls.

Tanner suddenly appeared at his side. "They've attracted attention," he said, pointing toward the road.

FOUR

Savanah

Jason looked like he hadn't slept in a week. Likely because he hadn't. Savanah hadn't either. Dark circles ringed his dark brown eyes, he needed a shave, and he wore the same rumpled, unwashed clothes he'd worn the day before. He wiped the perspiration from his brow with the bandana he kept in the back pocket of his jeans. His muscular arms glistened with sweat in the early morning sun. It was sure to be another scorching hot south Louisiana day.

From her window over the kitchen sink, she watched as he laid rifle parts out on the picnic table and set about cleaning them in preparation for what might be a battle between their group and Jason's family members. He had to be torn up inside. The men they'd be going up against were his brother and cousin, after all. Savanah poured Jason a mug of coffee, slid on a pair of bedroom slippers, and headed outside.

"Thanks," he said as she placed the mug beside him on the picnic table. "I can't believe how dirty these rifles are."

She didn't want to make small talk or beat around the bush. Not with Jason. She needed him to know that she didn't expect him to go to war with his family. "You don't have to do this, you know. This isn't your fight."

28

His head shot up. His gaze bored into her. She saw his jaw twitch and realized what she'd said had done the opposite of what she'd intended.

Jason got to his feet. "You want me to go?"

Her eyes grew wide and she moved back a step. "No! Not at all. I just don't want you to feel like I expect you to go to war with your brother."

His shoulders relaxed. The deep grooves in his forehead flattened. He looked past her toward the house. An awkward silence fell between them as Savanah waited for him to respond. He swallowed hard and turned to her. "I'm not going to let anything happen to those four kids."

Tears stung Savanah's eyes. Their father couldn't care less about them, yet Jason was willing to take on his own family to keep them safe. She'd felt so alone all these years while taking on the role of both parents. Not having family she was close to nearby made it even harder. She'd almost convinced herself that she didn't need anyone's help and she'd been doing pretty well before all this. But she was in over her head now, and she knew it. It terrified her. She'd hated feeling so helpless.

"I appreciate that so much. I can't even put it into words. I'm sorry that I said it wasn't your fight. I didn't mean to imply that you didn't care about the kids. I know you do. I see it in the way you've taken Karson under your wing and taught him all the things he needs to know to become a man—something his father should be doing—and in the patient way you handle Kylie's temper tantrums. I've noticed, and I'm sorry that I haven't always let you know how grateful I am."

Jason slowly lowered himself back onto his chair, picked up a rifle barrel and a white cloth, and continued to clean the weapon. "They're good kids. They deserve to grow up and have a great life."

Savanah looked away as tears spilled onto her cheeks. The relief in knowing she wasn't alone, that she had someone willing to step up and help her protect her children was overwhelming beyond words. It gave her hope that they might have a chance of making a life worth living for them.

"I'm going to gather the eggs. You want to wash up and give me a hand with breakfast?" she said.

"I should finish this first. Wouldn't be good to have gun parts lying all about if those hogs of yours decide to come tearing through here again."

Savanah wondered if it might be time to make sausage and bacon out of the adventurous animals. No matter what she tried, they still found ways to escape their pen. "All right. It'll be ready in about an hour. If you aren't finished by then, I'll set you a plate on the back of the stove."

Jason smiled. "I'll be finished."

Savanah walked past the solar panels her grandfather had set up several years before to operate the water pump and a few lights. She'd installed a larger array out in the back to power a small refrigerator and water heater. She was grateful for them. They were much better off than most. She was acutely aware of that fact as she lowered the door to the hens' nest boxes and gathered a dozen eggs. When winter approached and the days grew shorter, the hens would lay fewer eggs, and the fresh produce from the garden would be gone. She'd need to put in a winter garden in the green-house, or they'd be restricted solely to the food she'd canned or dehydrated.

"Mom!" her four-year-old called from the house. His tone said something was wrong.

She picked up the egg basket and quickly rounded the chicken coop. "What, Keegan? What's the matter?"

"Someone's coming across the back pasture."

Jason came into view. He picked up a barefoot Keegan and ran with him toward the house. Savanah dropped the basket of eggs and ran after them, cursing herself for not carrying her rifle and wearing only her slippers. Before she even reached the driveway separating the house from the barn, Jason had run inside and retrieved her rifle. He handed it to her as she reached his position at the back corner of the house.

"Halt right there," Jason shouted.

The man stopped in his tracks. His hands flew into the air. Around his neck hung a rifle on a two-point sling.

"What do you want?" Jason asked.

"I'm your neighbor. My family's property abuts your southern border."

"That's not Mr. Herbert, Jason. Herbert is seventy years old."

"What's your name?" Jason asked, stepping one foot toward the man.

"Blake Richards, Frank Herbert is my father-in-law. We came to stay with him till this mess passes."

"Does Mr. Herbert even have a daughter?" Jason whispered.

"Two. They live up north somewhere though."

"What's their names?"

Savanah thought for a moment. She'd only ever heard them called by their rank of oldest or youngest.

"Renae and Misty," Kendra said as she crept up behind them.

Savanah spun on her heel and jabbed a finger toward the door. "Get your butt back inside. You're supposed to be protecting your siblings."

Kendra's eyes grew wide as if Savanah had slapped her. "What's going on?"

Savanah wasn't usually so curt with her children, but the stranger in their field had her troubled. "I'm sorry," Savanah said softly. "Please go inside and make sure your brothers and sister don't come out."

"Why? What's wrong."

"There's a stranger in the pasture," Jason said.

"Should I get my rifle?" Kendra said, turning toward the door.

"No!" Savanah snapped. "Get your pistol. Put your holster on and keep it concealed from the others. I don't want to scare them."

"Okay. But if you need me to—"

Savanah cut her off. "We won't. We just need to see what he wants. He probably wants to trade for some eggs or something." Savanah didn't want to worry Kendra needlessly. If the man hadn't come alone, she might have had her daughter move the other children to the safe room, but she'd wait and see what he wanted before upsetting the entire household.

Savanah turned her attention back to the man. "What's your wife's name?" she asked him.

"Melissa. She's the Herberts' oldest," the stranger said without hesitation.

"Misty could be a nickname for Melissa. He might be telling the truth."

"What do you want?" Jason asked.

"I heard you were having issues with the folks from Sugar Hill," he said.

The gossip train was still running, even without telephones.

"What about it?" Savanah asked.

"I was hoping we could help each other," the man said. "I'm Blake. I'm a police officer in Cincinnati."

"What does he plan to do, go arrest them?" Savanah whispered.

"If he's telling the truth, at least he's had training and experience dealing with criminals. He might be able to tell us how to defuse this situation without bloodshed."

Savanah knew that was Jason's hope, but they'd need an entire police force to handle the Blanchards. With them firmly entrenched in town and others branching out to take additional territory, it might take the National Guard to weed them out. Savanah couldn't see a successful scenario where the Blanchards survived. She doubted seriously they'd allow themselves to be taken alive.

"How about you place that rifle on the ground and slowly move this way, and we'll talk," Jason said. He glanced back over his shoulder. "We should hear him out, at least."

Mrs. Bertrand brought a pot of coffee to the seating area beneath the old oak tree where Savanah used to have tea parties with her grandmother. Savanah's grandfather had built the house before her father was born and had been proud of his craftsmanship. After their mother died, and their father became a drunk—and worse—it was their grandparents that had raised her and Will. They'd done their best to teach them how to farm and live off the land and involved them in all their activities around the homestead so that someday, they could take it over. After their grandmother died and their grandfather's health declined, the house and barn's condition had deteriorated. The white clapboard siding needed a fresh coat of paint, and several pieces of the wood trim surrounding the six-over-six windows had rotted. Jason had helped her replace the shingles two winters ago. There were so many memories in this place. She prayed they weren't forced to leave it.

Mrs. B set the coffeepot and mugs on the wrought-iron table between Savanah and Blake. Jason lifted it and filled a mug. The officer eyed it like a kid would stare at a candy bar.

"You still have coffee?" he asked as Jason handed him the mug.

"It's cut with a little chicory to make it last longer. Not sure how far it'll stretch with this many folks," Mrs. B said, turning to head back toward the house.

"How many people are staying here?" Blake asked.

Savanah started to answer, but Jason beat her to it. "A few," he said. Jason cocked his head and eyed the man. "How many are at your place?"

The officer stared back at him. "My in-laws and my wife. Our daughter is back in Ohio at college."

"That sucks," Savanah said under her breath. It was all she could do not to worry herself sick about her brother and nephew. She'd go crazy if she didn't have all her children with her.

33

"Have you spoken to any of the neighbors on your road?" Jason asked.

"A few. Most are elderly, or at least older, and unwilling to take on a gang of thugs. They're just waiting for them to come at them. A few are just too cocky to think they need help."

"Cocky?" Savanah asked.

"Yeah. You know—all bravado. They have guns and dare anyone to trespass on their property. They don't realize these people will come while they're sleeping and burn their houses down around their families if they defy them."

He knew what kind of people they were dealing with. He'd probably dealt with the likes many times as an officer of the law. But they didn't have a police force behind them. Their tactics had to be different. Even Savanah knew that.

"You know you can't just go try to arrest them, right?" she asked.

Blake kept his dark brown eyes steady on hers. "No, ma'am, we can't."

"Well then, what do you propose we do to stop them from raiding and killing folks?" Jason asked.

"Band together. There's strength in numbers. We need to circle the wagons like in the old wild west days."

"We tried to get folks to help us set up barriers and guard them, but they're too scared."

"You have to make your perimeter as small as you can. Instead of blocking off the intersections, cordon off a few farms. Once you have your families and friends within a secure area, I'd start picking off those thugs one by one. When you've reduced their ranks, you go for the leader."

"Just ride up in there and shoot it out with him?" Savanah asked, shock evident in her tone.

He shook his head and leaned back in his chair. He stared out over the herb garden as he answered her. "No. You send in a sniper to take him out."

"Sniper?" Jason asked. "Yeah, we'll get right on the phone and get one out here."

Jason was being sarcastic, but Savanah doubted the man would suggest such a thing if it weren't a viable option.

"Are you a sniper?" Savanah asked.

The corners of the man's mouth tugged up. "I just need ammunition," he said, nodding his head to his rifle still on the ground in her field.

Savanah's gaze shifted to Jason. Until that moment, killing his brother had seemed theoretical. Blake had no way of knowing the people he was talking so casually about taking out were Jason's family members. Her heart broke for him. No matter how evil they were, they were still blood. And in southwest Louisiana, blood was everything. It must go against his DNA to turn on them. She searched his face, but he avoided her gaze. What an awful position he was in. She wondered if she should tell Blake or let Jason do it. Would it matter? For all their sakes, she hoped not.

FIVE

Will

DAY SEVEN

"There's Gus and Jaz," Cayden yelled above the shouting.

"We need to get the hell out of here," Tanner said.

Will's eyes never left the group of young men approaching them as he slid into the driver's seat. "Get in," Will said.

Isabella was still hanging out of her door.

Will turned the key and put the truck into gear. As he did, he prayed the wheels caught traction, and they didn't get stuck in the muck. The wheels spun, struggling to grip the wet, muddy pavement. Will heard shouting between the two groups but tried to remain focused on getting the pickup across the parking lot to get Gus and Jaz.

Will's gaze bounced between the teen girls and the approaching men. They'd both turned their attention to the running vehicle. Two of the young girls jumped in front of the vehicle, waving their bats and yelling for Will to stop. He stomped on the brake to avoid hitting them, unable to believe what was happening. They hadn't made it but a couple of miles.

Isabella screamed Will's name, and he turned to find a disfigured young man's face peering back at him through the open window. Scarface twitched the barrel of a small handgun.

"Out of the truck," Scarface said.

Will wanted to look to see where Tanner and Monte were. They had the pistols and were the only ones that could prevent the pickup from being taken.

"I said get out," Scarface repeated.

"Cayden, stay put until I'm out," Will said, without taking his eyes off the man beside him.

The back passenger side door opened, and Isabella screamed. Cayden shouted for someone to let her go. Scarface's attention turned to them. Will grabbed the handle and shoved with all his might, slamming the door into the distracted man, and knocking him off balance. He pulled it back and shoved it into the man a second time, knocking him to the ground. Will was out of the truck in seconds, lunging for the guy. He needed that pistol. He had to get control of the situation before someone got hurt.

The two young women raced over and jumped on Will's back as he and Scarface struggled for control of the weapon. Scarface somehow got his finger inside the trigger guard. Will forced his arm to the left with the barrel pointing over Will's shoulder. The gun went off. The weight of one of the girls lifted off his back as the other young woman began screaming. Gunshots rang out somewhere nearby. Will's heart raced. He was desperate to see where Cayden and Isabella were. Who was doing the shooting? The man yanked hard, nearly tossing Will over his head. Will had to keep his focus on the gun. Scarface rolled left, trying to throw Will off balance. As he did, the man spread his legs, leaving himself wide open for Will's knee to his groin.

Scarface doubled over in pain, and Will seized the opportunity to wrench the pistol from his hand. Will rolled to the right, landing face up, and grabbed the pistol in both hands. The man was still writhing on the ground, no longer an immediate threat. Will pushed himself backward with the heels of his boots and jumped to his feet. On the ground, inches from Scarface was one of the teen girls. Her lifeless eyes stared up at the sky. Only a trace of blood oozed from the bullet wound in her forehead. The second girl looked up, tears streaking her cheeks. She screeched as she lunged for him. Will stumbled back, trying to put distance between them. He did not want to shoot a kid. Tanner appeared out of nowhere and clothes-lined the girl. She bounced off his muscular arm and fell back on her butt, grabbing her throat.

Gus ran up behind them and pounced on the girl. He yelled something in Spanish and rolled her over onto her side. Will's attention turned to searching for Cayden and Isabella and his eyes scanned the area behind the truck. There were people on the ground.

Panic seized Will, and he ran around the vehicle, calling Cayden's name.

"Over here, Dad."

A sigh of relief escaped his lips as his eyes focused on his son standing beside Jaz and Isabella near a short row of hedges that lined the street.

Looking through the front sights of his newly found pistol, Will turned and took in the parking lot, making sure they'd taken care of all the threats. On the passenger side of the truck, Monte stood over two men who were face down on the pavement. Four men were lifeless behind the vehicle. All others had fled.

"We need to go before they come back with friends," Will yelled, gesturing with his hand for Cayden and Isabella to get to the truck.

"What about these four?" Gus asked as he rounded the back of the pickup. The teen girl was thrashing about, trying to dislodge his grip on her arm.

"I'll take care of them," a male voice called out.

Will pivoted, searching for its source.

Gus turned. "Are you sure, Father?"

Will spotted the priest dressed in the traditional black cassock and white collar and lowered his pistol.

The priest said something to the girl and she hung her head. "I'll take responsibility for them. They're not bad kids, really. They just lack proper guidance."

"If you say so," Gus said, releasing his grip on the girl.

She twisted and backed away, throwing her head back. "I told you, I ain't staying at the church, Father."

"Two Hispanic men dressed in blue dickies and white T-shirts stepped out from behind the priest. Gang tattoos covered their arms, faces, and necks. One was tall and broad-shouldered. He carried himself with authority. The second was shorter and thinner. He scanned the street, leery of being out in the open. They walked toward Gus with their chests out and heads cocked slightly to one side, stopping next to the two kids on the ground. Monte stepped backward several feet and lowered the pistol halfway.

"Get up," the broad-chested man barked. The men surprised Will by complying without complaint. The shorter man grabbed the girl's arm and shoved her toward the priest. She looked back as if to say something but turned and casually began making her way across the parking lot. Gus gave the two men a slight nod as he eased around to the driver's side of the truck.

"I'd walk if I were you. That truck is gonna do nothing but get ya'll killed," the larger man said.

Will was beginning to think he was right. All it would do was attract unwanted attention. He'd been stupid to expect otherwise, but they were kind of stuck now. Isabella couldn't walk and what were their chances of finding bikes close by?

"I got you. We're going to stick to the freeways. Thinking there'll be fewer people," Gus said.

Will doubted it. Evacuees stranded while trying to get away from the storm wouldn't have traveled far from their vehicles. It was just too dangerous. But now, with the water receded, they'd likely be traveling south using the freeways.

"We going?" Monte asked. He lowered his pistol and moved

toward Gus. The larger man's right hand whipped around to the back of his waistband.

"Let's get these kids back to the church. I'm sweating my balls off out here," the broad-shouldered man said.

"Let's go, Cayden," Will said, placing a hand on his shoulder.

More people appeared as everyone loaded back into the pickup. They gathered up the bodies and disappeared back the way they'd come.

"Well, that was scary as hell," Jaz said as she climbed back into the front passenger seat and closed her door.

"I sure hope that dude isn't right about this truck causing us problems," Isabella said. She held her injured left hand across her chest. The pain medication that the medics had given her had long since worn off and Will was impressed at how tough she was being. She had to be suffering.

Gus took the turn out of the parking lot a little too sharp, causing Tanner to fall off the wheel well. Will could hear him cursing Gus through the open back glass.

"What the hell happened back there?" Gus asked.

"I'm not sure. We split up to check the area for threats, and that group of girls came running after Monte."

"The church is full of people. They said there are groups of individuals camping out nearby. They're doing their best to feed everyone, but they're just about out of food," Jaz said.

"Monte said those girls had canned goods stacked up back there in the quad. I bet they took it from the school cafeteria," Will said.

"I'm glad they didn't get the truck," Cayden said.

"Me too," Jaz said. "Hopefully, we can avoid any more of that mess getting to my mom's."

They hadn't traveled two blocks before that notion had been put to rest. A middle-aged man and his small son stepped out into the street and stared at the vehicle as it passed by them. The truck was attracting way too much attention. The noise of the engine seemed to carry through the neighborhoods. Will hoped it would be better on the freeways.

Gus gripped the steering wheel tightly as they passed an apartment building where a few men and a woman were sitting on the hoods of cars. Each of them turned to face the street. One man slid down off the hood and took a step forward. Will glanced back. Tanner had his pistol pointed in the man's direction.

"This isn't good," Will said, tightening his grip on the pistol he held pointed between his feet.

"I see them," Gus said as he sped up before the man could have a chance to pull his own weapon.

A small group of people stepped between two cars in front of the truck, and Gus swerved to avoid hitting them. He hit the gas, slinging mud into the air, and sped past them. The interstate was up ahead, and Gus focused on reaching the on-ramp without crashing into abandoned cars or getting the truck's tires slashed by metal debris.

"I hope it isn't like this the whole way," Jaz said, pointing to the piles of twisted electric lines, pieces of wood, and chunks of what had once been someone's roof.

"It will get better the farther north we go," Will said. The further they traveled north, the less hurricane damage they'd encounter. At least that had been Will's experience. Without news reports, it was hard to tell what area had been hit the hardest.

Will was concerned about all the dead cars on the freeways. Making their way through them might prove impossible. From what he'd seen, the roads had been packed with residents evacuating when the EMP struck. Many had simply run out of gas and abandoned their vehicles on the sides of the road before that. There might not even be passable shoulders on the interstate. They'd likely spend all their time pushing vehicles out of the way.

"The debris will probably lessen, but there could be more people. All the evacuees stranded by the EMP could still be hanging out by the freeways. They likely didn't travel far from the vehicles," Will said.

Before they'd started their journey, Will had known it wouldn't be easy but seeing first-hand how rough it would be had every muscle in his body on high alert. He rolled his shoulders, trying to ease the tension building in them.

When they finally reached the on-ramp, Will was pleasantly surprised. Someone had already come along and pushed vehicles aside enough to clear the shoulder and right lane. Possibly the military had been through this way. It was likely too much to hope that they would have cleared the other freeways as well. If it was unobstructed all the way to the Crosby Freeway, they could make it to Liberty much faster. But if not, once they turned off of Interstate 610, at least there would be fewer cars to have to get past.

Despite being anxious to get to their destination, Gus kept his speed low in order to rapidly respond should anything unexpected pop up in front of them. Jaz leaned over and placed her hand on his shoulder. "If things stay like this, we could be there in an hour."

"I hope your crazy uncle doesn't shoot us when we pull in," Gus said.

"If he's still there. Mom said he was being moved, but with the storm, they may have waited."

"If they didn't move him, then he's screwed," Gus said.

Jaz leaned back and grew quiet.

"Why would your uncle shoot at us?" Isabella asked.

Jaz hesitated before answering, causing a knot to twist in Will's stomach. He needed to know how much trouble this uncle of hers was and if it was safe for him and his son to stop there.

"My uncle was supposed to testify against this dude, so he's supposed to be moving into witness protection soon," Jaz said.

"That sounds serious," Isabella said.

"My mom was scared. She told him if they didn't come for him that day, he'd have to go, so either way, he shouldn't be there now."

Will hoped that was the case. Regardless, he would plan on leaving as soon as they dropped Gus and Jaz off. He had no intentions of getting caught up in their family drama.

SIX

Will

DAY SEVEN

Almost immediately, Will spotted the Houston skyline from a gap between cars along Interstate 610. From that distance, it looked like downtown had been the center of a war zone. Instead of the shiny glass and metal, all he saw was black and charred buildings. Somehow it appeared worse than it did close up, seeing the scale of the destruction.

Isabella and Cayden leaned forward to get a look.

"It's bad, isn't it?' Jaz said, following their gaze.

"Yeah. We were down there when it happened. It was terrifying. Glass just rained down on us. The smoke was so thick. My lungs hurt just thinking about it," Isabella said.

"Wow. That sounds terrifying."

"It's a good thing the military picked you up and brought you home. I can't imagine walking all that way with all that destruction," Gus said.

"I guess so," Isabella said, lowering her voice. Her eyes dropped to her lap. She was likely remembering Betley. They hadn't had time to discuss his death. Maybe they didn't need to.

Will stared off to his right at the long rows of rail cars filled with petroleum products that now would likely never reach their destination. There were enough toxic chemicals on those tracks to take out a good-sized city if they fell into the hands of the terrorist insurgents. He couldn't seem to stop thinking about their battle with them. There were just so damn many. How had they gone undetected by the government? They'd known that *something* was going on. If only they'd moved sooner. Will sighed. It wouldn't have stopped the EMP strike, but it would have given them a better shot at fending off an invasion.

He recalled Stephens saying that they had military assets out in the Gulf of Mexico and the Fourth Fleet down in the waters off South America. How long would it take for all the US ships and personnel overseas to make it back to help defend the nation? With the capabilities the military had left, would they be able to hold out long enough? But he'd witnessed the fight from those brave men and women and he knew that they'd do all within their power to prevent foreign powers from stepping foot on American soil.

As Will looked toward downtown, thinking about what the rest of the country must be going through, Jaz gasped. Will looked up and followed her gaze. The road ahead was charred black. Smoke still circled above the tank farm to the right of the interstate. Husks of the tanks were all that remained with the Buffalo Bayou just beyond, the dark, debris-filled water still out of its banks.

As they crossed over the bayou, Will turned his attention to the road ahead. Abandoned vehicles stretched as far as the eye could see. He stared into the bed of another pickup as they slowly passed. It was loaded down with suitcases, furniture, and toys. Will spotted a cooler strapped to the back.

"You know, Gus. There may be some useable stuff in these vehicles," Will said. "It might be worth making a short stop to check them out." Will shifted his gaze to Cayden. His clothes were filthy. Will would almost kill for dry socks and clean underwear. There would likely be a treasure trove of snack food inside them. He'd loaded his Jeep down with chips, cookies, and Cokes for their trip to the lake house and imagined most other travelers had done the same. Some may have had the forethought to take it with them when they abandoned their automobiles, but it was doubtful they could have carried much.

Gus slowed the truck. "I guess it wouldn't hurt to take a peek."

He stopped between a loaded down pickup and an SUV with boxes and totes strapped to the luggage rack.

"Wait here," Will said as he climbed out. Cayden rolled his eyes.

"What's the problem?" Monte asked, hopping over the truck's bed rail.

"We just want to check out the contents of a couple of these vehicles to see if there's anything we can use," Will said.

Will dropped the magazine of the pistol and examined the ammunition. He counted fifteen bullets. He pulled back the slide and ejected the round in the chamber. After slapping the magazine back into the pistol, he chambered a round. He instinctually moved his thumb to flick the safety before shoving it into his back waistband and joining Gus at the back of the SUV. That's when he spotted four bicycles strapped to the back of a lime green Prius.

"Hey, Gus, you mind if I throw a couple of those on top of your stuff in the bed?" Will said, pointing to the bikes.

"If you can find something to strap them down, go for it," Gus said.

"Cayden, you want to come help me?"

As Cayden and Isabella followed Will to the Prius, Gus and the others pulled the tarp back on one of the trucks and began going through the owner's belongings.

"So you're still considering using bicycles?" Isabella asked, leaning against the SUV in the opposite lane. She held a pack of wet wipes in her hand. She'd let her hair down and was scrubbing off her drawn-on five o'clock shadow.

"I like to have a backup plan, especially after what just happened back there at the school."

"I guess that's smart, but if someone takes the truck, won't they get the bikes too?"

Will hadn't thought about that. His focus had been on if they got stranded or it became too dangerous to continue in the truck. They had no way of knowing what the roads would be like after they left the interstate. He'd rather have the bikes and not need them than not and have to walk all the way to Louisiana. He released a mountain bike from the rack and handed it to Cayden.

"Where will we put all our supplies?" Cayden asked.

"If we have to use the bikes, we'll have to pare down to only what we can strap to the backs," Will said, handing down the second bike.

Will stepped back to lean the third bike against the car and bumped into Isabella. "Sorry. How's the leg?"

A slight smile tugged at her lips. "About the same as the last ten times you asked."

They were in no shape to be out there on the road. He was pushing her too fast, he knew, but the longer they hung around the city, the more likely it was that they'd run into trouble they couldn't get out of. They'd been lucky so far. They'd been through hell and survived. He was afraid that, eventually, their luck would run out.

"Sorry. We won't use the bikes unless we absolutely have to," Will said. He pressed a thumb against the tires to see if they were aired properly. They were.

"Cayden, look around for straps or bungee cords. We need something to strap them down with."

While Cayden checked a nearby vehicle with a trailer attached, Will rolled two of the bicycles over and leaned them against Gus's truck. Isabella grabbed the other. She looked at it for a moment and then threw her uninjured leg over and climbed onto the bike's seat.

Will watched as she placed one hand on the handlebar grip and tried to push off and pedal. He caught her before she could fall over. "We'll figure something out if it comes to it," Will said, extending his arm to help her off the bike. Her foot caught on the pedal, and she lurched forward, nearly toppling them both. Will stepped back, lifted her up, and slowly lowered her to the ground. Their eyes met briefly before Will turned his gaze. As he backed away, Isabella slowly withdrew her hand from his, sliding her fingertips lightly along his palms. His breath quickened and electricity shot through his body. He fought the urge to pull her back into his arms. Will looked around for Cayden, but he was out of sight.

Isabella turned away. "What we need is one of those sidecar thingies."

Will leaned over and hoisted the bicycles up and over the side of the truck. "Yeah. That would be great. We'll have to keep our eye out for something like that," he said, regaining control of himself.

"Gus," Jaz said. Alarm rang in her voice. "Gus, there's people coming."

Will spun around, looking for Cayden. He felt the same panic he had when Cayden was three and had become separated from him and Melanie at the county fair. He spotted the top of his head between cars. Pulling the pistol from the small of his back, he ran toward him. "Cayden, get to the truck," Will called to him in a low voice.

Isabella yanked open the pickup's door and gestured for Jaz to get in. "Jaz!" Jaz stared at her for a moment and then took off running toward Gus. Monte stepped into view. "What?"

Jaz stopped abruptly and pointed over her back. "People are coming this way."

Will stood tall but couldn't see anyone.

"Where?" Monte asked, turning in that direction. He must have seen them because he raised his pistol and began backing toward the truck. "Tanner, we have company," he said.

Will grabbed Cayden's hand, and the two rushed between vehicles, staying low and out of sight. Cayden's eye fell to the gun Will was holding. He lowered it, pointing toward the ground.

The pack was within twenty feet of Isabella and the pickup when they spotted another group consisting of six to eight men walking toward them on their left. Gus poked his head out from inside a mid-sized sedan. He saw the look on Will's face and straightened.

"What?" he said, just a little too loud. Will looked past him. If they hadn't spotted Will and the others yet, they had now. The gang picked up the pace and was running toward them by the time everyone made it back to the truck. Will pivoted in his seat and stared at the group as Gus stomped the gas and sped away.

"This sucks," Jaz said. "I can't wait to get to my mom's. This is too stressful."

That was an understatement.

"We shouldn't stop again," Will said.

"No, shit!" Gus said. "That dude back there was right. This truck attracts too much attention."

"What choice do we have? I can't walk forty miles," Jaz said, rubbing her baby bump.

Isabella glanced back to the pickup's bed. "The way things are looking, we may end up on those bikes after all."

Will hoped they didn't lose the bicycles. He hadn't had the chance to strap them down. Tanner was sitting on top of one of them, but the other two looked like they could slide off the heap of suitcases and bags any moment. They couldn't risk stopping to tie them down. All he could do was hope that they made it to Jaz's mother's house. From there, he'd have to decide if it was worth it to take the truck.

SEVEN

Savanah

DAY SEVEN

Savanah watched as Blake picked up his rifle from the ground and walked off across the field. Before climbing back over the fence, he threw his hand in the air and gave a brief wave. Jason stood and gathered up the empty coffee mugs. He'd been quiet ever since they'd heard Blake's suggestion to deal with Jason's brother and cousins. She wanted to know how he felt about it but wasn't sure how to approach the subject. She couldn't just come out and ask him what he thought about Blake assassinating his brother.

"I'm going over to Pete's. We need to go back to all the neighbors and try one more time," Jason said as he turned toward the house.

Although Pete Ashby had agreed to work with them against the Blanchards who'd taken up residence at the Sugar Hill community, most of the other neighbors were too afraid. Savanah wasn't sure that Pete was the right person to take to convince them.

Mrs. B was standing in the doorway. She held the door open as Jason went inside then joined Savanah as she tried to salvage the eggs she'd dropped earlier. It had been a stupid mistake. Every egg was precious food. Savanah shooed away the cats and picked through the shells. They were all wasted. There'd be no eggs for breakfast. At least the mousers would enjoy them.

Luca and Jane stepped out on the front porch. Jane waved. Savanah raised her hand and returned the gesture. It was awkward having strangers living in her house and tiptoeing around people sleeping in every nook and cranny. She'd moved Keegan and Kylie in with her. There was plenty of room in her bed. Of course, Kylie was less than gracious about giving up her room to Luca and Jane, whereas Keegan was thrilled to have the Bertrands using his room. Jason was still staying in the barn, despite Karson offering his room.

Jason reappeared with a bandolier filled with ammo and a small pack. "I'll be back before dark," he said.

"Wait, I want to come with you," Savanah said.

"No!" Jason said, just a little too sharply. He lowered his voice. "No. You should stay and help guard the farm. I've got this."

Something was wrong—she could feel it. A knot formed in her stomach as she called after him.

"Jason."

He kept walking.

"Jason," she called again.

"Everything will be fine, Savanah. Just stay here and watch out for the kids."

She stared at his back with her mouth open, trying to think of something she could say to stop him. The thought ran through her head that this could be the last time she saw him. If he was going to see his family, he might never come back to her and her children. She took a step toward him, but Mrs. B caught her arm.

"You have to let him do what he feels is best."

Her forehead creased. "But—"

"He'll be back. He cares too much about you and those little ones not to."

"Where's he going, Mommy?" Keegan asked as he ran up to Savanah. He was barefoot as usual.

Savanah picked him up. "He's got something he has to take care of. He said he'd be back by dark."

"But he said he'd make me pancakes this morning."

"It must have been really, really important then. I can make you pancakes," Savanah said, turning toward the house.

"But you don't make them crispy like Jason does."

"That's because Jason's are more like the funnel cakes you get at the fair. They're totally bad for you."

"He lets me put a little sugar on them."

She'd allowed Jason to indulge the kids somewhat since the world went to shit, knowing the two-pound bag of sugar Mrs. B had brought with her wouldn't last forever. Especially as much as Mrs. B baked with it. If she'd known that there'd be so many things that her children would miss out on, she would have been a little more indulgent with them herself. She suddenly recalled the cookies Paul Broussard had given her for the children. She had placed them in her backpack before heading home from town. Keegan's birthday was in two days. They might be a little stale by now, but they'd still make a special treat.

"Let's go in, and maybe you can show me how Jason makes his crispy pancakes. I'll let you have an extra spoonful of honey on them. How about that?"

An ear-to-ear grin spread across his face.

After Kendra and June milked the goats and all the other animals were fed and watered, Savanah donned her tactical vest and grabbed her rifle to patrol the fence line. There was a ton of laundry and other household chores that needed to be done, but she couldn't seem to concentrate. "I'm going to walk the fence line. You want to come with me, Luca?" Savanah asked. Luca turned to Jane. She smiled kindly and nodded. He picked up his shotgun and followed Savanah out the back door.

"I think Jason is right. I think we should try to talk to all the neighbors again and convince them that we need to work together," Luca said.

Savanah said nothing as she held open the gate for him to pass through. "He didn't go to talk to the neighbors."

"He didn't?"

"No. He went to talk to his brother."

"How do you know that? Did he say so?" Luca asked.

Savanah latched the gate and headed south along the cross fence, heading toward the gully that separated their farm from Blake's in-laws. She considered going over and telling him what she suspected. If Jason let it slip that they had discussed taking him out, Blake and the residents of Sugar Cove Road might be in even more danger. The Blanchards would be more than eager to kill a cop. The farther she walked, the more she was convinced they should know. They needed to take steps to protect themselves.

When they reached the gully, Savanah stopped and stared through the trees along the Herberts' fence line.

"You're thinking of going over there and telling that officer?" Luca asked.

She was, but that could derail any plans that might come up to settle this thing with Sugar Hill's Blanchards. Jason would feel betrayed. Maybe he hadn't gone to visit his brother after all. How much did she trust him? Savanah turned back toward her house. She trusted Jason with her life—with her children's lives. She'd wait and see what he had to say. Maybe he could take care of things with his family. It was a long shot, she knew, but she could hope—for all their sakes.

EIGHT

Will

DAY SEVEN

It was an encouraging sign that the off-ramp for Highway 90 had been cleared of vehicles until Isabella spotted something odd as they neared the exit.

"Guys, do you see that?" Isabella asked.

"Who is it?"

"Stop! Stop!" Will shouted. "Stop the truck!"

Gus hit the brakes a little too hard, causing Tanner to smash into the back glass. "What the hell?" he yelled.

"Are they ours?" Isabella asked.

Will did a double-take. It wasn't every day that one ran into military tanks on an American interstate. After what they'd experienced the day before, the sight sent a chill down his spine.

"I think so," Will said.

"Definitely ours. Those are Bradleys—a mix of M2s and M3s," Tanner said through the opening in the back glass. "My dad is a veteran. Military stuff is like a religion to him and the old-timers he hangs out with."

"What are they doing out here?" Jaz asked.

"I have no idea," Tanner said.

"To stop the Chinese from heading north or east," Cayden said.

Jaz turned in her seat to face them. "What? Why would they need to stop the Chinese?"

No one answered her.

Will shifted his gaze to Isabella. He wasn't sure if they could answer that—or should.

"Isabella? What do you know?" Jaz insisted.

"The Chinese launched a nuke high in the atmosphere over the continental United States, causing an electromagnetic pulse capable of taking out the power grid and everything else," Cayden said matter-of-factly.

Will placed a hand on Cayden's thigh. He looked up, and Will shook his head.

"Is that true, Will? Did the Chinese do this?"

Will said nothing.

"What the hell. You know what happened and you won't tell us?" Jaz turned around in a huff, crossed her arms, and rocked back and forth in her seat. "We're at war, and you weren't going to tell us."

"When the military came for you, that's what it was about?" Gus asked, looking over his shoulder.

Will couldn't hold his gaze. He regretted not telling them, but what good would it have done for them to know just how screwed they were? Would they have done something differently? Could they have?

"We weren't sure how much we were allowed to discuss. We kind of got ourselves mixed up in some classified shit, and well, it really doesn't matter who did this. The results are the same."

"Yeah, if it doesn't matter, then why the hell are there tanks on the interstate?" Gus said.

"It's just insurgents right now," Cayden said.

"Insurgents?" Monte asked, his face appearing in Will's open window.

Tanner suddenly arrived next to Isabella's door, startling her.

Her hand flew to her throat. "What insurgents? Chinese?" he asked.

"Yeah. My dad and Isabella had to fight them yesterday."

Will lowered his head and rubbed his brow. "We needed to see if they've blocked the Crosby Freeway," Will said, reaching for the door handle.

Monte stepped back. "What? You're just going to march over there and ask them?"

"Yes. It would be nice to know before we get too far up the ramp. It might be hard to get turned back around."

"I'll go with you," Tanner said.

"I don't know—"

"I want to find out for myself what's going on."

"They're not going to tell you anything," Will said.

"I know how to ask nicely."

"Are you sure that's a good idea, Will?" Isabella asked.

"We'll be right back." Will handed his pistol to Isabella. "Hold this for me. I don't want to give them a reason to shoot." He turned to Tanner and pointed to his weapon. "You might want to leave that here."

Tanner hesitated and then nodded. "Good idea. We don't want to give them the wrong impression."

Will and Tanner walked slowly toward the roadblock with their hands held out to their sides, making it clear they had no weapons and weren't a threat. The soldiers didn't see it that way, however.

"Stop right there. Turn around and go back the way you came."

Will stopped. Tanner didn't.

"Hey, we're just trying to get to Liberty. We were hoping the Crosby Freeway was open."

"I said stop," a soldier barked.

Tanner slowed but didn't stop advancing. Will could barely see the soldiers behind their vehicles, but he was sure they had weapons trained on them.

"Tanner, you're going to get us shot," Will said.

"Can you just tell us if we're going to have an issue taking the Crosby up to Liberty? Did you clear the lanes, and are we going to get shot by insurgents—stuff like that?" Tanner said.

"Tanner, you shouldn't have mentioned insurgents. Now they're going to have to question us."

"Turn around and put your hands on your heads," the soldier demanded.

Will and Tanner complied, turning to face the truck. Will couldn't see inside, but he was sure that Cayden and Isabella would be freaking out about them. A moment later, they had rifles pointed at them and soldiers wanting answers. Will hated being right.

"What do you know about insurgents?" one of the soldiers asked. He was the older of the four. He reminded Will of Hollingsworth. He had a confidence and professionalism about him.

"Will told us that he was involved in a firefight with them back at Ellington. That's all I know," Tanner said. "I have no first-hand knowledge. I just met this group a couple of hours ago."

The soldier turned his attention to Will. "Ellington?" he asked, his eyes lasering in on Will. His scrutiny was intense, and Will wanted to look away.

"It's a long story. I don't have any new information for you. We haven't seen anything since we were dropped off at my friend's apartment yesterday."

"What were you doing at Ellington?"

"Um…" Will didn't want to get into trouble. No one had told him that he wasn't allowed to talk about what he knew. It just seemed right not to divulge details that at least should be classified. "I'm not sure I'm supposed to say. I was there with a CIA analyst and an FBI agent."

"Are you with intelligence?" the soldier asked.

"No!" Will said sharply. "My son and our friend were just in the wrong place at the wrong time, is all. You can ask Lieutenant Sharp. He can vouch that we were interviewed and released."

"Lieutenant Sharp?"

"Yes," Will said.

"Where did you say you were headed?' the soldier asked.

"Up a little past Liberty. We were hoping that you had cleared a lane on the Crosby Freeway."

"We did, but I'd advise against travel right now. You should turn around and go back home."

"We need to get out of the city. My friends back there in the truck have family in Liberty." Will gazed over his shoulder. "There isn't anything left for us back there."

The soldier glanced toward the roadblock and then back to Will. "We aren't going to stop you, but you're better off hunkered down somewhere for the time being."

Will heard the sound of several heavy vehicles. It sounded like the convoy had on the day they were first picked up by the military.

"Reynolds, they're coming," a soldier called from behind one of the Bradleys.

"You need to clear the area. Now!" The soldiers turned and ran back toward the roadblock.

"Who's coming?" Tanner asked. "Is it insurgents?"

"We have to go," Will said, turning toward the truck.

"This is deep shit," Tanner said as they sprinted back.

"We need to haul ass out of this city. I am not getting stuck in a war zone," Will said.

They'd been caught in the middle of enough of it already. They were civilians, and he had a kid. As they approached the driver's side of the pickup, Will shouted, "We have to get the hell out of here. Now!" He yanked open the truck's door and jumped in.

"What did they say?" Isabella asked.

He ignored her question as he glanced back to make sure Tanner had made it. "Drive, Gus!"

"Will? What did they say?"

"They said we'd better go. I heard troops coming this way," Will said.

"That's what that noise is?" Gus asked.

"Yeah, and a lot of them."

"Are they ours?" Jaz asked.

"I don't know. I couldn't see anything."

"I think they're ours. I believe I saw Abrams tanks."

Before Gus could get the truck into gear, a thunderous explosion up ahead was followed by a cloud of smoke. A second later, Will heard what sounded like a jet. His heart dropped into his stomach. It was an airstrike. Enemy aircraft were over Houston. They'd hit the convoy advancing to reinforce Ellington and secure the ports. Was it only a matter of time before Houston fell to the opposition forces? Were they too late?

"What's happening?" Jaz screamed.

"We have to get out of here!" Isabella shouted.

Gus sped up the on-ramp to the Crosby Freeway. He maneuvered into the cleared center lanes of the overpass above Interstate 10 as Will twisted, rising in his seat, trying to look back to see if he could tell if it was the United States military or something else. "Do you see them, Tanner?" He was practically standing in the truck's bed. At first, all Will could see was smoke.

"Damn!" Tanner said.

Monte got to his feet, blocking Will's view west. Gus stopped the truck, and Will opened his door to get out. His mouth dropped open. Military vehicles lined the interstate as far as the eye could see. The aircraft had struck the convoy close to the interchange, and the column had stopped.

"We shouldn't be here. We need to get as far away from them as possible," Will said.

Gus punched the gas and sped away. Will turned to see if Tanner and Monte were still back there. They were and were holding onto the stack of crates and suitcases with all their might.

"Were they heading east?" Gus asked. "Why are they headed east?" Fear laced his voice.

The military was headed east. Was that what the soldiers were warning them about? They needed to get ahead of that convoy if that was the case. Otherwise, they'd become trapped in the middle of the battle.

"They were being attacked by planes," Isabella said. "How are they going to stop an invasion now?"

Will reached across Cayden and took her hand. He leaned over and whispered, "Stephens said they were in contact with our ships. That has to mean they are close. They'll come. It will be all right."

"If they were out there, why didn't they stop that plane before it got here?"

Will didn't have any answers for her. He had no idea how crippled their armed forces were or if they could repel an invasion, but he wanted to avoid a panic. They had to stay focused on getting the hell out of Houston before an all-out war started.

"They're coming, Isabella. We have the best military on the planet. They know what they're doing. We have to trust them to do their jobs while we get the hell out of their way."

"Did those soldiers say if the Crosby was cleared all the way?" Gus asked.

"I think so," Will replied, though honestly, he couldn't recall that part of their conversation. His mind had fixed itself on the soldier's warning and the tone in which he'd said it. He'd wanted to warn them, but it was like he couldn't say more. It didn't really matter. There was no way Will was turning back now. He'd much rather keep moving toward their destination and hope they'd be able to avoid any trouble ahead.

As they approached an overpass, Will leaned forward, hoping to catch a glimpse south toward Channelview and the Houston Ship Channel. He wasn't sure whether he'd be capable of seeing anything from that position.

"Will," Isabella said, pointing to her right.

Thick black smoke rose into the air.

"The ports?" Cayden asked.

"Could be. Might be the fuel tank farms or even the pipelines," Will said.

Gus slowed, and they all stared off in that direction.

"Listen!" Cayden said. "You hear that?"

In their new world, void of man-made sounds, it stood out. Will tilted his head slightly and listened to the whine of an engine —a jet engine.

NINE

Will

DAY SEVEN

"It's one of ours!" Tanner shouted. The whole truck bounced as he jumped up and down in the back. "It's one of ours! Now those Mfers are in trouble."

"Are you sure?" Will asked, craning to see the aircraft for himself.

"I'm positive. My dad dragged me to every air show and exhibition for the last three decades. That's a B-52H Stratofortress."

Will hoped he was right, that it was a US aircraft. If not, what hope was there for Houston?

"We shouldn't stick around and find out," Jaz said. "It's just not safe near the city."

If they weren't able to repel an invasion, it wouldn't be safe anywhere. Will hated the thought of falling under Communist Chinese control. He'd always assumed with half the country owning guns, it would be foolish for another country to try to invade the United States but under the current circumstances, people were just trying to survive. If they showed up with food and humanitarian supplies, how many US citizens would just lay down their arms and give up? Will glanced over at Cayden. Could he resist if his son was starving to death?

Will took one last look south toward the ship channel. It could be the final time he saw Houston as a free state. It was then that he began thinking that maybe his sister's place in Louisiana may not be far enough away to not be drawn into the fight. It was foolish to think that enemy invaders would stop at the Texas state line. He'd need to prepare himself for what may come. He prayed he had time to recover from his injuries and arm himself before facing any more battles.

Everyone grew quiet as they drove east toward Liberty. Will became lost in thought, trying to console himself with how good it would be when they reached Calcasieu Parish. At least then, they could take the time to recover and assess the situation. All he, Cayden, and Isabella had been doing ever since the lights went out was reacting and surviving. There hadn't been the opportunity to consider their future. All he really knew was that this could not be it. This couldn't be what took America down. She was much too resilient for this to be the end. He was staring off into space when Jaz shouted, startling him.

"Gus!" she said, pointing ahead.

"No. No. No." Will said. "Can't we just catch a break, please?"

"Can we go around them?" Isabella said, leaning forward in her seat.

Gus slowed the truck and stopped two hundred feet from the group of people blocking the roadway ahead of them. The group had halted and turned toward them.

"They're blocking the only clear route, dammit," Gus said, punching the steering wheel.

Will scanned the lane beside them. The military hadn't cleared the lanes this far from Houston. How long had Gus been driving on the shoulder?

"What are we going to do?" Jaz asked.

Will eyed the ditch on the side of the road. Half a foot of water in it meant the ground would be soft—too soft for a loaded down pickup. They'd get stuck for sure.

"Can we back up, maybe take the feeder road," Will said.

He hadn't been paying attention, but if the exit wasn't very far, they could get off the freeway, take the frontage road running along the highway, and maybe get back onto the Crosby someplace ahead of this crowd of people. From where he sat, Will couldn't see how large the group was, but they could move faster in the truck, so they'd get ahead of them, eventually.

"Where are they all going?" Cayden asked.

"My guess, away from the city," Gus said.

"On foot? That would really suck."

"I agree, buddy," Gus said, putting the truck into reverse.

Before he could even put his foot on the gas, a couple of men began running toward them. Will heard Tanner shout for them to stop. He twisted in his seat to make sure he wasn't pointing his pistol at the pack. He wasn't—not at the ones in front of them. A small group had moved from between the abandoned vehicles and were blocking their exit.

"Stop, Gus!" Will shouted.

A woman stepped out from behind a sedan holding the hands of two small children.

"Tanner, do not shoot them."

Gus stopped less than twenty feet from them. They looked dirty and tired. Will wondered if they had been evacuating the city when the lights went out. If so, how had they survived out there for a week? The crowd stared back at them with blank, hopeless expressions.

"They're coming," Jaz said. Will turned his attention to the crowd in front of them. They were now trapped between the two groups, with the ditch being their only option.

"Please move from the roadway. We don't have any food or anything," Monte called to them.

They just kept coming.

"Gus, get us the hell out of here," Jaz demanded.

"I can't. What do you want me to do, run them over?"

"You can't take the ditch. We'll get stuck," Will said.

"What other option is there?" Gus said.

"We could give them our food. Maybe they'd move out the way and let us pass?" Cayden said.

"They won't, Cayden. They'll take the food and then take the truck," Will said. His kind-hearted son had so much to learn about human nature. Their sense of self-preservation won't let them not at least try to take the only running vehicle.

"I'm going for it. It's our only option," Gus said, putting the truck into gear and gunning the engine.

"Hold on, guys," Will yelled to Monte and Tanner.

As soon as the front tires left the shoulder of the road, Will knew it was not going to work. The truck tilted right and slid slightly as the back tire struggled to find traction in the soft earth. A second later, the truck lurched forward and took off across the median. Will thought he'd been proven wrong until they began the climb up to the frontage road. Mud flew into the air as the tires spun and spun, digging a deeper and deeper hole.

The engine revved as Gus stomped on the gas, but the truck wouldn't budge.

"Stay back," Tanner yelled. "I said, stay back."

"We're going to have to push," Will said. "Isabella, you should drive, and the rest of us will push."

Gus's door flew open, and he jumped out. "Izzy, stay there. Jaz slide on over here. Don't push on the gas until I tell you to."

"Cayden, stick by me, son," Will said, as he hurried out to join Gus at the rear of the truck.

Monte was already there with his hands on the bumper. Tanner was next to the passenger side, waving his pistol back and forth, attempting to keep the crowd from approaching.

They were shouting now—something about it being selfish of them not giving them a ride while others were begging for food. It was hard to hear, but he knew they couldn't help them. He wasn't heartless, but his responsibility was to Cayden and Isabella. He had to protect them.

Will, Cayden, Gus, and Monte pushed with all their might while Jaz floored the gas. The truck rocked back and forth, but the truck's tires only went deeper into the mud. They were covered from head to toe in filth, and Will's boots struggled to find traction.

"It's hopeless," Monte said. "There's no way this truck is coming out without a tow truck."

"We can help you get it out if you'll give us a ride," a middle-aged man dressed in a long-sleeved shirt and cowboy boots said.

"We don't have room for all of you," Tanner called back.

"You would if you dropped that load of stuff," the man said. "We can help each other if we work together." The man looked sincere.

Will counted at least fifteen people. There was no way that even if they left all their supplies behind, they'd be able to fit all of them in the pickup's bed. A small child moved from behind the man's legs. Will studied the group closer. They were mostly women and children. The scene reminded him of photos he'd seen of people during the dust bowl back in the 1930s. They had that same hopeless look on their faces. Could he turn his back on children? Cayden shifted his weight and stepped forward. What harm could it do to try? They didn't look that dangerous. He saw no weapons.

"Gus?" Will said. It wasn't his truck so, technically, it wasn't his decision to make. That fact did little to ease his guilt though.

"I don't know, man. It doesn't look like we're going to get this damn thing out of the mud with just the four of us pushing, but I'm not sure about leaving all our stuff behind to give them a ride."

"Can you carry it all if we have to walk?" Will asked.

Gus glanced back at the tarp-covered heap. "I guess not," he said, moving toward the driver's door. "Jaz, what do you say?"

Jaz stuck her head out the window and eyed the crowd. "We can't leave kids out here like this. I can move the stuff for the baby up here, and we can leave the rest, I guess. I don't like showing up at my parents' empty-handed, but I don't see as we have a choice, really."

Isabella and Jaz watched as eight strangers removed supplies from the truck's bed and piled them on the side of the road. Will was most upset about seeing the bicycles go. It seemed that somehow fate had determined that his plan to ride them to Louisiana wasn't in the cards. He hoped they could get the truck unstuck, or they might have to go against fate and ride them anyway.

A young mother stood back a way on the Crosby Freeway with her three small children. Her little boy, probably no more than three or four, stared cautiously at Tanner as he guarded the group as they unloaded the truck.

Once everything was unloaded, Jaz opened one of the boxes and held out a can of soup to the young mother. The children stared at the can eagerly, but the woman refused the offer and walked away.

Will took it, pulled the top, and held it out. "They're hungry, and we can't take all this with us. Let them eat."

"It's okay, Carrie. No one is going to hurt you or the kids. You can take the food," a woman in her late fifties said. She took the can from Will, walked over, and gave it to the boy. He held it out to his two sisters, and they scooped soup out with their fingers.

"Everyone, come help yourself," Jaz said, holding a can of stew into the air.

They just stood there looking at one another. Will didn't understand why they all seemed so reluctant to take the food.

"Forgive them, please. We've had a rough few days out here. Not everyone is a nice as you people seem to be," the middle-aged woman said as she took the stew from Jaz.

"We understand. We've seen some pretty bad stuff ourselves," Jaz said.

The woman distributed canned food to everyone in the group,

and they ate before turning their attention to getting the truck back on the roadway.

Will, Cayden, and Isabella huddled together off to one side, watching the poor souls scarf down what might have been the first food they'd had in a week. How many more refugees were out there, just like them? He didn't know exactly what kind of trouble they'd seen, but he knew that people like them would be easy prey for the unscrupulous and evil people who roamed the roads now.

TEN

Isabella

DAY SEVEN

"Where are you headed?" Isabella asked the young mother as she handed her a second can of soup for her children.

"I don't know. Away from the city. We were just following everyone else."

"Oh yeah, where did you come from?"

The woman looked up. Her big brown eyes were bloodshot and rimmed with the same dark circles common to everyone these days. Isabella's heart broke for the woman and her two small children. "We were pulled from the roof by the Cajun navy three days ago. Since then, we've just kept moving, trying to stay ahead of the men with the guns."

"Men with guns?" Isabella asked. With all the lawlessness that had broken out all over the city, a lot of good people were likely to become prey to them.

"The one's fighting the army," the woman said.

"The army?" Had she been over near Ellington? "Where?" Isabella asked.

"Channelview," she responded.

Was the fighting widespread? Were they safe anywhere?

"Were the other men Asian?"

"I don't know. Maybe. We were caught in the middle when the bombs started dropping. That man there." She pointed to a muscular young man in his late twenties. "He helped us get away."

"Bombs?" Isabella brought her right hand up to her throat. Her heart raced as she recalled being buried alive in the rubble of the flight museum.

"Are you all right?" the woman asked.

Isabella blinked several times, clearing away the images from the day before. Her eyes once again focused on the woman and her kids. The news that the fighting appeared widespread throughout Houston only strengthened her resolve to leave the city as fast as possible before they could become trapped in the battle.

Isabella studied the kids as they spooned carrots from the can with their fingers. Their frightened eyes stared back at her. The toll all the chaos was taking on the most vulnerable was almost too much to think about. She was glad that Gus and the others had agreed to help these people. But where were they to go? Isabella couldn't help but think that she would be in the same position if she hadn't met Will and Cayden. At least she had a farm to go to with food and clean water. What hope did this woman and her babies have? How long before they became victims of this new world?

"We're going to try to get the truck out now. You all might want to go stand up on the road out of the way of the flying mud," Will said.

Isabella couldn't help but laugh at him. He was covered from head to toe in the stuff. All she could see were the whites of his eyes. She wasn't sure how he was ever going to get clean.

"Do you need help with the children?" Isabella asked.

"No. They're leery of strangers. We haven't met many people as nice as you all."

"I'm sorry. I'm here if you need me," Isabella said, moving to the side and letting the woman and her children pass.

With all of Gus and Jaz's possessions and the supplies she and

Will had brought stacked up on the roadway, everybody who was able had assembled behind the pickup. Jaz was in the driver's seat, and as the engine revved, everyone else pushed. With grunts and shouts, they heaved and managed to lift the tires out of the ruts and onto the shoulder. After one last shove, to everyone's delight, the truck bounced onto the pavement and came to a stop in the opposite lane of the frontage road. The celebration was short-lived as the men, women, and children piled into the back of the pickup. Gus and Will shoved as much of the food and supplies as could fit around and between them as they could, though Will was still disappointed to leave the bikes.

Isabella handed Will and Cayden some wet wipes, knowing it would do little to clean the mud caking nearly every inch of them. She was almost glad that she had a broken wrist and hadn't been able to help in their failed attempt to get the truck unstuck. When they'd wiped as much as they could off them, she handed them fresh shirts from their backpacks.

After cleaning themselves up, Gus climbed back into the driver's seat and Jaz returned to the front passenger seat. She had one of the small children in her lap and looked content. She was going to make a great mom. Someone handed Isabella a toddler. She and the child were too exhausted to protest. With everyone loaded in, Gus drove east along the frontage road until reaching the next on-ramp to the Crosby Freeway.

The mood was somewhat lighter as they continued on their journey to Liberty. Jaz was talking softly to the toddler in her lap and the little boy Isabella was holding fell asleep about ten minutes after they got on the road. Isabella's mind raced with the information the woman had given her. That, along with the bombs back at the checkpoint, confirmed the fighting was not restricted to the base. She wanted desperately to believe that the military would quickly get things under control, but how? With limited technology, how would they coordinate and call for reinforcements? She couldn't bring herself to think about what other places in the country must be experiencing. It was overwhelming and made it very hard to remain hopeful.

"That young woman I was speaking to said that they fled bombing down in Channelview," Isabella said in a low voice.

"They must be fighting for control of the ship channel," Will said. He reached out and placed his hand on hers. "It's all right. We'll get away in time. We'll be at my sister's before dark."

She glanced at Cayden, who was staring out the front glass. He looked dazed and exhausted. They all were. She wanted to ask Will if he thought his sister's place would be far enough away that the fighting wouldn't affect them, but she didn't want Cayden to worry. He was a tough kid—and smart—he'd likely had the same thoughts.

Isabella gave Will's hand a gentle squeeze before he removed it. She thought about their kiss—more him kissing her. She'd been so shocked that she'd frozen. She still wasn't exactly sure how she felt about it, though it was likely just the emotions of the moment. She'd been ready to give up, and he had just been trying to comfort and encourage her. It likely didn't mean anything. It was clear he wasn't over the loss of his wife, and she'd just days ago lost her boyfriend. She shuddered at the image of his body. Neither of them was ready for anything like that.

Tanner rapped on the truck's roof, causing Isabella to jump.

"Hey, there's another roadblock up ahead."

ELEVEN

Savanah

DAY SEVEN

Savanah passed back and forth in front of the large windows in her living room. She stopped to see if she could see Jason coming down the drive every few minutes. At half past midnight, she'd waited as long as she could. The children and the Bertrands were sleeping. Jane and Luca were in the barn caring for a sick goat. If she left to find Jason, there'd be no one to guard the house but...

She had her hand on the doorknob when Mr. Bertrand spoke her name. Savanah stopped and turned, but the house was dark, and she couldn't see him standing near the hall. "You planning on going to look for him?" he said.

She hesitated. Was she? Should she? Even if she found him and he was in trouble, what could she do against so many? "I..."

"He said he'd be back. You have to give him time to work things out in his own way."

"But what if he's in trouble? I should have never let him go out there alone." A ball of fear formed in Savanah's stomach.

"That wasn't your call. It's between him and his family now."

"I don't think his brother would hesitate one minute to harm Jason if he got in their way. They will never forgive him for splitting with the family."

"He had to try something, and you tagging along would've only made things worse," Mr. Bertrand said.

"He should have been back by now, though. Maybe I could just check the road—look in the ditches. He could be hurt and lying out there bleeding."

"You ain't going to see much in the dark. Wait until morning. If he ain't back by then, I'll go with you."

Morning was only a few hours away, but those precious hours could mean the difference between life and death to Jason.

Daybreak. She'd wait until sunrise, and then she'd go find him. She prayed she was wrong and that he hadn't gone to see his brother.

Luca and Jane came in just before the first light shone over the horizon. They'd been up all night caring for sick animals. They would be sleeping most of the day. If she and Mr. B left, that would leave only Mrs. B and the children awake to guard the farm. She could make it the five miles to Sugar Hill in a little over an hour by herself, but with Mr. B in tow, it could take a couple of hours. That would mean they wouldn't make it back home until early afternoon.

The awful feeling in the pit of her stomach told her that she had to go. She had to find him. She'd checked her rifle and loaded spare magazines into her pockets and backpack. She was ready when Mr. B woke up. Savanah handed him a thermos of coffee and a rifle.

"I have to go now," she said.

"We should eat a good breakfast. We might be doing a good piece of walking today. We need energy."

Savanah handed him an energy bar and marched to the back door.

"Okay then," he said, sitting by the door and sliding on his boots.

"Where are you two going, Mommy?" Keegan was dressed in his overalls and straw hat, which meant he was ready to milk the goats. He'd been getting up early, trying to beat Kylie out there.

"We're just going to go check the fences again," she lied. She never lied to her children. Savanah smiled and tried not to let the worry show on her face. In her heart, she knew that something terrible had happened or Jason would have been back by now. How could she tell her four-year-old son that they were leaving to search the ditches for Jason's body?

"I'm heading out to get Matilda ready for milking. Kendra said I could do her first."

"You wait for your sister. Jane and Luca were out there all night with the babies. Some of them have belly aches, and I don't want you scaring them chasing their mom around."

"Aw, Mommy. Kylie will beat me out there if I wait."

"Keegan, just do as I say and stay inside." His little face scrunched, and she could see tears starting to form. She hated being short with him, but she didn't have time to deal with it now.

"We have to go. You go wake Kendra for me, all right?"

Without a word, Keegan turned and slowly walked away. "I love you, buddy. We'll be back in a bit," she called after him. Her stomach was doing flip-flops. She was so torn. Her concern was turning into anger—at Jason—for putting her in this position. It was stupid for him to go alone. She prayed she'd get the chance to tell him so.

"Ready?" Mr. B asked.

"Not really," she said.

"We could give him some more time."

Savanah looked him in the eyes. "You really think he's just going to walk back down the drive by himself?"

He said nothing.

"Let's go then," she said.

Savanah walked westbound on their two-lane road while Mr. B walked on the opposite side, each keeping an eye on the ditches for any sign of Jason. Savanah looked for drops of blood or anything that might indicate an injured person had walked by there. When Mr. B stopped, put both hands on his knees, and bent over, staring into the drainage ditch beside the Johnsons' driveway, her stomach lurched.

"What do you see?" she asked, rushing to his side.

"Just a shoe someone lost. I don't think that it's Jason's."

Savanah leaned down to get a better look. "It's a running shoe. Definitely not his." Relief flooded through her. She turned to cross back over to the other lane and froze.

"What?" Mr. B said, bringing his rifle up as he turned.

"I didn't mean to frighten you," Blake said as he stepped between the trees lining the road.

"What are you out here sneaking around for then?" Mr. B asked.

"I wasn't sure who you guys were at first."

"What are you doing over here?" Savanah asked.

"I was heading back from surveilling that subdivision. I was going to cross over Mr. Johnson's pasture to get home to my in-laws' place."

He'd been to Sugar Hill?

"Did you see Jason?" Savanah asked.

"No. Why?"

Savanah's eyes pivoted to Mr. Bertrand. She didn't want Blake to know that Jason had gone out there on his own. "He's patrolling the road." Her gaze dropped to the blacktop. Blake's boots were covered in mud. Her eyes cruised his pants legs. The knees were wet like he'd knelt on the ground. "What did you see over at Sugar Hill?"

"I saw a group of six young men riding quads with trailers

attached arrive at the gate. They were loaded down with stuff," Blake said.

"Did you see a tall, muscular man dressed in black jeans and a white button-up shirt?" Savanah asked.

"I did. He seemed to be the one in charge of things. He roughed up this one kid pretty bad. Seems he took a little something for himself and the punishment for that is a beatdown."

"He's their leader," Savanah said.

"And Jason's brother?" Blake asked.

She lowered her head and nodded.

"Where did Jason really go?"

She hesitated before answering. "He said he was going to talk to some of the neighbors again."

"But you don't believe that's where he went, do you?"

"He didn't come back last night," she said.

Blake moved closer to her and placed a hand on her shoulder. She stared at it while he spoke. "He didn't go to Sugar Hill. I can assure you of that."

"How can you be so sure?"

"I've been there practically since I left your place. I wanted to have all the information I could about the place and the people. You were right. They're using those folks. They're victims in all this. Until I saw it with my own eyes, I wasn't convinced. But they're as terrified of those Blanchards as we are."

"So, where's Jason?" Savanah said, turning to Mr. Bertrand.

He shook his head. "He said he was going to talk to the neighbors, right?"

She nodded. Fear seeped into every crevice of her mind.

"Then maybe that's what he did. We need to go back and start there, and we should get Pete to help us look for him."

TWELVE

Will

DAY SEVEN

Will spotted a crowd of people in the convenience store's parking lot fifty yards ahead and to their right. Tanner hopped down from the back of the truck and appeared in Will's passenger side window. He raised his rifle and peered through its scope.

"How many? Do they have weapons?" Will asked.

"At least a dozen, maybe more. I see one dude with a shotgun."

Will got out and stood beside Tanner. "I think we should try to find another way around."

"Do you know this area well enough to know the back roads?" Tanner asked.

"No. Not really."

Gus climbed out and joined them. "Jaz?"

"I don't know the streets. I didn't grow up around here. My mom moved here after she married my stepdad," she said.

"Maybe one of them knows," Gus said, nodding back over his shoulder.

Tanner took a step back. "Any of you know another way to Liberty from here that doesn't go through town?"

A wiry man in his late twenties threw a leg over the truck's bed and hopped down beside Tanner. His head swiveled, studying the convenience store. "What's the problem? Why can't we just keep going?"

"They might want a ride," Gus said.

Will jerked his thumb toward the crowd. "Or worse, try to take the truck and leave us stranded in that parking lot."

"You could turn left at the crossroad and go north," a young mother said. She moved her toddler to the opposite knee and shifted slightly to face them. "We could wind our way around to the other side of Dalton, but you have to get back onto ninety to cross the Trinity River."

Will turned to Gus. It was his truck, after all. Well, his now; he'd acquired it. The legality of it all had blurred, not that it even mattered at this point. "What do you think?"

"You think we can make the turn before they can rush in front of us and block the lanes?" Gus asked.

"I don't know. It's risky, but what choice is there?"

Isabella called Will's name. "The kids." She nodded toward the boy in her lap. "We can't take unnecessary risks."

He understood her concern. The last thing he wanted was a child's blood on his hands. This all sucked so badly. Now he was accountable not only for his son and Isabella but all these other refugees. He wanted to tell himself that they were not his problem, but as long as they were traveling together, he had to consider all their safety as well. "Gus?" That was a chicken shit thing to do, he knew. But it wasn't his decision to make alone. Gus had a girl-friend and a kid on the way. They all needed to be on board with whatever they chose.

Gus turned and stared off in the direction they'd just come. "What if we turn around? Do you think we could find another road?"

"We'd have to backtrack about three miles or so, go north another fifteen or so miles before cutting over to bypass Dalton and come out on the east side of town. All in all, it'll add thirty or more miles to the trip," the young mother said.

"That's an hour, probably," Will said.

"What if you just floored it and shot past them real quick?" Monte asked. He'd appeared out of nowhere. Will hadn't seen him get out of the back. "They have a bunch of women and children too. They might not want to engage in a firefight either."

Will's head rotated, scanning the parking lot. He was right. They might not want to risk it, especially if they saw Tanner and Monte brandishing pistols. He wasn't looking forward to adding another hour or more to the trip. He'd hoped to be at Savanah's by nightfall.

Gus looked torn. "I don't know. Even if we make it past this group, we are more likely than not going to encounter more people up ahead in Dalton."

"If we make it past them, I know a way around the south end of the city that will bypass the most populated areas," the young mother said.

Gus studied the crowd in the parking lot. "I could be doing at least forty miles per hour by the time we pass them. That might be fast enough that even if they fired, they'd miss, but what if they rush onto the highway and block the lanes? This truck is loaded down with people. I can't just swerve to miss them. I might throw people out."

"Drop those guns to the ground! Do it now!" a man shouted.

Will dropped low and searched in the direction of the voice.

Tanner whipped around and raised the pistol as he slumped to a crouch by the left front tire. "Where are they? Anyone have eyes on them?"

Monte flattened himself against the cab of the pickup. "They're in the tree line along the road. Bastards snuck up on us."

"Get down, everyone! Get down!" Will shouted, slapping the air with his hand.

People were scrambling to get out of the truck's bed. Children were crying.

Will heard Isabella's voice. "Get out of the vehicle," he yelled back to her. He moved backward, yanked open the back driver's-side door, and pulled Cayden down to the ground. "Stay down."

"We don't want to hurt anyone," the voice called from the trees.

"We're just passing through. We don't want any trouble," Gus yelled.

Will moved around Cayden to take the child from Isabella. His mother appeared at Will's side and snatched the boy from him.

Isabella pointed to the westbound lanes as she slid from the seat. "We should get across the median and hide the children behind that mover's truck."

Will glanced back at the rental van. It was large and would provide better cover for them, but to get there, they'd have to go out into the open. "I don't know. It might—"

Isabella didn't wait for Will to answer. She grabbed the boy from his mother and took off running for the van. The child's mother followed after her, screaming her son's name. In seconds, Isabella disappeared around the back of the moving van.

"Let's go," Will said. "Cayden, take that child's hand." He pointed to a six or seven-year-old boy standing by his sister. "You two, hold hands." Will looked their mother in the eyes. "I'm going to get you and your kids over there where it's safer." The frightened woman nodded, tears slipping over her eyelids and streaming down her face. "Ready?" Will asked, and then he grabbed the woman's hand, and they ran across the median just as the first shots rang out.

Will didn't look back to see who was doing the firing. He continued on around the van and deposited the woman and her children by the front tire. Isabella was crouched by the back, clutching the boy to her chest. Will pointed. "Cayden, stay down right here. I'm going to check on Isabella." Cayden opened his mouth to protest. "Stay here."

Will moved quickly toward the back, stepped around the boy's mother, and placed a hand on Isabella's shoulder. "You okay?"

"Jaz and Gus?" she asked.

"I'll get them," Will said.

He risked a peek around the rear fender. Everyone back at the pickup had dropped to the ground. Parents were covering their children. Will's eyes cruised the length of the truck before finding Gus and Jaz near the front tire. The shooting had stopped. The only sound was the children whimpering. Will looked for Tanner or Monte. He still couldn't be sure who had fired the first shot. Surely it wasn't Tanner and Monte. Would they put the kids at risk like that? Will didn't think so. They'd come to Texas to save lives. They didn't seem like the type of people to be so careless.

"Monte?" It was Tanner calling for him. Will shifted, trying to locate him among the bodies on the pavement.

"You have eyes on them?" Monte called back.

"Negative," Tanner said.

"I think they are at your two o'clock, by that mound of gravel," Monte said.

Will spotted Tanner when he raised his head and repositioned himself onto his elbows. "Got 'em."

"How many?" Monte asked.

"I see two sets of boots."

"Toes pointing to the sky?" Monte asked.

"Nope."

"Shit fire." Monte got up onto all fours and crawled toward Tanner's position at the back of the truck. "You boys might as well go on back to your loved ones. We ain't giving up this truck," he yelled.

The men answered by firing a round into the truck.

Will ducked back behind the moving van. "Stay down. Stay down." When he looked again, Monte was crawling on his belly toward the side of the road. "On me, Tanner," he said, disappearing into the tall grass. Tanner took off slithering to the shoulder of the road on his belly. Rifle rounds kicked up dust in the gravel along the road, and Tanner hurried to follow Monte into the grass.

Will looked for movement or any sign of the two in the brush but saw nothing before the gunmen suddenly appeared near a mound of gravel some twenty yards away. Will wanted to shout and warn Tanner and Monte, but he didn't want to give away his position. He had a clear shot at both men, if only he had his rifle. If only he had ammo for it. The damn thing was useless without ammunition. He cursed the soldiers for not returning the magazines.

A shot cracked, and one of the gunmen dropped to his knees while the other dove behind the gravel pile where Will lost sight of him. He returned his attention to the other man. He'd dropped his rifle and was holding his stomach. Monte appeared beside him, kicked his weapon away, and pressed the barrel of his weapon against the side of the man's face. Will stiffened, anticipating Monte firing a bullet into the man. The man fell sideways just as Tanner rushed behind the gravel mound. He bent, and when he straightened, he was holding the second man's rifle. "They're both down," Tanner called back.

Will blew out a breath and ran the back of his hand across his forehead. He moved around the bumper and took in the scene back at the Valero gas station parking lot. The people who'd gathered there had scattered, and he hoped they were no longer a threat. He was sick of the violence.

"Let's get the hell out of here before someone comes looking for them," Tanner said, hurrying back toward the truck.

Gus helped Jaz to her feet, and she rushed around to the passenger seat. "Cayden, Isabella, let's go," Will said, not wanting to get left behind.

"Give me my son," the mother shouted.

Isabella turned and handed the boy to her. "Come on. We have to go."

"No. I'm staying here. I'm not getting back in that truck. That thing is just a giant bullseye. I'd rather walk."

Isabella stared at her for a moment before nodding and turning her back to them.

Will grabbed her hand, and they followed Cayden back across the median and climbed into the truck. Tanner handed a rifle through Will's open window.

"Here," he said. "He only had one extra magazine for it though." Will inspected the AR-15 as Monte handed Isabella a shotgun and a handful of shells. It wasn't much, but at least they were no longer defenseless.

The other evacuees must have concluded the same thing as the young mother as they chose to stay behind. They hadn't made it far, and Will wondered how they intended to survive out there on foot. They were five miles from town, and there was no telling what dangers awaited them there.

"Keep an eye on that parking lot. People may have scrambled for cover, but they could still pop out and get a shot off," Tanner said.

"You guys hold on tight back there," Gus said. "I'm about to floor this Mfer and haul ass away from here. If you fall out, I ain't stopping."

THIRTEEN

Will

DAY SEVEN

Gus stopped the truck just outside the city limits of Dalton, Texas. Will leaned forward, placed his hand on the back of the driver's seat, and peered through the windshield. Alongside the westbound lane sat a long train that had been heading for Houston. Will wondered how many millions of barrels of petroleum product sat on idle trains like that one. He began to think of what other commodities were shipped by rail. Grains for sure. What about the food? How great would it be to come upon a whole freight car full of canned foods? He doubted weapons or ammunition would have been moved across the country that way, but they were transported somehow. The way things were going, a person would need a shit ton of it in order to survive.

"What do you think?" he asked.

"I say we floor it and get through town as fast as possible and don't stop for anything," Gus said.

"Might be safer to go around," Will said.

"And it might not. May just as likely get shot taking a wrong turn down some ole boy's driveway."

That was true. Without GPS or a decent map, they could get hopelessly lost and wind up stuck on a dead-end road.

"Floor it then," Will said.

Gus did just that. They approached the city of Dalton doing sixty miles per hour. It was a good thing that traffic there must have been light on the day of the EMP and few cars remained on the road. Several men were standing around the auto parts store's parking lot, but none attempted to stop them. Will's stomach growled as they sped past all the fast-food restaurants. He wished he'd eaten when everyone else had. It was hard to say when they'd get a chance now, and most of the food was stacked up back on the roadway where they'd picked up the refugee group earlier.

They were almost out of town when the first sign of trouble appeared. Two men riding all-terrain vehicles suddenly pulled out of the Jack in the Box parking lot, blocking their lane. Gus swerved into the turning lane to avoid hitting them.

"That one is a cop," Jaz said.

"I'm not pulling over for no cop on a four-wheeler," Gus replied.

Everyone was looking behind them. When Will turned back to face the road ahead, two more ATV riders blocked their lane. "Gus!" Will yelled. Gus turned and cursed as he stomped the brakes. They came to a stop within twenty feet of the officers who had their rifles pointed at the truck.

"Hands in the air," one of the officers yelled. Everyone in the cab of the pickup complied. Will resisted the urge to turn to see if Tanner and Monte had.

The second officer moved to the driver's side of the vehicle. "What's the hurry?" he asked.

The hurry was that they didn't want to get their vehicle confiscated or into a gun battle again, but that wasn't what Gus told the man.

"Some folks back there shot at us. We were just trying to get as far away from them as possible," Gus said.

That wasn't what Will would have told the cops. Now they

might want to question them about the incident and take witness statements or something.

The officer stepped back and examined the bullet holes in the side of the truck. "What'd they look like?"

Gus looked back over his shoulder to Will. "Um…"

Tanner spoke up. "The one ole boy had on a long beard. He wore a white cowboy hat and some fancy boots."

The officer moved toward the bed of the truck, and Will shifted in his seat to watch him.

"And he just shot at you as you were driving by?"

"Sure did. Scariest shit I have ever been through," Tanner said.

"Where ya'll headed?"

"Liberty," Gus said out the window.

The officer moved back to the driver's side window. He leaned forward and looked at everyone. Will smiled, as did Cayden and Isabella. Jaz crossed her arms and glared at him.

"What's in Liberty?"

"Her parents," Gus said, nodding toward Jaz.

"So you're just passing through?"

"Yep."

"You got a license and the registration for this truck?"

Will's stomach flip-flopped. He had no idea where Gus had found the vehicle, but his name would not be on the registration, Will was sure of that.

"I don't have my wallet. It was stolen back in Houston. But the registration is in the cubby." He pointed. "Jaz, you want to get paperwork for the officer?"

Without a word, Jaz opened the glove compartment, pulled out a sheet of paper, and handed it to Gus. He smiled and then handed it to the officer. Will held his breath as the cop unfolded the paper and read the name.

"You're Stefan Kowalski?"

"Yep," Gus lied.

Will almost laughed out loud. Kowalski?

The officer eyed him with suspicion before returning the document.

"What about the rest of you? Your wallets stolen too?"

Will shifted and fumbled for his billfold. It wasn't there. He had no idea when he'd lost it. He shook his head. "I don't have mine either."

"I never had one," Cayden said. The officer smiled and then glanced over to Isabella. She batted her eyelashes and heat surged beneath Will's skin. She reached into the front pocket of her jeans and pulled out her identification then leaned across Will and Cayden and handed it through the window.

"Isabella D'Angelo," he said. "How long have you been in Texas?"

"Oh, a few months. I've been meaning to get my license updated."

He handed it back to her. "I guess it don't much matter now."

Everything seemed to be going so well that what he said next surprised Will.

"I'm going to have to ask you folks to exit the vehicle."

"What? Why?" Gus asked.

"By order of the Mayor of Dalton, we are authorized to seize all working vehicles for use by emergency personnel."

Jaz lost it. At first, she spoke something in Spanish and then lit into him in English. "Hell to the freaking no! No way! I'm not giving up this truck until I reach my mama's. I am not walking in this heat. Not going to happen," she said, waving her hands in the air wildly.

Gus was doing his best to calm her down, but she just swatted his hands away and kept on.

Will turned toward the officer who just stood there with the rifle across his forearms, waiting for her to stop. He wasn't fazed by it at all.

"You three in the back, go ahead and crawl on out of there."

Will's hand dropped to the door handle, but before he could

open his door, Gus stomped on the gas. The officer near the ATVs jumped back just in time as Gus swerved into the turning lane and raced away. Will grabbed Cayden's arm and pulled him down, covering him with his own body. "Get down, Isabella." He expected bullets to crash through the back glass at any second. He waited and then waited some more.

"Dad, I can't breathe."

Will sat up and turned to look in the direction they'd just come. The officers had jumped on their quads and were taking chase after them, but they couldn't outrun the truck. "I think we're in the clear," he said as they exited the town.

"That was close," Isabella said.

"Too damn close," Gus replied.

As they approached the Trinity River, Will was more concerned than ever about making it to Savanah's in the truck. It was great to be able to move quickly, but it had nearly got them killed numerous times. He was beginning to think it just wasn't worth it. He stared at the old rusty bridge that ran alongside the new one. How long would it take before all the country's infrastructure looked like that?

After the way the trip had gone so far, Will was sort of in shock when they were able to drive through Liberty without encountering trouble. They'd crossed the bridge of the Trinity River, and there wasn't anyone waiting for them on the other side. The truck proceeded east, past a small seafood restaurant and a tire shop without seeing a soul. On first impressions, Liberty looked like any other small town in Texas that you'd drive through and nothing would stand out. It had all the fast-food chain restaurants, convenience stores, and pharmacies of every other town.

"Turn left up there at Main Street," Jaz said.

Gus turned, and they drove over the railroad tracks where an old train depot sat as a reminder of a bygone era when the town likely bustled with activity and commerce. Will stared back as they passed the library. Reading was now one of the few ways to pass the time. Books had almost become obsolete in the digital age, but they were sure to make a big come back now that the internet was gone.

"Which way?" Gus asked at the non-functioning traffic light near the Liberty County Courthouse.

"Just stay straight," Jaz said, eyeing Liberty County's seat of justice as they passed it.

"Where is everyone?" Cayden asked.

"I don't know. It's strange to drive through town and not see anyone out," Jaz said.

"I expected to be stopped like we were in Dalton," Isabella said.

They saw the first signs of life as they passed the Veterans of Foreign Wars post. The two older gentlemen standing in front of the VFW waved as they drove by. As they neared the Walmart, Gus spotted two police cars and called out. "Do I stop?"

"No. They'll take the truck," Jaz said.

"Will?"

"It doesn't matter now. We've made it to your destination," Will said.

"But you need it to get to your sister's," Jaz said.

Will turned to Isabella. "I'm not sure it is a good idea to take the truck. Look how much attention it has attracted so far."

"But Izzy can't walk on her leg."

"I'll be fine. It hardly hurts anymore."

"We'll try to find some bikes or something, but we'll be better off without the truck. I do appreciate the offer though," Will said. He was abashed and looked away. He should have discussed it with Isabella before making a decision that affected her. But regardless of what she thought about it, he wasn't taking that risk with Cayden. They were better off on foot where they could slip in and out of towns unnoticed, even if they had to do so under the cover of darkness.

When Gus slowed the truck, Tanner rapped on the glass. "What are you doing? Just floor it."

"No. We have to stop. We didn't come all this way to get shot a couple of miles from Jaz's mom's."

Gus stopped twenty yards from the police cruiser blocking the side road. They were stopping traffic from turning toward Walmart. Could it be possible that the store had not been completely looted out by now?

"Step out of the truck," the officer yelled.

Gus turned off the vehicle and pocketed the keys before opening his door and getting out. Jaz followed suit, and then Will, Cayden, and Isabella got out and stood beside them. The broad-shouldered officer approached with his gun drawn. He stopped and lowered the pistol. "Jaz? Is that you?"

"Manny, what the hell are you doing pointing a gun at me?" Jaz scolded him.

"How was I supposed to know it was you? Who's truck is that?"

"We borrowed it from a friend," Jaz said, taking a step closer to the officer. "Guys, this is my baby brother, Manny."

Jaz and Manny hugged, and Gus shook the man's hand. "How's Mom?" Jaz asked.

"Bossy as usual. She's over at the store, giving the mayor and city council a hard time."

"Where is everyone? The town was empty when we drove through."

"Everyone's at the Walmart for the distribution."

"Distribution?"

"Yeah, the town distributes food and hygiene items once a day," Manny said.

"You can go on home. I'll let Mom know you're here. She'll be so glad to see you. She's been threatening to go get you every day since the lights went out, but George wouldn't let her. He said that the city had turned into a war zone."

"It has. I'm glad she didn't come. It's pretty bad there."

"I'm glad you got out. I'll see you when we finish up here. I'll bring you some potato chips."

"I knew there was a reason you were my favorite brother." Jaz laughed.

"I'm your only brother," Manny said.

"Not true. Our dad has a son, remember?"

"Nope. Don't claim him," Manny said as he walked back to his police cruiser. He turned back. "Hey, you might want to call out before you go inside. We have a visitor with an itchy trigger finger."

"Visitor?" Jaz said.

"You'll see. Just announce yourself."

FOURTEEN

Will

Gus drove the pickup to the outskirts of town and pulled to the curb in front of a red brick ranch-style house. Will took in the neighborhood. Jaz's parents lived in an older middle-class subdivision north of Liberty. The lawns were all well-kept. A few had trash cans at the curb like they still expected it to be picked up, or maybe the homeowner hadn't made it home after the EMP. It looked safe enough, but you just never knew. It wouldn't have been the place he would have chosen to stay during this crisis. Even if you knew and got along with all your neighbors, how long before they'd turn on you once their kids start going hungry?

A man dressed in a white cowboy hat and boots stepped from the front walkway. He held a pistol in his right hand, and in the other, he had a star-shaped badge. The Texas Ranger wore a pair of khaki pants, a white dress shirt, and a tie.

The "Don't Mess with Texas" slogan came to mind as the lawman stared them down. He wasn't all that tall, but he looked well-built. Will guessed him to be around forty years old, which probably meant he'd been in law enforcement a while.

"Jaz, why is there a ranger at your mother's house?" Gus asked as he put the truck into park in front of the house.

"What do you want?" the lawman asked, still pointing the pistol at the pickup.

"My mom lives here. Who the hell are you?" Jaz asked, totally disregarding the weapon in the man's hand, and opening the door.

"What's your mother's name?" he asked as Jaz exited the vehicle.

"Listen, this is my mother's house. I've had a very shitty day, and I'm tired, so if you ain't going to shoot me, get the hell out of my way so I can go inside."

The ranger looked perplexed as Jaz brushed past him and headed up the walk toward the front door. Gus exited and walked around the bumper with his hands in the air. "I'm with her," he said, continuing up the pathway. Everyone else got out and stood on the sidewalk. The lawman lowered his pistol and watched Gus and Jaz. Will wasn't sure what to do. He hadn't been invited inside and Gus had taken the keys to the truck. The ranger holstered his weapon and pocketed his badge as he approached the pickup. "What about the rest of you?"

"They're my neighbors," Isabella said. "This is my friend, Will, and his son." She nodded to Tanner and Monte. "They're with the Cajun navy. They got stranded here after the EMP."

"The what?"

"After the lights went out."

"You're thinking an EMP did this?" the ranger asked.

Cayden stepped around Will, who had been blocking him in case the lawman's pistol came back out. "We know it did. An FBI agent told us so."

Will's stomach tightened at the memory of the last time he saw Betley. The images of Kim and all the others flooded his mind.

The ranger's eyebrows raised as he pursed his lips and nodded. "Oh yeah? Where was that?"

"Houston."

The ranger leaned forward slightly and eyed Will. "You guys going in or what?"

Will shrugged. "We're not staying."

"Where are you heading then?"

"Louisiana," Will said.

"You guys can come in and get a bite to eat before you run off," Jaz called from the front door.

Isabella didn't hesitate. She grabbed Otis from the back seat and limped toward the door with Cayden right behind her. The ranger nodded toward Monte and Tanner, who were being uncharacteristically quiet. "What about them?"

Will glanced behind him and gave a half shrug. "I don't know what their plans are. We just met out on the road here. I imagine they'll be heading back to Louisiana. You'll have to ask them."

The lawman took a few steps to his left and addressed his question to Monte and Tanner.

"I think I'll wait out here with the truck. Wouldn't want anyone getting any funny ideas and taking off with it," Monte said.

"I'll wait with you, but I'd love a to-go plate of whatever you're having though, Will," Tanner said, opening the front passenger side door to the pickup and taking a seat.

Will followed Isabella and Cayden inside the house, where Jaz and Gus were already pulling food off the pantry shelf. "Beef stew or canned tamales?" Gus asked, holding out two cans.

"Canned tamales? Gross!" Jaz said, shoving the can back at him.

"What about you, Cayden?" Gus asked.

"I don't mind tamales," he replied, and Gus handed him the can.

"You can't eat that. Those aren't tamales. My mamá makes the best tamales in the world," Jaz said, licking her lips.

"Your mamá hasn't made tamales in years," a male voice said from the doorway into a back room. "She practically quit cooking when she moved to Liberty."

Jaz turned and put her hands on her hips. "Well, Marco, you don't look like you've missed any meals."

The man patted his round belly and stepped into the room. He was short and stocky. A bulge under his black T-shirt near his right hip told Will that he was concealing a weapon.

"What are you still doing here? I thought you were going away," Jaz asked.

"The feds never showed up," the man said.

"What's up with the ranger outside?" Gus asked, stepping over and extending his right hand to the man. They shook and then bumped shoulders. Gus didn't appear too concerned about the man's presence. Despite the lack of introduction, Will assumed he was the troubled uncle Jaz had spoken about.

"He showed up right before the lights went out."

"Why? What's he doing here?" Gus asked.

The man pulled a bar stool out from the island and took a seat before answering. Jaz pointed to a small kitchen banquet, and Will, Cayden, and Isabella slid in and began opening cans as Gus placed them on the table in front of them.

"Was he here to arrest your ass again?" Jaz asked when he didn't answer.

"No! He was here to interview me. He wanted info on a couple of cases before I disappeared, and he couldn't get to me."

Jaz cocked her head to the side and glared at him. "He wants to know where the bodies were buried?"

Marco tore the lid off a can of Vienna sausages, pulled one from the container, and popped it into his mouth.

"Have any of Arturo's people been around since the lights went out?"

"Nope. They probably think I'm long gone. I put the word out that I was going to Honduras."

"You should have left by now. If you get my family hurt..." She turned her back on Marco and walked over to the pantry, pulled a small bottle of apple juice from the shelf, unscrewed the lid, and took a drink. "You should leave with Will and Izzy. They can drop you off in Beaumont. You got baby mamas there, right?"

Will stiffened. He hadn't agreed to take the man anywhere. If he was in some kind of trouble, there was no way he was getting in the middle of it.

"Can't. That ranger said I had to stay put until the feds get here."

"The feds ain't coming, Marco."

"Tell him that. He keeps talking like the government is coming to help any day now."

"He has to. He's part of the government," Gus said.

"Everyone around here thinks they're still coming too."

"And you don't?" Gus asked.

"No! We haven't seen a single FEMA worker or anyone from the government. Some folks came through a few days ago saying that this was all across the state. I figure if that is the case, the government is overwhelmed with folks needing help. It could be months before they show up. We'll all have starved to death by then."

The front door opened, and the Texas Ranger entered the kitchen. "What's things like in Houston?" he asked, pulling out a barstool and plopping down next to Marco. He poked his fingers into the Vienna sausage can and popped one into his mouth.

"It's hell. What the hurricane didn't destroy, the bombs are taking care of," Jaz said.

"Bombs?"

"Yes, bombs. The whole damn place is like a war zone. But you'll have to ask them." She jerked her thumb over her shoulder toward Will and the others.

The ranger turned in his seat to face them. "What do you know about the bombing?"

Will wasn't in the mood to go into all they'd been through. He especially didn't want Cayden reliving it. "The city is under attack from Chinese insurgents."

"Insurgents?"

"They've been here a while from what we were told. They've

blown up fuel farms and highway interchanges and attacked Ellington Joint Reserve Base. We saw explosions on our way out of town. That's all I know about it."

The ranger looked like someone had punched him in the gut as he slumped forward in his seat. He removed his cowboy hat and ran a hand through his salt and pepper hair. His tie was already loose around his neck, but he tugged it off and stuffed it into the front pocket of his khaki pants. "So it was an enemy attack. I was afraid it was something like that. What about our military? They're fighting back, right?"

"They are. We saw one of our planes fly over as we were leaving," Will said.

"Well then, it won't be long, and they'll get it all sorted."

"Unless the Chinese invade," Cayden said, wiping chili from his mouth with the back of his hand.

"It's going to take a very long time to get everything back to normal after the EMP, even if the military can defeat the enemy quickly. The power grid is fried, and everything electronic will have to be replaced. That could take months, even years," Isabella said.

Everyone in the room turned and stared at her. No one spoke. The thought of enduring that kind of hardship even for months was difficult to swallow, but years were inconceivable. It would be devastating. Many, many people could die from starvation and disease. And then there was the lawlessness that would descend upon them.

"I guess everyone will have to prepare to endure a while longer," the ranger said.

After everyone finished eating, Will was anxious to be on their way. He needed to get Gus alone to discuss Jaz's suggestion that he take her uncle with them. That was not happening, and he needed to make that clear.

Will whispered to Isabella. "We should say our goodbyes now and head out. I would really like to get to my sister's before dark."

"You still planning on leaving the truck?" she asked.

"No. As concerned as I am about all the attention the vehicle draws, I just want to get to my sister's sooner rather than later." He didn't want to continue on in the truck, but most of their supplies had been left behind when they'd picked up the group back on the freeway. All they had now was what they each carried with them in their backpacks and it wouldn't be enough if they had to spend days walking.

"Could we just get off the freeway and take back roads?" Isabella asked.

Will took time to mull it over. In normal times, she might have been right, but they didn't have a map of the back roads, and he sure didn't know how to get them across all the bayous and rivers without going through cities.

"She has a point," the ranger said, suddenly appearing behind Will. "You'll want to avoid Beaumont for several reasons. The population, the refineries—those are a big problem. You'll want to head north, cross the Neches River at around Silsbee and then drop back south to say around Mauriceville and then east to Deweyville to cross the Trinity River into Louisiana."

Isabella leaned across Cayden. "You know those roads?"

"Sort of."

"Can you tell us which ones to take?" Isabella asked.

The ranger scrunched up his lips and looked to the ceiling. "Oh, I don't know." He dropped his gaze to Isabella and smiled. "Maybe I can just show you, if you have room for one more, that is?"

"Where are you headed?" Will asked.

"I got me a little hunting spot up north of Silsbee along the Naches River. I thought I'd go hang out there till all this blows over." The ranger stepped back and extended his hand. "I'm Ed Sudeski, by the way. I'll get you to the Louisiana border. If you'll have me."

"What do you think?" Will said, turning to Isabella.

"I think we won't make it without someone who knows the roads. Besides, he knows how to shoot."

She had a point. Having someone with law enforcement training would be an asset. But would it hurt them in their effort to find food if they needed to? He might not be too willing to take things without paying. Will studied him for a moment. It was worth the risk. "Sure, we can give you a ride to Silsbee."

FIFTEEN

Will

DAY SEVEN

Will managed to get Monte and Tanner alone to talk about their plans. It hadn't been discussed, but since they were both from Louisiana, Will had assumed they'd be traveling with them to get back home. Their presence on the trip would make him more comfortable. They seemed to know how to handle themselves in challenging situations. Monte appeared to have some sort of formal training, maybe military, and having them come along increased their odds of making it to Savanah's.

"I'm from around Lake Charles, and Tanner is a bit east of there. We'd like to tag along. We sure weren't looking forward to walking all that way," Monte told him.

"The ranger is going. He knows some back roads and can get us around the towns that we need to avoid. He'll be getting off at a place called Silsbee. He said it isn't too far from the Louisiana border. I know my way once we get across the river."

"It appears we have a sound plan. With that route, though, we aren't going to make it by dark. I prefer rolling into unfamiliar places when I can see far ahead."

"I was hoping to drive straight through. The more time we spend out on the road, the more likely we'll encounter trouble."

Will didn't want to go into detail, but he wanted to put as much distance between them and Houston as possible.

"I'd suggest waiting, but it's your ride, so I'll do whatever you decide," Monte said.

"I think there's enough daylight to get you there by dark," the ranger said. He held his hand out to shake hands with Monte.

"So, you really a Texas Ranger? You know all that martial arts shit like *Walker Texas Ranger*?" Tanner asked as he approached.

The ranger turned. Tanner was at least a head taller than him. "I know a little, but I'm no Chuck Norris."

"Well, let's hope we don't need to karate chop anybody then, Walker," Tanner said as he climbed onto the tailgate and slid back against the cab of the truck.

Monte extended his hand to the ranger. "Glad to be riding with you, Walker, and don't worry. Tanner can handle himself in hand-to-hand combat if it comes to that."

If the nickname offended the lawman, he didn't show it. Maybe he got that a lot. It had been a popular television show back in the day—one of Will's grandfather's favorites. He'd been a huge Chuck Norris fan.

They shook hands, and Monte joined Tanner in the rear of the vehicle. Will climbed into the driver's seat and adjusted the mirrors. He was a little taller than Gus. Isabella and Cayden were in the back seat while the ranger rode shotgun in the passenger seat. Will was pleased that the goodbyes were quick. Jaz and Gus stood in the doorway and waved as the group pulled away from the curb and drove off. Will glanced into the rearview mirror. A single tear spilled over Isabella's eyelid and down her cheek. Will hadn't thought she and Jaz were that close, but he must have been wrong.

"We could go back and get him," Cayden said, placing a hand on her shoulder.

Will hadn't noticed that she hadn't brought Otis. He'd been preoccupied with planning their route.

"No. He's better off there. It's too far for him to travel," Isabella said.

"Are you sure?" Will asked. "I don't mind turning around."

She shook her head. "I..." She choked back a sob. "I'm worried if we get carjacked like back in Houston that I wouldn't be able to get his carrier out in time. I couldn't bear to think of what some crazy person might do to him."

The memory of their carjacking was traumatic for them all. It had been the scariest moment of his life, watching that criminal drive off with his Jeep with his son still in the vehicle. He could understand her fear. It was a selfless thing to leave her beloved Otis behind and he admired her for being able to make that sacrifice for the feline.

"I'm sure that Jaz's mother will take great care of him. She's a special lady. I wish you could have met her. She's nothing like her brother," Walker said.

"I know he'll be fine there. Someday soon, he'll be a loving companion to Jaz's baby." She sniffed and wiped her tears.

Isabella was quiet as they drove back through town and Will kept glancing back to check on her. She'd lost so much already. Leaving her cat behind seemed like a cruel blow.

"Take that left there before the roadblock." Walker pointed as they approached the intersection where the Liberty Police Department had their checkpoint.

The road wound around, avoiding the Walmart store and the population of Liberty gathered there, eventually coming out near Highway 90 and the little Creole community of Ames, Texas. Walker gave them the history of the town as they turned east on the outskirts of the city. Will hadn't known that such a large community of Creoles lived outside of Louisiana. He was lost in the conversation as they passed three elderly African American men standing outside an old white-clad church. The men waved as the pickup passed them. Walker returned their greeting.

"How long have you been a Texas Ranger?" Cayden asked.

"About fifteen years. I joined after I left the army."

"So you were a soldier too?"

"For a while."

"Did you ever kill anyone?"

Will cringed. He was about to scold him when Walker answered. "That's what the army trained me to do. Doesn't mean I enjoyed it."

"My dad and Isabella had to kill people."

Walker's head pivoted toward Isabella.

"We were involved in some trouble back in Houston. It was self-defense, I swear," Isabella said.

Walker said nothing.

At that point, Will felt the need to explain, so he filled the lawman in on how they'd met Kim and Betley and what led up to the fight with the Chinese Mafia.

"It's like another nine eleven, but nationwide. I can't believe our intelligence community missed a plot like this," Walker finally said.

"Analyst Stephens said she'd been working on it for a while. I guess they were too late to stop them," Isabella said.

"And this CIA analyst and FBI agent were at Ellington when it was hit?" Walker asked.

"We all were," Cayden said. "Isabella was buried under the rubble when they bombed the flight museum."

"That where you got your injuries?" he asked.

"Yes. Mostly," Isabella said.

Walker grew quiet, likely trying to take it all in. The section of highway they were on turned rural quickly and Will was grateful to be away from people and the potential for trouble. That was until five miles later when they approached a small convenience store. In its parking lot sat an old beat-up pickup truck, a side-by-side utility vehicle, and several all-terrain vehicles. An overweight man with a bushy beard sat on one of them with a beer in one hand and a cigarette in the other. He wore a surprised expression as Will stomped on the gas to quickly get past him.

Rounding a curve in the road, Will could see that the road ended at another highway. "Quick, which way?" Will asked.

Walker pointed. "Take that left turn."

"Left! Are you sure?" Will repeated.

"Yes. Left."

SIXTEEN

Will

DAY SEVEN

Will took the turn a little too fast and veered off the roadway slightly but managed to move back onto the highway without over-correcting and tossing Monte and Tanner out of the bed of the truck. A moment later, Monte rapped on the back glass. Will looked into the rearview mirror to see three ATVs racing up behind them. Will glanced down at the speedometer. He was doing forty-five and accelerating. They should be able to outrun them pretty quickly. He heard a shot.

"Did he just shoot those men?" Isabella asked, turning in her seat.

Will glanced into the side mirror. All three quads had left the roadway.

"Did you shoot them?" Isabella repeated, her voice high-pitched.

"I sure as shit did. I fired at them before they could shoot my ass," Monte said.

Isabella turned back around in a huff and crossed her arms. To Will's surprise, Walker was quiet about the matter. Will glanced back at Cayden. He seemed unfazed by it all. That almost concerned Will more than if he'd been upset by it. He didn't want his son so desensitized to violence.

A desolate length of road stretched out before them and Will's thoughts drifted back to the battle at the storage unit and Kim Yang's death right there in front of his son. Before he knew it, they were on the outskirts of another small town. The Daisetta Fire Station's bay doors were up, and the fire engines missing. He pointed. "They must have been out on a call when the EMP hit."

"Must have," Cayden said.

Monte was standing in the bed of the truck facing the town. All Will could see was his legs as he leaned against the rear sliding window. He banged on the roof of the pickup. "Roadblock ahead."

Will leaned forward to look for it.

"Take that right turn there. We'll take the back streets and avoid it," Walker said.

Will was amazed the lawman knew the streets of all these small towns. He was even more glad they'd run into him. They wound around and finally came out back onto the highway and continued north for several more miles before turning east again near a little place called Batson.

They were forty miles from Silsbee when they approached an old Chevy truck stopped in the middle of the road with both doors open. Will slowed to pull around it. Blood trailed from the driver's seat onto the pavement, and the windows were all smashed. Someone had encountered trouble.

"See anyone?" Will asked him.

"No. Someone must have come by and taken them to the hospital," Walker replied.

"Don't look, Cayden," Will said, expecting to see a body or two off in the ditch up ahead with that much blood.

A few miles later, as they approached the bridge, a figure appeared in the roadway in front of them. "Don't shoot!" Isabella cried out. She slid open the rear window and repeated it.

Walker drew his pistol and held it in his lap as Will slowed the truck. He stopped twenty-five yards from a middle-aged man with his arm around a woman's waist. Her foot was bandaged. Before Will could say anything, Isabella was out of the truck and limping toward them. Walker and Monte were right behind her. Walker had holstered his pistol. Monte, however, held his at the low ready, prepared to respond if necessary.

Will put the pickup in park and told Cayden to stay put before exiting the vehicle and approaching the couple himself.

"Let's get her into the truck," Isabella said. "Will, help me." Isabella put her arm around the woman's waist and tried to take her from the man. He looked like he was going to protest but didn't.

"What happened?" Will asked.

Walker slid his arm around the woman from the other side. "Let me help, Isabella," he said.

"They attacked us for no reason. They appeared out of nowhere and just beat the shit out of my truck," the man said, gesticulating with weathered hands. He adjusted his cowboy hat and looked toward the west.

"I never even saw them. They had my door open, and I was on the ground before I knew it," the woman said. The petite woman's sandy blonde ponytail stuck out of the back of a ball cap.

"How many of them were there?" Walker asked as he moved the woman toward the pickup.

"Four," the woman said.

"They were hoodlums from town. They must have gotten stranded like Glory."

"I didn't see anyone on the road as I drove home, Alan," Glory said.

"They dragged us both out of the truck and tried to drive off, but I had the keys in my hand."

"I tried to run, but I twisted my ankle. I think it's broken."

"How did you get away?" Isabella asked as she and Walker placed Glory into the back seat.

"We were forced to defend ourselves," Alan said, climbing in beside his wife and placing her foot in his lap.

Will stood with his hand on the door, ready to close it. "Which way did your attackers flee?"

"They didn't. They're still back there in that field near my truck. They won't be bothering anyone anymore," Alan said.

Will's gaze turned to Walker. He was the law officer.

"Were they armed?" Walker asked.

"With crowbars," Alan said.

"She needs a doctor. Is there one in town?" Isabella asked.

"There's a medical clinic but I doubt it's open with the electric out. All we got is Doc Townsend."

He'll be at his ranch north of town," Glory said. She shifted in her seat and winced in pain. "Just take me home, Alan. I'll be all right."

"Would you fine folks mind giving us a ride back to our ranch? It's about ten miles north of here."

Will poked his head into the cab of the truck, turned the key, and checked the gas gauge. They were at half a tank. The way the old truck guzzled gasoline, Will wasn't sure they'd have enough fuel to get to Savanah's as it was.

"I have fuel—lots of fuel. I'll fill your tank up and send you on your way with a couple of gas cans," Alan said.

Will couldn't pass that offer up. It was only a few more miles out of their way, but something tugged at the back of his mind. Wasn't that what he'd said when he'd offered to detour to take Isabella and Kim to the hospital? He surprised himself when he said yes to the man but hoped he wouldn't regret it.

"I need to pack up camp and get my rifle," Alan said, slowly easing out from under his wife's foot.

"I can help," Tanner said. Where are you camped?"

"Down by the creek."

"How long have you been out here?" Will asked.

"Since the first day after all the technology failed." Alan stopped and turned. "Glory had gone into town and when she didn't return, I went looking for her. We were on our way home when those thugs stopped us. After that, Glory couldn't walk, and I've got bad knees so I couldn't carry her. We've been waiting for someone we knew to come by. They never did."

Alan and Tanner returned with a large army drab-colored pack with tons of tools hanging off it and an AR-15 rifle. Tanner threw them in the back of the pickup and he, Monte, Isabella, and Cayden loaded up into the bed. Alan pointed as they passed his abandoned truck. "That's where they ambushed us."

"What happened?" Walker asked.

"They shot my tires out as I drove by. When they shot through the side glass, I ducked, and I guess I hit the brakes because they were on us in a flash, smashing the windshield and side windows. When they pulled Glory from the truck, I went for the pistol I carry concealed and shot at the guy. He dropped her and took off running. But one of the son-of-a-bitches hit me from behind. It was lights out for a moment."

"I was able to get my 9mm pulled and fired," Glory said.

Alan stared out the side window. "I was struggling with one of them for the keys when I heard the shots. I released my grip on the keys and raised my pistol. The guy backed up, raised his hand, and pitched the keys into the woods. That's when his buddy sucker-punched me from behind. I fired when I saw the guy raise the tire iron."

Glory's forehead wrinkled, and she looked down at her hands. "We spent ten minutes looking for the keys before deciding we'd never find them in the marsh. We didn't want to stick around and wait for them to come back, so we started toward town."

Alan patted Glory's hand. "About the time we reached the bridge over the creek, we heard the ATV and went to hide, hoping they wouldn't see us. Well, they did. This time, though, I didn't hesitate. I took the shot and dumped their asses in the creek."

"It sounds like a clear case of self-defense, but you should report it to law enforcement as soon as possible," Walker said.

The two looked at each other for a long moment. Will could

see they were worried about the legal consequences of their actions, but he wasn't sure how the justice system would function in such chaos. He'd likely be leery of self-reporting the incident as well. He couldn't imagine being stuck in some jail awaiting a trial that may never come.

Minutes later, they arrived outside a wooden gate crossing a gravel drive. Above it was a wrought-iron sign that read, "Rockin D Ranch." Will could see a two-story house, an old wood barn, and a newer metal pole barn in the distance. As Alan got out and unlocked the gate, a dog barked in the distance and then raced down the drive toward them. The dog followed the truck to the house and leaped inside the back of the pickup the moment the doors opened. Alan tried to pull him away, but he jumped up and began licking Glory's face. "Good to see you too, Rosco!"

SEVENTEEN

Isabella

Alan and Glory's two-story home was decorated in traditional farm style. A Texas flag was framed and hung over the sofa and two well-worn recliners faced a large-screen television.

Alan placed Glory down on the sofa and propped her foot on a stack of cushions. "I'll get the medkit and put you on a clean splint."

Isabella picked up a framed photo of the couple with two young boys—a happy family playing on the beach. Seeing the picture made her homesick. The way things were looking, it might be a very long time before she would see her family again. Once Glory was comfortable, Alan led Will and the guys out to his shop to fill the gas cans.

"That door to the left of the refrigerator is our walk-in pantry. If you look on the second shelf on the right, there should be some MREs," Glory said.

"Some what?"

"Meals ready to eat. I don't think they taste all that great, but Alan insists on stocking them. There are plastic grocery bags in that doohickey over the back of the door. You take some for you and your group."

Isabella's mouth fell open as she entered the pantry. There had to have been enough food in there to last for months, if not years. There were canned goods and stacks of five-gallon buckets of rice, beans, wheat, sugar, and numerous other things. One whole wall had jars of vegetables, likely from their garden. Isabella loaded six MREs into grocery bags and placed them by the front door.

"It's very generous of you to share your food with us," she said.

"I like to repay kindness when I can. There's not much of it left in the world and I am truly grateful that the Lord sent you our way. I was getting so tired of eating rice and beans out there by the creek."

Isabella took a seat in the recliner next to the sofa. "I'm glad we could help. I hope your ankle heals soon."

"Me too. Alan is already talking about heading out to find our boys. I'll need to stay back and take care of the ranch. I got too many chores to do to be laid up in bed."

"Where are your boys?"

The door banged open before she could answer and Alan flew past them. As he disappeared down a hallway, Will and the others hurried through the door.

"What's wrong?" Isabella said, getting to her feet.

Will grabbed Cayden and shoved him to the floor near the sofa. "Stay down," he said.

"Will, what's wrong? What happened out there?"

Alan returned with an armful of rifles. Will grabbed two and shoved one into her arms. Alan handed a third to Walker. As Alan disappeared again, Will, Walker, Monte, and Tanner all began checking and loading ammunition into their rifles.

Glory sat up. "Isabella, open the top of the coffee table for me."

Isabella pulled on the top, and it hinged open. Inside were two ArmaLite style rifles and several pistols, all laid out on black Polyethylene foam.

"Give me the AR-15 on the right and one of the handguns. I'll need a couple of magazines for the rifle too."

Who are these people? thought Isabella. They weren't the sweet old couple she'd thought them to be.

"You better take a couple of mags for yourself," Glory said. She pointed at Cayden. "Can you shoot?"

Cayden nodded and reached for a pistol. Isabella grabbed his arm. "No. You need to ask your dad."

"I've been shooting since I was five years old. I know how to handle a weapon. My dad taught me the four laws of gun safety."

"Will?"

"Take the 9mm but keep it on safety until I tell you to take it off," Will said.

Isabella straightened and clapped her hands loudly several times. "Stop! Someone better tell me what the hell is going on here."

"There is a car at the gate," Monte said.

"A car? What about it?"

"Men with guns got out of it," Will said, matter-of-factly.

"That would be Ricky and the rest of Lyle's family," Glory said.

"Who the hell are Ricky and Lyle? Why are they here with guns?" Isabella said, moving toward the window.

Tanner stuck his arm out and blocked her. "Stay away from the windows."

"The guys we killed out on the road were Ricky's brothers. They must have been waiting here for us to return or something."

"Let's just go, Will," Isabella said.

"We can't. They're blocking the gate."

Alan rushed through the living room and flung open the door. "I'm going out to the barn. I'll draw their fire. You guys go around the back of the house and try to get to your truck. Drive through the field. Knock down the fence if you have to."

Glory tried to stand. "Alan, no. You can't go out there alone."

"They aren't going to just go away, Glory. I have to draw them away from the house. I'll lead them off toward the Muellers' barn. You go with them. They can drop you at Doc Townsend's, and I'll be in town shortly."

"Hell no!" Glory said, hopping across the floor toward him. "I go where you go. It's been that way for twenty-five years, and it ain't about to change now."

"I don't have time to argue with you, woman. You have to go with Will and Isabella. They'll get you to town."

"She's right. You can't go out there alone," Walker said.

"What are you going to do, ranger? You going to stroll out there, flash your badge and arrest them?" Monte asked.

His tone took Will aback. He wasn't sure where all that antagonism was coming from.

"You've got the right idea about drawing them away from the house. If you draw them out into the open, Tanner and me can pick 'em off," Monte said.

"That's murder," Walker said.

"No, that's self-defense. The man has a right to protect his family and property—Castle Doctrine."

Will suddenly realized the lawman's morals and ethics were still grounded in the pre-attack-on-America world.

"I ain't got time to stand around here debating. You're free to arrest me, ranger, but I'm not going to let those asshats hurt my wife or take what's mine," Alan said as he exited.

"I'm coming with you," Tanner said. "I ain't running like a scared kid. You coming, Monte?"

Monte glared at Walker as he stepped past him. "Hell yeah!"

"Alan!" Glory called after him but received no response before the door shut.

Isabella grabbed Will's arm. "Will?"

"I think we should hunker down here. It's too risky to try to get to the truck."

Glory hopped over to the window and parted the curtain. "We

need people at the windows and doors then. If they don't go after Alan, they'll likely set the house on fire and smoke us out. We need to see them before they get close enough to do that."

"What makes you think they'll do that?" Walker asked.

"Cause that is what they've been doing for the last decade to settle feuds."

Isabella moved to the kitchen and peered out of the window over the sink. There were very few trees or shrubs near the back of the house. She found that unusual. Their cooling bill must have been expensive without trees shading the house from the brutal sun. Isabella pulled the rifle up to her cheek and checked the scope. At about two hundred and fifty yards, there was a barbed-wire fence. Hanging on it was a metal target with several bullet holes. It seemed that Alan had sighted in his rifle for that range, so she knew she could be accurate to the distance. She scanned back and forth and saw no one.

"You should move your son to the bathroom down the hall. That's the safest place—no windows," Glory said.

"Cayden, you—" Will started to say.

"I'm not hiding this time. I can shoot. I'm thirteen, not three."

Will blinked a few times and stared at him in silence for a long moment. "Let me see that pistol," he said finally, holding out his hand. Cayden held it out, and Will took it, flicked the safety off, dropped the magazine, and ejected the round in the chamber. He reinserted the magazine and snicked the safety back on before handing it back to his son.

Cayden defiantly took the pistol off safety and chambered a round. "Cocked, locked, and ready to rock," he said as he pushed the safety back up with his thumb. "I'll take the back door."

Everyone stared at him as he walked into the kitchen. He placed himself against the wall between the back door and the wall of the pantry. He nodded to Isabella. "I've got from twelve o'clock to three. What do you have?"

Isabella looked back over her shoulder. Will was still standing there, staring at Cayden with his mouth agape. Walker had moved to the front door. She could no longer see Glory. Isabella returned her gaze to the window and the backyard. "I've got nine to twelve o'clock." She scanned through the scope and once more stopped at the target on the fence. Her gaze traveled a well-worn path to about fifty yards out, where a lonely bird bath sat surrounded by flowers. She was ready but unsure about the rules of engagement.

"Um—ranger?" She couldn't recall his name and didn't feel comfortable calling him Walker. She wasn't sure if Monte had meant it in a derogatory way or not. "If they have a gun in their hands and I shoot, is that legal?"

"If they've got a gun, you better shoot. They won't hesitate to fire at you," Glory called from down the hall.

"I—" Shots rang out, and Walker never had the opportunity to finish his sentence.

"Two down on the south side near fifty yards from the barn," Will called out from the side door.

"Alan's up in the loft," Glory said, glee in her voice.

"They've got rifles," Will said.

A second later, a round shattered the front window. Everyone dropped to the floor. Isabella scrambled over to Cayden and threw her arm around him. "We have to move."

He shook her off. "We have to guard the back door. We can't let them get inside."

"Cayden, get to the bathroom. This shit is serious," Will yelled.

Cayden stood and returned to his post by the back door. "The backyard is still clear."

Walker moved to the broken window and returned fire. That was when the seriousness of their situation hit Isabella.

"Fire! Fire!" Glory called out. "The bedroom is on fire."

Isabella dropped down and pulled open the door to a cabinet under the sink. She groped around and grabbed the fire extinguisher before racing down the hall meeting Glory just outside the entrance to the back bedroom on the right. "I heard a crash and then saw the room go up in flames."

"You open the door and I'll spray," Isabella said, holding up the extinguisher.

Glory turned the knob slowly and then shoved open the door. The heat was intense already, and the smoke stung Isabella's eyes. She pulled the pin, pointed the nozzle into the room, and released the locking mechanism. Isabella squeezed the lever and sprayed into the room, sweeping from side to side before moving toward the opposite wall. Within a minute or two, the flames were out, but the smoke and fine powder from the extinguisher made it hard to breathe. Isabella backed out of the room and closed the door.

When she returned to the kitchen, Will and Cayden were missing, and the back door stood open.

EIGHTEEN

Will

DAY SEVEN

"I've got one on the west side coming out from behind the barn. He's armed with a pistol," Will called out to Walker.

"There's two out by the truck," Walker said.

A shot rang out, and Cayden yelled. "Dad! Tanner's hit."

Will ran to the back door and pushed Cayden back toward the pantry. "Stay down." He scanned the side yard to the stables and spotted Tanner on the ground, attempting to crawl back to the house.

"We have to help him," Cayden said.

Will couldn't see a shooter and assumed they'd moved back around the barn. He ran back to the side door to see if he could tell where the man had gone then shifted to the left side of the door to get a better view of the side with the lean-to and heard the back door open. "Cayden!"

Will got there just as Cayden sprinted off toward Tanner firing his pistol as he ran. He screamed his son's name and ran after him. Will reached him just as he was helping Tanner to his knees. Two gunshots rang out, and Will dove on top of Cayden and Tanner. He rolled off and scrambled to his feet, pulling on Cayden's arm as he did. Tanner tried to stand but only made it up on one knee before a round struck him in the torso. Will grabbed Cayden by the shirt and ran for the shed.

Anger mixed with fear as he shoved his son back against the side of the weathered building. Will raised his rifle and peered around the corner to see if the shooter had followed them. Will stepped out and fired when he spotted a man sprinting from the front of the barn to the back of the truck. The first round struck the man in the arm but didn't seem to faze him. The second round struck him in the leg. He turned to fire at Will, and when he did, Will squeezed off another shot, hitting the man in the chest.

Isabella screamed, and Will dropped back behind the barn. A previously unseen shooter fired, hitting the side of the old wooden structure only inches from where Will had just been standing. He pushed Cayden to the ground and covered him. When the shooting stopped, Will pointed to the west corner. "Stay behind me. We're going to try to make it to the shop." He needed to get Cayden out of the line of fire. They were cut off from the house. The only other structure was the metal shop building over a hundred feet from the old wooden barn. The galvanized steel building wouldn't stop a bullet, but Will hoped something inside could provide them with sufficient cover.

His thoughts were a jumbled mess. His first priority was to Cayden, but Isabella's scream continued to ring in his head. Not knowing if the men had made it into the house was torture.

"Where are Alan and Monte?" Cayden asked.

"I don't know. Stay close. We have to make it to the shop."

Just as they reached the edge of the barn, Will heard Alan calling for them. "Will, over here."

Will stuck his head around the corner. There weren't any shooters visible but the range between the buildings would put them out in the open too long. It was too much distance to cover.

"Will, I'll cover you," Monte yelled.

Will looked up. Monte's face appeared in a loft window.

"Do you see them?"

"Two are by our truck. The others are dead. Come on over. They can't see you from where they are."

Relief washed over Will. If Monte had eyes on the only two gunmen left alive, then Isabella was safe. He reached down and took Cayden's right hand. The two ran to the side door as quickly as possible. When they reached the metal building, Will rammed his shoulder into the side of it and nearly passed out from the pain. He pushed through it, reached for the doorknob, and turned. It was locked. They were exposed where they were and would need to go around to the front to get inside, but that would put them in the line of fire for the shooters.

"Monte, the door is locked."

A second later, it opened, and Alan appeared. "Get in."

"Tanner's gone," Will said, moving through the shop. His eyes journeyed the space, landing on the 1951 Chevy truck parked in one of the bays. "There, Cayden. Go sit over there behind the truck." Will moved to the front of the building and pressed back against the wall between the bay doors and a window. He leaned slightly to take in the area between the shop and the driveway. Their truck was about one hundred and twenty-five feet away. Will scanned the space around the back of the vehicle. He saw no one. "Monte," he yelled. "Do you still have eyes on them?"

"No, they dropped down on the passenger side out of view."

Shit!

"Would you see them if they made a break for the house?"

"Yeah, I think so."

You think so?

"I'm going to go around the back of the barn and try to make it to the house," Alan said. "You two stay here."

"Monte should go and cover you. I've got this side."

"Good idea," Alan said. "Monte, follow me back to the house."

"Coming down," Monte said. A second later, his legs appeared on the ladder leading to the loft.

"We need to get back inside and make sure they can't get to the women," Alan said.

Monte dropped his magazine and inserted a fresh one before moving toward the side door.

"Monte, Tanner is down. He's near the lean-to." Will hated to tell him that his friend was dead, but he didn't want him coming across him in the middle of bullets flying and get distracted.

"Dead?"

Will nodded.

Monte hung his head and shook it. Without a word, he made the sign of the cross and pulled open the door. "All clear," he said and stepped outside.

Alan looked back at Cayden and then at Will. "We're going to finish this, don't you worry." He took off running, leaving the door standing open.

Will returned his attention to the truck. He still couldn't see anyone. He waited and listened. Seconds passed that felt like hours, and then one of the men rose slightly. He was near the front passenger door. He raised his rifle and steadied it on the hood of the pickup. He was aiming toward where Tanner had fallen. Was he waiting for them to come retrieve the body?

The report of a rifle boomed, and the man dropped out of view. A second later, another man stood and took off running toward the road. Walker came into view. He was giving chase. The man turned to fire when Will was halfway out the door. Walker was still running toward the man, his pistol gripped with both hands. Will raised his weapon, lined up the shot, and began moving his finger toward the trigger guard. He heard the sound of the rifle a second before the man dropped. Walker looked back. The shot had come from behind him.

NINETEEN

Isabella

The rifle shook in Isabella's hands but she did her best to keep her sights on the torso of the man on the ground in front of Walker. It had all happened so fast. From the moment she realized that Walker hadn't seen the man raise his pistol until she'd squeezed the trigger had occurred in a fraction of a second. Isabella hadn't had time to think. She'd just reacted.

She felt Glory brush against her, and then her hands slide down her arm. "It's over now," Glory said, pushing the barrel of Isabella's rifle toward the ground. Isabella slowly looked up and met Glory's gaze. "Let's go back inside, and I'll get you something to calm your nerves." Isabella was trembling so hard that she was almost immobile. Glory had to help her turn back toward the door. She didn't recall going inside or taking a seat at the kitchen table. Somehow she glanced up, and Will and Cayden were standing over her each with a hand on her shoulders. Tears began to flow when she saw the concern on their faces.

"It's all right. They're all gone. You got the last one," Will said.

She scanned the room for Walker.

"He's outside with Monte."

"Where's Tanner?" Isabella asked.

"He didn't make it," Cayden said, his voice cracking.

Her head pivoted. "Are you hurt?" she asked, pushing back from the table to look at him.

"I'm fine." He didn't look fine. His eyes were moist and he was gnawing on his thumbnail.

"When I ran into the kitchen, and the two of you were gone, my heart stopped."

"He ran outside to help Tanner and nearly got himself killed," Will said, anger lacing his voice.

"Cayden!" Isabella stood and took his hands in hers. "Don't you ever scare me like that again." She grabbed him into a hug and squeezed him tight, suddenly feeling inadequate. How on earth were they going to keep Cayden safe in this crazy, violent world? She'd only known the kid a week, but she couldn't imagine her life without him.

"I'm sorry I scared you. I just had to help Tanner. He was down and trying to crawl to safety. That's what my dad would have done."

"You're a kid," Will snapped. "You could have got us both killed. You have to do what you're told. It's my job to keep you safe. I can't do that if you're going to be impulsive and run into danger like that."

Cayden stiffened and stepped away from Isabella. He turned his back on them, crossed his arms, walked across the room, and stared out the side door.

"Cayden, your dad and I just don't want anything to happen to you. Your dad couldn't bear it. I…" Isabella swallowed hard. "I couldn't take it. Can you just try to be more careful—for us?"

He said nothing.

Isabella knew it sucked to be at that in-between stage of life when you are not quite a kid and not yet an adult. The impulsive nature of a teen could be dangerous in this new era. Isabella looked at Will. It was hard enough to be a parent before the world fell apart.

Glory walked up with two shot glasses and held them out to Isabella and Will. "You just need to do some training with the boy. He'll learn when and where to take the fight to the enemy. Won't do no good to try to shield him from it. If this doesn't get fixed real quick, the world is going to be full of takers, and he'll need to be able to defend himself."

Isabella studied Will's face, looking for a reaction. He was so protective of his son. It was hard to imagine him letting go of that attitude. But Glory was right about him needing to know how to defend himself. All they'd seen since the EMP was violence. What would happen to Cayden if Will wasn't there to protect him?

Will dropped his head. "You're right. As soon as we get to my sister's, we'll do some training. He already knows how to handle weapons. I've taken him to the range with me, and we've hunted together since he was little. We've never trained on shooting people though. It's something we'll have to discuss for sure."

"No offense, but you might want to start now 'cause he might need it before you get to your sister's."

Isabella had hoped that with all the extra people with gun experience, Cayden was safe, but realized none of them were. Tanner could handle himself, and he'd still gotten killed out there. "I could use a refresher course myself," Isabella said. "I don't know how I was able to be accurate with that shot. I was shaking so much the sight was bouncing all over the place. I could have just as easily hit Walker."

"I'm grateful you didn't," Walker said from the front door. "Thanks, by the way. The sun was in my eyes as I ran. I didn't see him raise his pistol."

"That's why you take them out on sight. You can't take chances like that anymore," Alan said behind him.

Walker turned on him. "You can't just murder people either."

"Is it murder?" Alan stopped in the middle of the living room, rested his rifle across his forearms, and glared at Walker. "Did you have any doubt what those ole boys' intentions were? I sure the hell didn't. They've wanted to gun me down for twenty years. The only thing that stopped them before was the law but there doesn't seem to be any law enforcement around to stop them now."

"We can't turn into a lawless society along with them. We can't let it become a 'kill-or-be-killed' world. Someone has to stand up for the rule of law."

"Well, ranger, that's your job. Not mine," Alan said as he turned and walked into the kitchen. Glory poured a shot glass full of single malt whiskey and handed it to him. Isabella stared at the glass in her hand. She wasn't much of a drinker. When she did, it usually had an umbrella sticking out of it. But her nerves could use something. A shot of the amber liquor might just be enough to give her the courage to get back out there to face the evil, lawless world.

TWENTY

Will

DAY SEVEN

"You sure you should rush off now? What's the hurry? You could stay the night and head out fresh tomorrow," Alan said.

They'd all just returned from burying Tanner near the back of Alan and Glory's property. Everyone was solemn and quiet, especially Cayden. Will was concerned about what all this was doing to his son and vowed that when they arrived at Savanah's, he'd find a way to shield him from all the ugliness the world had become.

Will was worn out. He'd never felt so drained in his life. All he wanted was for this nightmare to be over. He knew it wouldn't be for a very long time, but the next best thing would be to arrive at Savanah's. The thought of curling up and sleeping in the house his grandparents built was comforting. But Alan was right. They were too exhausted to go on. If they encountered any more trouble, they would be in no shape to defend themselves. He hated to admit it, but it was just too risky to head out now. "If the others don't mind, I guess it would be okay to get a little rest and leave first thing in the morning."

Isabella nodded. "I agree. I'm beat. I would love to just sit and watch the sun go down and pretend the world hasn't gone to shit."

Will turned to Monte.

"I'm good either way," Monte said, his voice low and face expressionless.

Will hadn't known Tanner, but he seemed to have been a good man, and Monte would surely miss him.

"Walker?"

"I agree. We should rest up tonight. It is very kind of you two to offer your home to us for the night," Walker said, tipping his hat.

He hadn't said much since his discussion with Alan about the morality of Alan's shoot-on-sight stance with the men that had attacked his ranch. Will was sure that it went against all the ranger's training, but they were alive because of it. Will's issue was that he couldn't be sure that he could make snap decisions about who posed an imminent threat and who were just fellow survivors like themselves.

While Cayden followed Glory out to the barn to help tend to some of their animals, Will joined Isabella on the swing under a shade tree near Glory's rose garden. Neither said a word as they watched the sun slip over the horizon. Will's eyelids grew heavy with the rhythmic rocking as the sound of crickets relaxed him. It reminded him of nights spent sleeping under the stars in his grandfather's backyard as a kid. He laid his head back, and as he started to drift off, images of all the violence of the last few days invaded his brain, and he jumped. Isabella flinched and then gently slid her hand into his.

"That's what happens when I close my eyes too," she whispered. She paused. "Tell me it will get better."

He wished he could. He'd give anything to be able to assure her that everything would be all right, but he didn't believe it. This was just the beginning. There were so many scenarios that played out in his mind, the scariest among them, the military's failure to prevent the Chinese invasion. If that happened, nowhere would be safe.

"We're going to do everything we can to make it better. We have to try to think positive and not dwell on all that we've been through so far." He stroked his finger over the top of her hand. "We can use it to learn to be stronger and more prepared for what comes next."

"I'll try," she whispered.

"Dad?"

Will jumped to his feet. "What's wrong?" He moved toward his son's voice, and then a flashlight flicked on. Cayden was standing near the barn with a galvanized bucket in his hand.

"Nothing. I just couldn't see you. I wanted to know if you and Isabella would like some hot chocolate. Glory let me milk her cow. She said they have plenty for cocoa."

"I'd love some, son."

"Me too," Isabella said.

It was the little things now that made a world of difference. In the midst of all the horror, he could enjoy a cup of hot cocoa and hear his son describe how he milked a cow to get it. He'd cherish these little moments and do his best to focus on them and not the cold, lifeless look in the eyes of the dead that now haunted him day and night.

TWENTY-ONE

Savanah

DAY EIGHT

Pete's son, Beau, called out to them even before they reached the gate crossing their driveway. "Good morning. What are you folks doing out so early?"

"We're looking for Jason," Mr. B replied.

"Ain't seen him."

"Is your daddy around?" Savanah asked.

"Nope."

"Where is he?"

"Don't know."

He knew. He just wasn't allowed to say, or he wasn't telling them. But why? "We need to talk to him. Can you tell him we came by?"

"Sure thing." He shifted closer to the gate, and Savanah could sort of make out a human form under his leafy camouflage. "You think I could stop in sometime and visit with Kendra? It's boring as heck hanging out here all day."

Savanah wasn't ready for boy problems. Kendra was fourteen and it would be completely natural for her to be interested in spending time with Beau, but with all that was going on...

"Mrs. B has her pretty busy, but I imagine if you don't mind pitching in cleaning stalls and such," Mr. B chimed in.

At first, it pissed Savanah off. It wasn't his place to consent to her daughter having male company, but Beau's silence told her she had nothing to worry about. Cleaning stalls hadn't been on the kid's agenda.

"Well, we have to get going," Savanah said, stepping back onto the blacktop road. Instinctually, she looked both ways before moving to the middle of the street. "Where to now?"

"We should check with Rod and then stop by the Masters and Herberts. Jason might have tried to get through to them one more time."

Rod's wife flung open the door and greeted them with red-ringed, puffy eyes. Her hair was a mess. Her hand flew up to her throat. "Is it Rob? Is he dead?"

Savanah blinked several times. "We just came here looking for him. Obviously, he isn't home. Did he go out yesterday and not come back?" Savanah was seeing a pattern, but not one that made any sense. Jason, Pete, and now Rob were missing. According to Blake, they didn't go to Sugar Hill. Where did they go then?

"No. He didn't come home. He said he wouldn't be long."

"Did Jason stop by here yesterday? Did they leave together?"

"No. Pete came by. He said he needed help with something. Rob grabbed his rifle and gear and took off on the quad."

"Erin, was there anyone else with Pete?" Mr. B asked.

"He didn't come up to the door, but I saw someone out by the road. He was in one of those side-by-sides. I didn't recognize him."

Savanah turned to Mr. B. "Could that have been Blake?"

"Blake from over on Teartop Road?" Erin asked. "It wasn't

him. I went to school with his wife. I know what he looks like. This guy didn't look like a cop. He looked city."

"City?" Savanah asked.

"Yeah. Polo shirt and khaki shorts."

"Sounds like someone from Sugar Hill," Savanah said, more to herself than anyone. It didn't make sense. Who was this man, and why had Pete and Rod gone off with him?

"They could be from town—maybe from the mayor's office. That planning and zoning guy was always dressed pretty preppy," Mr. Bertrand said.

"You think?" That made more sense. He could live nearby or know Rob or Pete somehow.

"But you didn't see Jason at all yesterday?" Savanah asked Erin.

"Jason? No. Not yesterday. Only Pete. I want to go out and look for Rob, but I got nobody to look out for the little ones."

"We'll keep an eye out for him. If we see him, I'll let him know you're concerned," Mr. B said.

"Thanks, Mr. B. I'm just really worried. My Anna is sick and Rob wouldn't stay gone this long if he could help it."

"What's wrong with Anna?" Savanah asked.

"She got stung yesterday. Her arm is swollen up something awful. She just cries and cries."

Savanah turned her head back toward her farm. She had several herbal remedies that might help, but it would take time to go get them and she needed to find Jason. Her eyes journeyed an overgrown side yard full of native plants. Seeing the ones she was searching for, Savanah walked over and picked a handful of plantain and yarrow leaves.

"What are you doing?" Erin asked.

Savanah handed her the yarrow. "Crush these leaves." She held out the plantain leaves. "Chew on these and then combine it with the crushed yarrow and apply it to her arm. It should help reduce the swelling."

Erin looked at her sideways but took the plants and thanked her.

"We have to get going. If you see Jason, will you tell him that we were looking for him?"

Erin nodded. "You do the same with Rob."

"Will do," Mr. B replied.

Once they were back on the road, Savanah stopped and faced Mr. Bertrand. "Something strange is going on. Either that stranger is from Sugar Hill or Vincent. Either way, I have a feeling it isn't good. Jason has to be with them, but where?"

"We could hitch up the horses and ride into town and have a look-see."

"I don't think Jason would go all the way into town without stopping to tell us," Savanah said.

"Well, there is only one way to find out."

"I think we should go back and alert Blake and then Luca and Jane. We need to be ready if something bad is headed our way. That is the only reason that I can imagine that Jason would have gone off like this."

"Let's hope that isn't the case. We're not all that well prepared to defend the farm."

"Tell me about it."

Blake looked like he'd been sleeping. His mother-in-law had been reluctant to wake him. Maybe it was something in Savanah's tone that changed her mind. She'd tried not to sound panicked, but from the woman's abrupt turnaround, she hadn't been convincing enough. He entered the room, rubbing his eyes. After being out all night spying on Sugar Hill, he was likely dead tired, but Savanah wasn't sorry. He needed to know what they'd learned. She was hoping that he would come to a different conclusion and ease her anxiety.

"So, you didn't find Jason?" he said, taking a seat on the sofa.

Savanah and Mr. B were still standing just inside the door. They hadn't been invited to take a seat. It was strange and unneighborly of Mrs. Herbert, but Savanah pushed it from her mind.

Savanah started filling him in. "Rob and Pete are missing as well. Erin, Rob's wife, said Pete arrived at their door and there was a guy she didn't recognize waiting in a side-by-side at the road."

"You think that means trouble for us?" Blake asked.

"I don't think Jason, Rob, and Pete would go off and leave their families alone at a time like this unless it did have something to do with a direct threat to us."

Blake stood and motioned for them to follow him. They crossed the living room and entered the kitchen at the back of the house. It was large with an eat-in dining area. He pointed. "Take a seat. I need to get something in my gut while we talk this through."

While Blake ate soup from a can, they discussed all the alternative theories they could come up with, but in the end, Blake agreed that something was likely amiss. "The quantity of goods I saw moving through the gates at Sugar Hill leads me to believe they came from a store or warehouse of some kind. It was way too much for one house or even several. Besides, by now, they've cleared out most of the farms around here. I doubt there's much left."

"It could have come from the grocery store in town. The chief and his officers were guarding it when I left there the day all this started but if the Blanchards have control over the town, they have all the food in the stores."

"Why would they move it all the way out here? They don't give two hoots about the residents of Sugar Hill and I doubt any of it will be fed to them," Mr. B said.

"Maybe there's trouble in town," Blake said.

Savanah ran her hand down the length of her braid. It was so frustrating not knowing what was going on. How could they prepare if they had no idea when or how trouble was coming? Her anger at Jason for leaving was boiling to the surface.

"What about Pete's kin?" Mr. B said.

Savanah raised her eyebrows. "What about them?"

"They got tons of guns, ATVs, and know-how. Why don't we ask them to go check out the town and see if that's where everyone went?"

"We could ask, but why haven't they already if they were concerned?" Savanah asked.

Mr. B shrugged one shoulder. "His kid didn't seem all that concerned. Staying gone may not be new for Pete. Maybe they don't know that Rob and Jason are missing as well."

"If they're well armed and have transportation, I don't think it would hurt to at least fill them in on what we're thinking. Let me grab my boots and I'll go over there with you."

"We want to speak with your uncles, Beau," Savanah called from the Ashbys' gate.

She waited, but no one answered.

"Hello?" Luca yelled.

To Savanah's surprise, he hadn't hesitated to join them after Savanah had filled everyone back home in on the situation with Jason, Pete, and Rod going missing. Mr. Bertrand agreed to stay behind to help defend the homestead and Savanah's children. She was grateful to him for that.

"Where are they? They'd never leave this gate unguarded," Savanah said.

"Something must have drawn them away. Maybe trouble on the other side of their property," Blake said.

"Should we go in?" Savanah asked.

"Let me," Luca replied. "I can run up to the house and see if anyone is home."

Savanah's gaze turned to Blake.

"I think you're likely to get yourself shot."

"Then what do we do now?" Savanah asked.

"I don't think it's a good idea to go into town without backup. Even if we discovered Jason and the others were in some type of trouble there, we'd be powerless to help without the Ashbys or someone more than the three of us."

"So we do nothing?" Savanah couldn't fathom going home and waiting.

"Not nothing. We go home and prepare the best we can," Blake said, turning toward the road.

Savanah stared at his back as he walked away. The not knowing was killing her. She just couldn't walk away and not try to find out what had happened to Jason and the others and what might be coming for them next.

"I'm going to go up to the house and see if I can tell if they had some sort of trouble or what. I'm not sure what I'll find, but at least I'll know that I tried," Savanah said, stepping on the middle pipe of the gate and hiking her other leg over the top.

Luca grabbed her by the belt. "Savanah, wait. I should go. You got kids."

Savanah glared at his hand and he removed it.

"Let's both go then," she said, nodding toward the house.

Blake facepalmed. "Shit, you guys. This is a dumbass move. You said they were a shoot-on-sight kind of group."

Savanah landed solidly on the other side of the gate. "You can wait here for us." She was fifty feet down the driveway when she heard Blake's footfalls behind her.

"We should spread out. Maybe walk in the tree line so we'll have cover if they start firing," Blake said.

"Kathy!" Savanah yelled. "It's me, Savanah Fontenot. Don't shoot!"

Blake scrambled behind a row of bushes lining the narrow lane. "It might not be the Ashbys that shoot at us, Savanah."

"What do you want, Savanah?" a female voice called out.

"Kathy?"

"No. This is Kathy's sister, Mary. What do you folks want here?"

"We need to speak with Kathy and Pete's brothers."

"They ain't here."

"Can we come up? Something strange is going on, and I'd like to talk to you and find out what's happened here."

"Just you. I don't know those other two fellows."

Savanah sprinted up the drive. After rounding the last turn, the two-story vinyl-clad house came into view. Mary stood on the porch that ran the length of the front of the home. The rifle in her hand said she wasn't taking any chances.

"What do you want to talk about?" Mary asked.

"Jason took off yesterday, saying he was going to speak with some of the neighbors about those folks at Sugar Hill. He never came home. We stopped at Rob's and he's missing as well. Beau told me earlier that Pete was gone. Do you know anything about that?"

"I don't know anything about Rob. Jason stopped by here yesterday and Pete left with him. When he didn't come back by nightfall, the guys went out looking. They didn't come back either. Beau and Kathy lit out this morning."

Savanah's heart leaped into her throat. Her head began spinning. She'd known in her gut that something was wrong, but now her worst fears were being confirmed. There is no way that the Ashbys would go off and leave their place unguarded. Not unless something huge had occurred. Something more than just the Blanchards. Her stomach began to churn as her last meal tried to make its way back up. She drew in a breath and closed her eyes, willing her gut to calm.

"Are you here alone?" she finally asked in between breaths.

"I got all the kids."

Shit!

There was little she could do to protect them and her own family. "You're welcome to bring them and come stay with us until everyone gets back."

"Nah, I best stay here and do what I can to hold down the fort," Mary said. "I appreciate the offer though."

Savanah stared at Mary for a moment, unsure what more to say. She turned and slowly walked away. Before she was out of sight, she called back over her shoulder. "If you need us, we are just down the road."

As she walked back toward Blake and Luca, Savanah tried to make sense of what she'd learned. By the time she reached them, she'd determined she was no closer to knowing what had happened or how to respond than she was before.

Heading back toward Savanah's, the trio walked in silence. Each had agreed that something major had occurred, but its implications for them were unknown. Their next course of action was hotly debated. It was risky, but one Savanah believed was necessary. Blake had wanted to go alone, but Savanah knew that wouldn't work. He was a stranger in these parts. The Blanchards knew her. They were more likely to speak to her than Blake. Blake had objected to her proposal.

"If you go in alone, there is very little I can do to help you."

"I know. That's why I think you should stay here and protect our families. I don't think Jason's brother will hurt me. I really don't. If he doesn't know what has happened, he'll want to hear me out."

"For the record, I think it's a crazy idea," Luca said as he climbed Savanah's gate.

"I know. I hate to ask, but please watch over my children. Keep them in the house until I get back, okay?"

"I'll try. Kylie can be a handful," Luca said.

Kylie was obstinate and defiant at times—most of the time!— but Mrs. B could handle her. She had a way with strong-willed children, it seemed. "Ask Mrs. B to have her help organize the can goods. That will keep her busy."

Furrows lined the skin of Blake's forehead. "Are you sure, Savanah? We can talk about this some more and come up with something else."

"I'm sure. You said you saw them bring in several loads of stuff last night. Meaning they were out somewhere," she said, sweeping hair back from her eyes. She stared off in the direction of the gated community, her fear of them muted compared to the unknown danger lurking out there wherever Jason and others had gone. "They may know exactly what is going on. I'm going to get them to tell me."

Blake tilted his head back and exhaled. "Okay, then I'm going with you."

Savanah threw her hands in the air. "They aren't going to let you in."

Blake's head tilted slightly. "You'll have to convince them."

TWENTY-TWO

Will

DAY EIGHT

Will smelled bacon frying. At first, he thought he was dreaming, and then he heard voices in the kitchen. He rolled over to check on Cayden, who'd been sleeping beside him in one of the spare bedrooms. He was missing. Will sat up and bent to find his shoes. When he reached the door, he heard Cayden's voice. He was laughing. The sound made him tear up. He opened the door and stepped into the hall. The smell wafting in from the kitchen was heavenly and made his stomach growl.

"There you are, sleepyhead," Glory called down the hall. "Breakfast will be ready in about fifteen minutes."

"It smells wonderful," Will said. He was going to ask how she could cook with the electricity out but then recalled seeing the propane tanks outside.

"That's enough time for me to show you something out in my shop," Alan said.

Will ran a hand across the top of his hair and smoothed his wrinkled T-shirt before following Alan out to his shop. Monte and Walker were already there. In front of them were a long table and several disassembled weapons.

"Gotta keep those rifles clean, or they'll jam on you at the most inconvenient times," Alan said. "I can't spare much ammo, but I'll load you a few extra magazines. I have an extra tactical belt I could loan you too. I bought it for Glory, but she didn't like black, so we had to get her a girly one."

"I appreciate that, Alan," Will said.

"I also have this night vision scope. I'm surprised as hell that it still works. I'd thrown it into one of the half-empty ammo cans and forgot about it. It's not the best one on the market, but it's better than nothing."

"I can't thank you enough, Alan. It's very generous of you."

"You folks picked Glory and me up on that road and then engaged in a gun battle because of your good deed. It's the least I can do. I just wish I could do more, but it looks like this is going to be a long-term problem, and I won't be able to get a resupply of this stuff any time soon."

"I understand," Will said. "Have you considered leaving?"

"And go where? No, we'll just make our stand here," Alan said. "My boys will make it back soon, and we'll do a better job fortifying this place."

"You guys going to stay out there all day playing with guns or what?" Glory called.

"We better get in there, or she'll feed our breakfast to the hogs." Alan laughed.

After breakfast, all Will wanted to do was go back to bed. It was the first time his stomach had been full and satisfied in a week. He wasn't sure he was at all ready to face what came next out on the road. He prayed that life at Savanah's resembled the one here with Alan and Glory—without the gun battle they'd had yesterday, of course.

Walker climbed behind the wheel while Monte got into the passenger seat. Monte had suggested that Walker drive and it made sense. He knew the roads. If a route change needed to be made on the fly, it would save time not having to relay directions. In his lap, Monte held a pair of binoculars Alan had given him. In theory, he'd be able to spot trouble from a distance, giving them time to avoid it. Will hoped he was right. Cayden sat between Will and Isabella in the back seat. Glory had packed them a few MREs and filled a five-gallon jug of water for their trip.

Alan extended his hand through Will's open window. "It was nice meeting you, Will. I hope that someday you'll come back this way—when all this is over."

"We'll do that. I appreciate the supplies. It will make a huge difference," Will said.

Alan pointed at Cayden. "Make sure you keep this crew in line there, young man."

Cayden smiled. "I'll try."

"Keep that safety on," Alan said, pointing to the pistol holstered at Cayden's side.

Alan had spent two hours instructing him on gun safety and practicing shooting various targets. Will knew Cayden was responsible and a very good shot—at the range. But he was still only a thirteen-year-old kid. Handling a weapon was a huge responsibility, and knowing when to pull it was difficult, even for an adult. But in the end, he'd recognized that he might not always be there to protect him in the present danger they faced. He couldn't bear the thought of him defenseless against the type of enemies they'd seen so far.

"I'll keep it on safe, Mr. Alan," Cayden said.

"Isabella, I know I'm not exactly your size, but I packed you a few items of clothing. Sometimes just putting on a clean shirt can make you feel like a new woman if you know what I mean," Glory said. She placed the tote in the bed of the pickup and then patted Isabella's arm. "You're tougher than you know. You'll do fine."

"Thanks, Glory. And thanks for the clothes."

"Cayden, I sure thank you for helping me out with the animals. It can get to be quite a chore when you get behind from being gone like we were. You're a good kid," Glory said.

"I enjoyed it."

"Safe travels," Alan said as Walker put the truck into gear.

"Thank you for your hospitality," Walker replied.

Monte waved as they pulled down the drive.

Apprehension crawled up Will's spine as the truck's wheels hit the blacktop. He'd been naïve, thinking things would be better once they got away from Houston. Something in his gut told him that the worst wasn't over.

Walker turned the truck north just before coming into the city of Silsbee. The street was narrow and lined with houses that sat close to the road. It would be easy for someone to rush out and block their path without much notice. Will did not like the situation. He sat erect, eyes scanning the homes ahead, his hand on the rifle resting between his knees. His shoulders were tense and muscles ready to react to any threat that might arise. He let out an audible sigh of relief when the residential area gave way to a tall pine forest and then pasture lands. He wasn't looking forward to white-knuckling it the whole trip to Savanah's.

"How long have you had your place on the Neches River?" Monte asked.

"A decade or so. I don't get up there much anymore."

"And you think you're going to hunt and fish to survive?"

"Something like that," Walker said.

"Right," Monte scoffed. "There'll be a lot of folks that think like that. Those woods will be crawling with city folks trying to take down big game to feed their families. They're more likely to get themselves lost and die out there."

"It's that or go home to Beaumont. Which would you choose?"

"Sure as shit wouldn't be Beaumont or any city for that matter," Monte said.

"What's your plan?" Will asked.

"My folks have been living off the land for three generations. We know how to survive. The bayou will provide."

Will envied him in some ways. He seemed to have all the skills that it would take to make it long term without modern conveniences while Will was still wandering in the dark. He'd have a much better outlook once they reached Savanah's and could assess their chances of feeding themselves and what the security situation was there. He hated all the unknowns they still faced. It was hard for his mind not to imagine all sorts of dire scenarios.

"Walker, you should come on down to Lake Charles with me," Monte said. "We could use someone with your skills. I imagine lots of folks will think they can just run down to the bayou and take what they want. I doubt they'll survive a day out there. My family's camp is so far out that even I get lost sometimes."

A left turn took them through another residential area and across a set of railroad tracks. Eventually, it came back out on a highway heading east. As they reached the north side of Silsbee, Walker sped up, passing quickly by a washateria and a small strip mall before exiting the commercial area for a more rural setting. Walker relaxed in his seat and slowed a bit. They'd made it through Silsbee without incident and were back out on the freeway driving toward Evadale.

Walker was quiet for a moment, and then he asked, "Are you serious about that offer?"

"As a heart attack," Monte said.

"I'll have to consider it a bit."

"You better hurry up. Your turn is coming up soon, right?"

Walker was about to speak when Will spotted something on the road ahead. He leaned forward and pointed. "Slow down, Walker."

"What is it?" Isabella asked, poking her head between Walker and Monte.

"Looks like a body," Walker said.

A tight knot formed in Will's stomach. His head rotated back and forth, looking for signs of anyone else around. He saw no one.

"Maybe they're hurt," she replied.

The odd way they were positioned told Will they were likely dead. But how? Why had they been left on the road, and by whom?

"I don't like it, Walker," Monte said. "I think we should haul ass around it and get the hell out of here, pronto."

Will agreed. If the person were still alive, there wouldn't be anything they could do to help them. It smelled an awful lot like an ambush.

"You aren't going to stop and see about them, are you?" Isabella asked.

What a turnabout she'd made. Was this the same woman that had chastised him when they were downtown and had left the dying man in the street? Maybe she was finally beginning to realize they couldn't save everyone even if they tried. They had to look out for themselves. It had become the survival of the fittest.

Walker gripped the steering wheel tighter and sped up. As he did, Will pushed Cayden's head forward. "Stay down." He pulled his rifle into his lap and readied himself to fire at the first sign of trouble. Will thought about the Humvees they'd ridden through town on their way to the joint reserve base. How he'd love to be traveling in one of those. He'd feel much more comfortable up in the turret where he could see and respond to threats more readily.

Before reaching the figure on the pavement, Walker swerved onto the soft shoulder of the roadway. Will closed his eyes for a second, praying the tires didn't slip off into the mud and get stuck. Will looked back as Walker steered them back onto the highway.

It was mere seconds before their suspicions were confirmed. Three men and a woman ran into the street, waving their fists in the air. The shorter of the men aimed and fired his pistol, but the truck was too far away for his shot to reach its target. They'd dodged a bullet, literally.

"That was close," Isabella said.

Will wiped the sweat from his forehead. "Too close."

In minutes, they reached the Neches River, which wandered over four hundred miles through the East Texas Piney Woods and emptied into the Gulf of Mexico. Walker didn't have it all wrong. A body could disappear into the thick woods and feed off the abundance of the land—if they knew what they were doing. How many Houston residents would flee the city to try? Hundreds? Thousands? Not many would survive, but it would beat the hell out of staying in the war-torn city and starving to death.

"What's it going to be, lawman?" Monte pressed.

Walker stopped in the middle of the highway and placed the truck in park. He stared off down a lane to his left.

Will's head pivoted, looking for threats. He hated to rush him. It was a big decision, but they were exposed just sitting there like that.

"Aw hell. I might as well ride on with you guys. I wouldn't want you to become lost before you get the boy to your sister's," Walker said, placing the truck back into gear.

Will was surprised how relieved he was that Walker had agreed to continue on with them. More people did make it safer.

"All righty, then," Monte said. Let's put the pedal down and get to Cajun country."

"Great, I'll get to introduce you to Aunt Savanah and my cousins," Cayden said.

Walker twisted in his seat and smiled back at him. He opened his mouth, about to say something, when he heard the clang of something hard hitting the rear of the truck.

"What was that?" Monte yelled, twisting to get a look.

Everyone turned toward the rear left side of the truck. Isabella gasped.

"Let me see hands," a male voice said in broken English. He

was dressed from head to toe in black. Half his face was covered in a balaclava mask.

"What do you want?" Walker asked.

The man thrust his rifle in Walker's direction. "I say let me see hands."

Another man came into Will's view. "Get out!"

Without taking his eyes off the men, Will reached under the driver's seat, pulled out the Colt 1911 that Alan had given him, and stuffed it into the back of his waistband. He twisted toward the man, putting his body between the attackers and Cayden. Isabella's door opened, and Will's head pivoted in that direction. A third man had her by the hair and was dragging her from the vehicle.

"Let her go!" Cayden yelled as he grabbed hold of Isabella's waist.

The man hauled back to punch Cayden, but Isabella landed a blow to the man's groin with a fist, and he stumbled backward, with Isabella landing on top. Will grabbed Cayden to stop him from going after them then felt the cold steel of a rifle barrel against the back of his neck and froze.

"Get out! Now!"

The door opened, and Will pulled Cayden out with him. Walker was already on the ground, arms and legs spread apart. The first man was going through his pockets.

He held up Walker's badge and said something to the others in Chinese.

The man closest to Will and Cayden turned his back on them to look at it. Will reacted, pulling the 1911 from his waistband. He shoved Cayden to the ground and fired until the man went down before turning the pistol on the guy standing over Walker. Two down. Unknown numbers still to go.

TWENTY-THREE

Isabella

DAY EIGHT

"Will!" Isabella screamed as hands wrapped around her hair.

Cayden grabbed her by the wrist. His look of terror only fueled her anger at whoever had attacked her. She was face up, sliding toward the pavement, when she saw the man's other hand form a fist. When he leaned forward to hit Cayden, Isabella threw her right hand back and punched the man in the groin. He let go of her and she hit the ground hard, knocking the wind out of her for a moment. The attacker was less than five feet away, facing the front of the vehicle. If she attempted to stand and run, he'd be sure to grab her. He took two steps toward her with both hands balled into fists. Isabella ignored them. Her eyes were on the blade attached to the man's right leg. He took another step, and Isabella readied herself.

Boom!

Someone fired, and the man reacted by turning toward the shooter. Isabella lunged and grabbed the knife from his side. The man didn't appear to notice. All his attention was still on the commotion on the driver's side of the pickup.

Isabella plunged the man's knife up and under the man's vest and into his abdomen with all her might and withdrew it, quickly crawling away. The guy's mouth opened, and he dropped to one knee.

Boom!

After the second report from the deep throaty handgun, Isabella tried to stand, but her legs were like wet noodles. A hand grabbed her by the right arm and hoisted her to her feet. She spun around, ready to fight.

"It's me, Monte!"

Isabella dropped the knife and turned, looking for Will and Cayden. "Will!"

He appeared near the truck's hood on the driver's side with the pistol gripped in both hands. He lowered it when he saw her. "Any more over there?"

Monte pivoted and pulled his rifle up to look through his scope. "I don't see any."

Isabella rushed around the front of the vehicle, passing Walker and Will, and ran straight for Cayden, who was leaning against the back fender. "Are you all right? Are you injured? Did they hurt you?" she said in quick succession.

"I'm fine," he said flatly. "Dad got 'em."

Isabella pulled him into her arms and held him tight. Tears stung her eyes but she fought them back. Now was not the time. She would not fall apart.

"Are you okay?" Cayden asked, pulling back from her. He pointed to her hands.

Isabella stared at her blood-soaked right hand. The blank look on the man's face replayed in her mind. "It's not mine."

"I tried to stop him," Cayden said.

"I know. You shouldn't do that. You could get hurt."

"I'm not a little kid. I can fight too. I may be short for my age, but I can fight. I've fought bullies at school many times."

Isabella was filled with a mix of emotions—a sadness that he'd experienced bullies and a sort of pride that he was willing to stand up for himself. But this was different. The world was different.

Those were regular schoolyard bullies. The people they were encountering now were killers.

"We better go before more of these assholes show up. Those gunshots are sure to attract attention," Walker said.

"Where are the rest of them, Will? They don't travel in threes."

"Maybe these are just scouts," Will said, standing over one of the insurgents.

"These aren't dressed like the others," Isabella said. "They look more military. Look at their gear."

Will rifled through the pouches on the man's tactical vest, pulling out ammunition and finally a map. He spread it out on the hood of the truck, and everyone crowded in to see it.

"I can't read Chinese, but these marks here must be targets."

"That's the rail line between Beaumont and Houston," Walker said.

"You think that's their target?" Will asked.

"It's certainly of interest to them. It's highlighted in red."

"Why'd they attack us?" Cayden asked.

"Opportunists," Monte said. "They saw the truck. It's a much quicker way to travel. Dressed like that, I'm sure they weren't prepared for the heat and humidity here in Texas. They seemed pretty tired and slow."

Will grabbed the man's canteen and shook it. "Empty. They were out of water and probably dehydrated."

"Let's not stand around here and wait for more to show up," Isabella said.

She still couldn't believe that the insurgency had spread this far from Houston. What valuable targets could there be out in the Piney Woods of East Texas?

"We'll have to be more diligent from here on out," Walker said.

"And not stop for nothing," Monte added.

Will helped her up into the truck as Cayden ran around to the passenger side. He stopped and looked down at the dead man and then looked up. "You think I could have his knife?"

"That's up to your dad," Isabella said.

"Dad?"

"Only pull it if we are attacked," Will said.

Cayden nodded. Monte unstrapped the scabbard from the man's leg and placed the knife inside it before handing it to Cayden. "It's going to be a bit big on you, I'm afraid."

"It's okay," Cayden said, wrapping it around his thigh.

Monte, Will, and Walker stripped the gear from the insurgents. The vests were too small for the guys but fit Isabella perfectly.

"It's too hot," she complained. "I can't breathe in this."

Will pulled his over his head and strapped it, but it left half his abdomen exposed. "It'll be cooler when we're moving and the wind is whipping through here."

"Here, little man. There ain't no way this will fit me," Monte said, holding up the bloody tactical vest.

Cayden scrunched his face. "That's gross!"

"It'll still stop a bullet," Monte said, pulling it down over Cayden's head and fastening the Velcro straps tight.

"Can I have his pistol?" Cayden asked.

Monte picked it up off the ground and looked it over. "You ever see one like this?" he said, handing the gun to Walker.

"Not personally. That's Russian made."

"So is all this 7.62mm ammo, I bet," Will said.

"Russian?" Isabella said. "They're Russian?"

"The Chinese buy a lot of Russian weapons. These guys are Asian, not Russian," Monte pointed out.

"How do you know all this?" Cayden asked.

Monte smiled. "Google."

"Should we at least drag them off the roadway?" Isabella asked.

Monte looked at her like she had two heads. "Why?"

"Conceal them. In case others are close behind," Isabella said.

"Won't matter," Will said. "We'll be long gone."

Isabella couldn't quit thinking about the implications of insurgents out in the Texas countryside. There were only three, not the hundreds that she and Will had fought against in Houston, but why were they there? What did it mean? Were they scouts like Will had said? It was so very hard to wrap her head around. Enemy forces were on American soil.

"Why didn't they just shoot us all if they only wanted the truck?" she asked, thinking out loud.

"Maybe they wanted directions." Cayden laughed.

Isabella elbowed him with her broken arm and immediately regretted it as pain shot up her arm. "Funny guy."

"He might have something there. They might have wanted information," Walker said, "if they were on an intelligence-gathering mission. They likely thought we were locals and might very well have intended interrogating us for local information."

"Well, whatever their intent, they found out the hard way not to mess with Texas!" Isabella said.

Isabella was so lost in thought about what the world could look like if China achieved their goal that she didn't notice as Walker weaved around Evansdale and finally arrived on the outskirts of Deweyville. She was surprised when the truck came to a stop just before the bridge crossing the Sabine River.

TWENTY-FOUR

Will

DAY EIGHT

Will stood in the middle of the bridge spanning the Sabine River, which divided Texas from Louisiana. They'd somehow made it out of Texas alive. There was no turning back now. They'd have to keep going and face whatever was ahead of them.

"Now what?" Isabella asked.

A well-armed group awaited them on the Louisiana side.

"What do you think, Walker?" Will asked.

"I think maybe I should go over and speak to them." He reached into his pocket, and pulled out his crimson-stained Texas Rangers' badge, wiped it on his pant leg, and opened the door.

"What if they start shooting?" Monte asked.

"Shoot back."

Walker held out his badge and walked to the middle of the bridge. Will couldn't hear what was being said. Walker gestured over his shoulder. Next, he bent and placed his gun and badge on the pavement and stepped back as another man approached. The man retrieved them from the ground and thrust his thumb back over his shoulder. Walker turned and gestured for them to get out of the truck and join him.

Will was hesitant, unsure what the group's intentions were.

They could take the truck or disarm them and kill everyone. In the end, he decided the only way to find out was to join Walker. Will exited and held his hand out to assist Isabella.

"Are we sure this isn't a trick?" she asked.

"No, but we have to cross here, so we have to take the chance."

"I ain't disarming. That's all I got to say," Monte said, still sitting in the front passenger seat.

Will and Isabella met Cayden at the front of the pickup. He wrapped his arms around Cayden and Isabella and slowly walked toward the checkpoint on the Louisiana side of the river. He looked back, and Monte was standing beside the truck, his rifle at the low ready.

A young man stepped out from behind a road closure sign. In his hands was a rifle pointed toward the ground. Will took it as a good indication that they weren't just going to shoot them on sight. He glanced down at Isabella and then at Cayden and stepped forward. They were within fifteen feet of Walker.

"You can stop right there," the man said, his hand outstretched in front of him.

They stopped seventy-five feet from the end of the bridge. Will shifted his gaze to the guardrail and the water below. He was trying to determine how quickly he could shove Isabella and Cayden over the short rail if shots rang out.

"We aren't accepting refugees," the man said.

Refugees? What the hell? Were they now some third-world country? There was something familiar about the man, but Will couldn't place it. Maybe it was just the deep southwest Louisiana accent.

"We aren't refugees," Will called back. "We're just passing through heading home."

"Heading home? Where to?"

"South of Vincent," Will said.

"What's your name?"

"Will Fontenot."

There was a pause and then another man stepped forward.

"Will? I didn't recognize you," the man said. "I'm Kale. I used to do some work on your granddad's place when I was in high school."

Will squinted, trying to get a good look at the man. "I recall that now," Will said.

"Come on over," Kale said.

Will and the others slowly approached, still cautious as the other men at the roadblock hadn't lowered their weapons. He looked back and gave Monte a thumbs up before continuing.

"Good thing that guy knows you because they were going to take our truck and weapons and send us back across the river," Walker said.

"They said that?" Isabella asked.

"As you were walking up, I heard one of them say so."

"You think they still will?"

"Not if Will's buddy there vouches for us."

"It's fine. This here is Will Fontenot. He was the star quarterback the year Vincent took the championship," Kale said, turning back to the other men at the checkpoint.

"Quarterback?" Isabella asked, nudging him.

"That was a long time ago."

"Seriously," another man said, lowering his rifle and stepping forward. "You look different, Will."

"It's probably all the dirt and blood." Cayden chuckled.

"This is my son, Cayden, and this is Isabella."

"You guys look like you've been through hell and back," Kale said.

"We've come from Houston," Isabella said, attempting to smooth her uncombed hair.

"Shit. It's bad there, huh?"

"It's bad everywhere."

"Who's the dude back there with the AR?" Kale said.

"Monte. He was down in Houston with the Cajun navy helping

out after the hurricane. He got stranded. He's heading down Cameron area."

"I got folks down that way. He doesn't want to head down there."

"Why?" Isabella asked.

"My in-laws came up a few days ago and said they were run out by a fight between the police and some foreigners in military uniforms."

Will and Isabella stared at one another. That was too close—way too close to Vincent.

Will reached one hand out and braced himself against the road sign. They'd come all this way to find a safe place at the farm. Now to learn that there was trouble seventy-five miles away was beyond disheartening. His whole body hurt. He was exhausted, physically and mentally. He wasn't sure how to keep moving, yet they'd have to. They had to get to Savanah's and somehow convince her to leave the farm. But go where? Where would be safe?

"So you're headed home. You going to your grandpa's place?" Kale asked.

"Yeah. My sister took it over." His head was reeling and trying to accept this new information. "How far north is the fighting?" Will asked.

"From what we hear, it's between Beaumont and Cameron, but they're telling folks to evacuate. Of course, people had already headed north before the hurricane came in, so there ain't many folks still down there. Most headed to Shreveport and ain't made it back."

"Any word from the sheriff? What about the National Guard? Did they move toward there?"

"They moved toward Beaumont after the storm. That's probably a lot of the fighting around there."

"What're folks saying up this way? You feel safe staying put?"

"For now. I heard tell of a FEMA shelter that they set up before the storm that some folks have headed to. Thought we'd see how things go and if need be, head there."

"Where's that?" Will wanted to keep all their options open at this point.

"Texarkana," Kale said.

That was well over two hundred and fifty miles.

"Why so far away?"

"That's where the overflow from the one in Dallas and Shreveport went, so they set up a shelter there. That was the day the hurricane came in though. After the lights went out, I don't know if it's still operating. Everyone just keeps heading that way."

As they walked back to the truck, Will filled Monte in on what Kale had told him was happening around Cameron. The man's face went pale. As he climbed into the vehicle, he lowered his head and shook it. "I gotta try. I have to get to my family and move them out of there."

Will understood that perfectly. If it had been his family, nothing would have stopped him either.

"Walker, you're welcome to stay with us," Will said.

His head pivoted to look at Monte. He paused before speaking. Will knew what he was going to say.

"Nope. I was looking forward to a good ole crab boil, and some of his wife's famous gumbo Monte was bragging about. I'll just tag along and make sure he stays out of trouble until we find his family."

"Why didn't they evacuate with everyone else?" Cayden asked.

"Cause my daddy won't leave and let thieves loot the store," Monte said. "Besides, we all knew it wasn't going to hit Calcasieu Parish. Daddy was right. It hit somewhere between Galveston and Freeport from the damage I saw."

"So they should be safe, at least from the storm," Cayden said.

"They'll be safe from those damn commie bastards too. They'll head out to the bayou and stay at our camp."

"I hope you find them," Cayden said.

Will placed a hand on his shoulder. "If you run into trouble down there, you head on back up here. My sister won't mind."

The men guarding the checkpoint moved the barricades and allowed them through. Kale waved. "It was good seeing you, Will. Tell Savanah I said, hey."

Will waved. "Will do."

Walker pulled on through and headed east, eventually turning south just past Starks. The road was rural, two-lanes, lined by trees and occasional rice fields. They were all on edge after learning that the Chinese military might be along the Louisiana coast. Their scouts had gotten the drop on them once. Will wasn't going to let that happen again.

"They won't be at Savanah's," Cayden said after a long period of silence.

Will wasn't sure if he was trying to reassure Isabella or himself.

"No. They won't come up that far," Will said. However, he wasn't at all sure.

"If they do, will we all go to Texarkana?"

"Maybe. Or somewhere else safe."

"At least we'll be there to protect Aunt Savanah and the kids," Cayden said.

"It will be good to all be together. I know you've missed them."

Cayden just nodded.

As the miles passed, Will's thoughts turned to food. He could practically smell bacon cooking. He was dreaming of fresh farm eggs sprinkled with herbs from his sister's garden. And boudin. Something that had once been a staple of his diet. His sister had shied away from traditional Cajun dishes in her move to more organic, healthy fare, but he thought he might be able to persuade her to make a few of their favorites for Isabella.

~

Walker stopped the truck at the T-intersection just outside the city limits of Vincent, Louisiana. Will had traveled these roads thousands of times over his life and knew it like the back of his hand, but now it looked somehow foreign. Maybe it was the silence. He listened hard for the familiar sounds. No tractors. That was what was different. Farmers should be harvesting this time of year. He wondered how they would bring in the sugar cane, sorghum, and rice without tractors and all the other equipment. He thought about all those rice fields. That would be a vital food source now. Unfortunately, most of it likely had been harvested in the summer and shipped to places like China. What remained of the late-planted rice would be needed to feed the farmers and their families.

The Cormiers' tractor sat deserted in their field. Will leaned out the window to see if he could spot anyone outside. He wanted to know how the town had fared so far and if they'd seen his sister, but he saw no one. Even Mr. Cormier's old Bassett hound was missing from their front porch.

"Maybe they went to stay with their son in town," Cayden said.

"You're probably right," Will said. It wouldn't have been very safe for the elderly couple out there by themselves, especially with their house so close to the road. There'd be no warning before someone was upon them. Will wasn't sure how much better the town would be, but at least they'd have their son to watch out for them.

As they drove past the Cormiers' neighbor's place, Will noticed their gate was open. They usually kept it locked. On closer inspection, it appeared that someone had broken the lock, and the gate was off its hinges and resting on the ground leaned up against the post. That wasn't a good sign. Will stopped and inspected the scene. Red shotgun shell casings littered the driveway. It looked like there'd been a fierce battle there.

"Let's go," Will said, pounding on the back of Walker's seat to get him to speed up. He wanted no part of whatever trouble was down that driveway.

A quarter of a mile down the road, Will caught sight of his third-grade teacher's barn through the trees, or what remained of the structure. He sucked in a deep breath, fearing what he might see when they reached it. He couldn't believe his eyes as they approached the driveway. Everything was gone. Everything. The house, most of the barn, the sheds. Everything had been burned down. An open suitcase was on the ground in the middle of the front yard. Clothes were strewn all around it. Even from that distance, he could see the blood on them. He lifted his rifle.

"Dad?"

"Don't look, Cayden," Will said, even though he couldn't take his eyes off the scene. "Keep going, Walker."

"Will, what is it?" Isabella asked.

"Nothing. The house burned," Will said, trying not to alarm them.

As the truck continued down the road, Will scanned the front of the house through the rifle's scope. He tried to convince himself that it wasn't blood, but there was just too much of it to be anything else. *Maybe it was animal blood.*

The pickup stopped again at the Vincent city limits welcome sign. It felt odd returning to his hometown like this. It had been a few years since he'd been back but still, he hadn't expected it to look so different. The tire shop on the corner of Fontenot Drive was boarded up, as was the cell phone store across the street. Had they been preparing for Hurricane Epsilon too?

"We're going through town, Dad?" Cayden asked.

Will hesitated. That route was shorter, but he'd never been a fan of the chief of police and wanted to avoid any possible issues with the man. Mayor Thibodeaux might have issued some order confiscating vehicles or even weapons. He wasn't about to give up either. The alternative to driving through downtown Vincent would add a mile more to the trip. Was it worth the risk? The ache in Will's ribs and the hunger gnawing at his belly said it was.

"Just keep your eyes out for Barney," Will said.

"Barney?" Cayden asked.

He was too young to remember the nickname. Everyone called Chief Benoit Barney Fife because he looked just like him.

"Chief Benoit," Will said.

"Barney's from the Andy Griffith show, right? I love that show," Monte said. "My grandad had the series on DVD."

Will smiled. "So did my grandmother."

"Are you anticipating trouble with the police?" Isabella asked.

"No. Not really."

Isabella shook her head. "Why am I'm not convinced?"

"We just don't get along well, so I'm hoping not to run into the man."

Isabella tilted her head to the side and lowered her chin. The corners of her mouth curled up. "Were you an outlaw when you lived here, Will?"

"Not exactly."

"My mom used to tell stories about all the trouble Dad would get into."

Isabella pointed at Will and wagged her finger. "Aw, I knew it. You were the town rebel."

Will waved his hand dismissively. "Let's just try to keep a low profile, okay?"

As they rode east through town, Will began to think maybe they'd evacuated the city. It was deserted, eerily quiet, and he hadn't seen a soul out on the streets.

"Where is everyone?" Cayden asked.

Will shrugged. "I don't know."

"Maybe they all ran out of food and left," Isabella said.

As they approached the grocery store, Will spotted movement near one of the cars in the parking lot. He leaned forward and pointed. "Watch there." The person exited the vehicle and looked in their direction. Will watched the man's hands as he raised his pistol.

"Cayden! Isabella!" Will shouted as the first round slammed into the truck.

As Walker threw the truck into reverse and sped backward, Will pushed Isabella's head down and grabbed Cayden by his shirt. "Get down!" he yelled.

The truck's engine whined as Walker accelerated backward. Will heard what sounded like an explosion, and then he was thrown back in his seat, his head hitting the rear glass.

TWENTY-FIVE

Savanah

DAY EIGHT

Savanah stood across the street from the exclusive Sugar Hill community's main gate and waved a piece of white cloth over her head. Blake was hidden behind a row of bushes that lined the road, his rifle trained on the guard on the other side.

"What do you want?" the guard called out.

"I need to talk to Valson. It's about his brother, Jason."

An extended period of silence followed. She narrowed her eyes and tried to see beyond the gate but couldn't. Were they getting Valson or deciding whether to shoot her?

"What about Jason?" the guard asked.

"I need to talk to his brother. Now!" Savanah said, trying to be as forceful as she could. Jason's family understood strength and preyed on weakness. She would not show them fear.

A moment later, the gate opened, and Valson stood next to two of his henchmen. He was dressed in a tank top and swim trunks as if he'd just come from the pool. "What do you want, Savanah?"

"Jason's missing." She waited for a response, not wanting to divulge that Pete and Rod were too—not yet.

"Missing? Maybe he got tired of playing house with you and

163

found a new ho." The two clowns with him laughed and smacked each other on the backs.

Savanah turned as if she were leaving and then called back over her shoulder. "Fine, if you don't care if he's lying out there injured somewhere, then I'll go into town and see if your dad will help me find him."

"Aw, Savanah, you know I was just teasing you. How long's he been gone?"

She stopped and turned. "Twenty-four hours now. He was going to talk to one of the neighbors and hasn't returned."

"Did you check there? Maybe he got to drinking and forgot his way home?" one of the goons asked.

She scowled. "I checked. They're missing too. Pete Ashby left with Jason and didn't return. Rob left with some dude in a polo shirt, and he hasn't returned either. Something bad is going on, and I was hoping that maybe your crew might have heard or seen something while they were out last night."

Valson stepped into the street. When his henchmen tried to follow, he motioned for them to hang back. Savanah matched him step for step as she moved toward him, a tight knot forming in the center of her chest as they converged in the middle of the road.

"Seriously, Savanah, what was he up to? He wasn't going to make some dumb move on the old man, was he?"

Savanah stiffened. She'd never considered that. Why would he? Valson and Sugar Hill had been their immediate problem. She could see him appealing to his father to call Valson in and stop his reign of terror, but not Jason challenging his father for control of Vincent. No, that wasn't it.

"No way. Are you sure your guys didn't do something to him?" Savanah glanced over Valson's shoulder.

Valson followed her gaze. "Those clowns." He laughed. "They can't wipe their asses without me telling them to. They wouldn't mess with my brother without my permission."

Savanah lifted an eyebrow. "What about Pete and Rob?"

"They're fair game, but my crew would have told me if they'd been into it with anyone out here."

"You're sure?" Savanah asked, a growing concern spreading in her gut. She'd somewhat hoped Valson was holding them somewhere and that she could negotiate for their release, but she was starting to believe that he didn't know anything about their disappearances.

Valson gestured. "Stinky, get over here."

"Yeah, boss?"

"Did you see my brother or anyone from Sugar Cove when you guys were out last night?"

"Jason? No. We were east of the city. Why?"

"He's late coming home."

"Did you see anyone you didn't recognize?" Savanah asked. "Maybe some outsiders coming through the area?'

"My crew didn't but Buddy claims he saw little Chinamen slinking around the school out by the interstate. We blew him off because he was stoned and not making any sense."

Valson dismissed him with a wave. "I'll ride into town and check with the old man. Maybe some of his crew saw Jason and the other two."

It was too foreign—standing there having a semi-civilized conversation with a brutal killer about the wellbeing of his brother. Could she trust him? No. But she was now confident that he wasn't holding Jason, Rob, and Pete, and that was what she'd come to find out.

"If you find him, please tell him that the children and I are worried about him," Savanah said.

"I will. Don't worry. He's just fine. He's a tough son-of-a-bitch."

Savanah nodded and turned to go. He was right. Jason was tough, so was Pete, but they were both missing. Not knowing where they were or what had become of them was unbearable. And now, she was no closer to knowing than she was when she started.

"You believe him?" Blake asked as they walked toward Savanah's farm.

"I do. He has no reason to lie about his brother or the others. He'd brag if he'd done something. He'd be full of bravado and inflammatory words for the rest of us. That's just who he is."

"What about the theory that Jason and the others went into Vincent?"

"I don't buy that—unless something came up that we don't know about. Jason doesn't trust his family. He wouldn't go to his dad for help—with anything. Buzz Blanchard beat his kids into submission. He's pure evil. Jason would expect nothing else from him than that."

"So we're back to square one. We still have no leads on where they might have gone."

"The only lead is the guy in the polo shirt and the fact that Pete's family took off looking for them. What that means, I have no idea."

"Well, do we know who wears polos around here?"

"Just those guys from Sugar Hill," Savanah said, gesturing back over her shoulder.

She paused and then stopped in the middle of the road. She looked skyward and then at Blake.

"Pete's uncle owns a used car lot a mile south of town. Maybe he was the one in the UTV with Rob."

When they reached the farm, Savanah stopped and leaned against the gate. "What do you think? Should we go check out that lead?"

Blake turned his gaze to the ground. "I know you're concerned about your friend, but we really should stay put and prepare in case something is coming."

Her head said he was right, but her heart wanted to find Jason —and she wanted answers.

Savanah placed her foot on the gate and threw her leg over. "Okay. I guess we don't have any choice."

"I'm going to take the long way home, do a perimeter check of the neighborhood. Get some rest, Savanah. I'll be back later on today, and we can regroup and come up with a plan."

Savanah waved goodbye and headed up the driveway.

"Where have you been?!" Savanah yelled as she ran toward the entrance to the barn.

Jason smiled, making her anger boil.

"I'm sorry. It wasn't like I could pick up the phone and call," Jason said, approaching her with his arms open wide.

"I was so scared," she said, slapping him on the chest.

Jason pulled her in close and wrapped his muscular arms around her. "I'm sorry. Really, I am."

She melted—all the anger fading away. Once the tears started, she couldn't stop them.

"It's all right. Everything's going to be all right," Jason whispered, stroking her hair.

She was a little girl again, with her grandfather comforting her after she'd fallen off her horse. She wanted to believe Jason just like she'd believed her granddad, but things were not right in the world, and she had a feeling they never would be again.

"What happened?" she asked, this time without the angry tone.

Jason released his grip on her and stepped back. The somber look on his face made her heart jump into her throat.

"Outsiders," Jason said. "They're camped five miles from here along the Spring Gully. They are heavily armed and well supplied."

"Outsiders? Like from Lake Charles or Cameron?"

"Like I have to no idea where they're from. They were some type of military or maybe military contractors."

"Military? That's a good thing, right? Maybe they're getting ready to get services restored." Savanah was hopeful for the first time in over a week. She looked into his eyes. He did not share her optimism. "What, Jason?"

"I don't think they're with *our* military."

Savanah's knees buckled, and Jason reached out to steady her. He led her through the barn door and grabbed a crate, lowering her gently down onto it before continuing.

"While Pete and I were talking yesterday, his brother came running up with some tale about men in black—"

Savanah cut him off. "Couldn't they be from Fort Polk? It's only like seventy miles from here or something. Maybe they were out on some kind of patrol."

"I don't think they are American, Savanah. There were only about a dozen of them, so it's not an immediate threat."

"You saw them? They're not just some wannabe militia types playing military?"

"I did. Pete, Rod, and I went to take a look for ourselves. Whoever they are, I think they're on some scouting mission. They broke camp and took off at first light. Pete's brother and brother-in-law followed them while some of Kathy's relatives took off toward Fort Polk to warn them. Her cousin's retired from the air force. He said he knew someone up there."

She was confused. "So, should we be worried or not?"

"I think we need to be aware and expand our perimeter. We need scouts ourselves looking out for any more foreigners moving into the area. We should be prepared to bug out if it comes to that."

"Bug out?" she asked.

"Leave in a hurry."

A tear slid down her cheek. Jason knelt in front of her and wiped it away with his finger. He leaned in and kissed her forehead. "Only if we're facing an overwhelming force. Otherwise, we'll stay and fight. But I don't want those kids in the middle of some freaking war."

She nodded. It was incomprehensible. Where on earth would they go? How would they eat? Where would be safer than home? The thought of leaving the farm was too much. It was a part of her.

"We should go talk to the others," Jason said, helping her to her feet.

Savanah wrapped her arm around his waist and followed him towards the house. "We should send Keegan over to get Blake. He's going to want to hear this."

TWENTY-SIX

Isabella

DAY EIGHT

Isabella's broken arm struck Will's shoulder as they crashed into the truck behind them. Pain shot up her forearm and brought a wave of nausea. Her door opened and Monte pulled on her arm. She reached for Will, but it was too late. Men were at his door, guns raised. "Let's go," Monte yelled. Isabella's head rotated, looking for Cayden. She spotted him two feet in front of Walker, rounding the corner of one of the stores and heading for an alley.

Monte grabbed her right forearm, his hand gripping the burn. He was practically dragging her toward where she'd last seen Cayden and Walker. Her gaze was back on the truck and Will.

"Will?" she screamed.

"We can't help him. We have to go," Monte said, pulling harder and moving faster.

"We can't leave him," she cried.

"We'll get him back. I promise. But we won't be of any use if we get ourselves caught too."

Walker and Cayden were at the end of the alley, waving them on. Cayden had his pistol in his hand. Fear framed his face. She ran as fast as her injured leg would allow, finally reaching them just before Walker set off running across the next street toward a church parking lot. She was exhausted already. She didn't know how it was going to be possible to keep up. Monte ran behind her, prodding her to keep going.

"Don't look back. Keep running. Faster, Isabella! Faster!"

As hard as she fought, she couldn't help herself. She turned her head and gasped. It appeared the whole town was chasing after them. When they reached the church, Monte shoved her from behind, and she fell forward on her knees. She stuck out her right hand, but it slipped in the grass, and her chin bounced off the ground. Her teeth slammed together, and she was sure she'd chipped them. She didn't have time to check before Walker had her by the hand and dragged her behind the building. Round after round struck the stone facade and shattered the stained-glass windows. Monte returned fire as he dove and rolled, barely missing the round that dug a divot of grass where he'd just been. Cayden stepped around Isabella and fired two shots before leaning back and pressing himself against the building.

"Let's move," Walker said, tapping Cayden on the shoulder.

They ran across the street and down the block to the back of a warehouse where several old boats were stored.

"In here," Monte called, gesturing for them to hurry.

A row of bass boats, bay boats, flat-bottom boats, and various marine engines lined one wall of the building. In the middle were two lifts where boats were hoisted into the air. Tools and equipment were everywhere. Isabella spotted a back room filled with upholstery materials. She grabbed Cayden by his shirt and ran toward it while Walker and Monte secured the door they'd entered.

"What about my dad?" Cayden asked as Isabella searched for another way out.

"We'll go back for him. We need to lead them away from the truck and then lose them." She had no idea what the hell she was talking about. They didn't have a plan—at least one she knew about. She just wanted to give the boy some hope.

"Did you find any other exits?" Monte said, appearing in the doorway to the upholstery room.

"No." Isabella pointed to the door to her left. "That door goes to a long storage room with more fabric and parts for seats and such."

"Are there windows in there?"

"No."

"Good. You two go in there and shut the door."

"What?" Isabella's head turned toward the storage space. "I'm not hiding in there with no way of escape."

"Me neither," Cayden said, stepping in front of her. "I'm going back for my dad."

He gripped his pistol in both hands and started around Monte who stuck out his muscular arm and blocked him. "Just hold on there, son. Your dad would not want you rushing out there and getting yourself killed. We have to be smart about this. We're outnumbered—that's clear. We can get out of this and get your dad back, but not if we go running off half-cocked."

"What's your plan then?" Cayden asked. "He's hurt. They could have him right now."

"Let's discuss this and see what our options are," Walker said from behind Monte.

Monte moved deeper into the room and away from the door to allow Walker inside the cluttered space. Monte pulled up a roll-around office style chair and pointed for Cayden to take a seat. Isabella leaned back against a workbench that ran the length of the back wall. She wiped the sweat from her face with a white towel she found in a stack on the bench. The heat inside without windows was near unbearable.

"From what I could tell, there were maybe twenty people that came after us," Monte said, starting the discussion.

"They were on us so fast," Isabella said.

"They saw us coming," Walker said. "They likely had lookouts. As soon as that guy popped up and started firing, that truck roared up and cut us off. I didn't even have time to turn the wheel and avoid crashing into it."

"And they were at our doors in seconds. It's a miracle we got away," Monte said.

"Most of them weren't from Vincent," Cayden said.

"They weren't?" Walker asked. "Are you sure?"

"I recognized some of them. They're from Sulphur, a town about ten miles away. The others are from around here. They're all druggies."

"That makes sense," Monte said. "They likely moved in to steal the town's resources."

"How does this information help us?" Isabella asked.

"Well, for one, we know we are dealing with people who might not be in the best physical or mental state. For another, only half of them had firearms. The rest were carrying baseball bats and clubs."

Isabella's brow furrowed. "Those are still deadly."

"Yes, if they get close enough to hit you with them. I don't plan on letting them get that close," Monte said.

"What that tells us is they have a limited supply of firearms and hopefully not much ammunition."

"Where are the town's residents?" Isabella asked.

"Hopefully hiding," Walker said.

"Okay, how does this help us get to my dad?"

"We create a diversion. Draw them out, pick off the ones with guns, and..." Monte's eyes shifted to Walker.

"I'll do it," Walker said. I'll be the diversion, and you guys go and get Will."

"They might not buy it if they only see one of us," Monte said.

"I'll go with him," Isabella said. I can't do much to help carry Will, anyway. I can shoot, though."

"You can't run—not fast anyway. If we get overrun and need to exfiltrate..."

Everyone was quiet, contemplating all the possibilities. Cayden stared at the floor. Her heart hurt for him. He had to be so scared for his father, but he seemed to be handling it in such a mature manner. His dad would be proud.

"What's on your mind, Cayden?" Walker asked.

Cayden slowly looked up. "I thought I saw a face in the window at the church."

"A face you recognized?" Walker asked.

"I think it was Earl. He owns a tow truck company. I was thinking..." He paused. "I was thinking maybe some of the residents might be hiding at the church."

"The church? Why?"

"Because Earl's an atheist. He'd never go to church."

"Cayden, I'm sorry, but we can't rescue everyone," Monte said.

A silence fell over the group. Isabella wasn't sure they could rescue anyone.

Walker lifted both hands. "Why not? There's our army."

Monte dropped his chin and glared at the lawman. "They're hiding in a church." He punched every word. "What makes you think we could convince them to fight back against those thugs?"

"Maybe they just need the right leader," Walker said, pointing to Monte.

"Oh, no. No way. I'm not a leader. Besides, I'm not willing to be responsible for a bunch of citizens getting killed. Maybe they're right where they need to be. Obviously, it's working for them so far."

Cayden stood erect, shoulders back. He looked so much like Will at that moment. Fear ate at Isabella, not knowing if Will were okay.

"Don't you think they deserve a chance to get out from under the tyrant that has them all terrified?" Cayden asked.

Monte eyed him sideways for a moment. "Deserve? Do any of us deserve this? We have to play the hand we're dealt. Right now, our concern has to be getting your dad back. If we can accomplish that, then maybe he can be their so-called leader."

Isabella's nervous stomach was calling for a bathroom. She turned in a circle, hoping one was close by. She'd only turned her back for a moment, but it had been enough. "Where are you going?" she called as she ran after Cayden.

"To the church. I think we should find out what we're up against. Don't you?"

"Cayden, wait a minute. They're still out there." He was at the door. She was still ten feet from him. Her heart skipped a beat as light shined through the crack in the door. She stopped and stiffened, expecting bullets to be fired or bad guys to rush in.

"I'll be right back," he said as he threw back the door and disappeared.

She gritted her teeth, reminding herself why she'd never had children. "Cayden!" she called to the empty room.

TWENTY-SEVEN

Will

DAY EIGHT

Will's head was throbbing, and his vision blurred. He was disoriented but could discern that he was being carried.

"Put him in there," a gruff male voice said.

Will was confused. The voice wasn't Monte's or Walker's. Who was it? Where were they taking him?

He was dropped hard onto the concrete floor then saw a flash of a face before the door to the storage closet slammed shut and he lost consciousness again.

When the door opened again, he wasn't sure how long he'd been out. The light hurt his eyes, and he tried to raise his hand to cover them, but they had cuffed him behind his back. A man rushed in, grabbed his arm, and pulled him to his feet. He shoved Will through the narrow doorway into a corridor he recognized.

"Bring him in here," Mayor Clarence Thibodeaux said.

He was in Vincent at the city hall. How had he gotten there? Why was he handcuffed? For a moment, he was eighteen again and being hauled in for racing his 1970 Pontiac GTO down Main Street. Was that it?

"Welcome home, Will," a male voice said as they shoved him into the mayor's office.

Behind the desk sat Buzz Blanchard, his feet up and a cigar in his hand.

"Sorry about the lack of a welcome home parade. No one knew it was you. I told them the former star quarterback deserved a better homecoming than that."

"What's going on here, Buzz?" Will asked.

"The world went to shit, or don't you know?'

"I've seen. I came from Houston."

"Really?" Buzz put his feet on the floor and sat erect. "You know what's happened then?"

Will nodded. "We were attacked. They let off a nuke high up in the atmosphere capable of taking out everything electronic—well, most things."

"Well, I'll be damned. I told you. Didn't I tell you, Thibodeaux? I said it was some foreign assholes."

"Chinese, from what I know about it," Will said.

"China? Shit!" Charlie Blanchard, Buzz's son, walked around Will and approached the desk. "We're screwed then."

"The military is fighting back," Will said.

"Hooah!" a voice said behind him. Buzz's nephew Willie appeared at Will's side.

"Can I get these off?" Will nodded toward his cuffed hands.

"Not just yet. We need to find out who all came rolling into my town with you and where they ran off to."

Cayden!

Will lunged forward toward Buzz, but Charlie caught him and spun him around. "If you hurt my kid, so help me…" Will spat, punching every word as he tried to wrestle free from Charlie.

"You got a kid? I didn't know that. That woman with them yours too?"

They got away. Cayden will lead them to Savanah's. Will just needed to get out of the cuffs and escape somehow. "They are no threat to you or this town. We were just heading home." He could feel one of the cuffs sliding over the knuckle of his thumb. Will relaxed his shoulders.

"To your granddaddy's farm?" Buzz asked.

There was no use in lying. Buzz knew where it was. Will worked to pull the cuff down over his right hand.

"My sister took it over after..." Will cast a glare at the mayor.

"After she left that piece of shit son of Thibodeaux's," Buzz finished for him.

Thibodeaux stared at Will, expressionless. It was plain to see who was really in charge of the town now. Thibodeaux and his henchmen had run the city for decades. Everyone knew how corrupt he was, but they were too afraid to vote him out of office. People that had crossed him had their homes or businesses burned down or their pets killed as a warning. It would have been satisfying seeing him in this subservient position if the man who'd brought it about wasn't holding him and looking for his son and friends.

"Still, we can't just let people drive up in here like that. It sets a bad example for the town. We have a reputation and standards to uphold. Now, what we're gonna do is take you out on the steps of city hall and have you tell your people to give themselves up. That way, nobody's got to get hurt."

"They're no threat to you, Buzz. We just want to get quietly through town and make it to the farm. We won't come back, I promise."

Will knew there was nothing that he could say, but he was buying time—for what, he wasn't sure. Buzz gestured for Charlie to grab Will, and he was hauled out of the building. Will stood on the top step, flanked by Charlie and Mayor Thibodeaux.

Charlie held a megaphone up to Will's mouth. "Do it. Tell them to turn themselves in. If you don't, it won't be good for you, and it won't be pleasant for them when we do locate them."

Just as Will's right hand slid free from the handcuff, a shot rang out. Thibodeaux dove and rolled down the steps. Charlie just stood there, unmoving. Will dropped and ran in a low crouch to the end of the landing and dove behind the bushes on the side of the steps.

The door opened, and someone rushed out and grabbed Charlie, dragging him back inside. Will heard shouting, and then someone inside returned fire. Will crawled behind the shrubbery to the corner of the building. He poked his head out, trying to see where his group was firing from. It had to be Monte or Walker that had fired. They'd come for him. He prayed that Cayden and Isabella were tucked away someplace safe. He swept his view across the lawn of the library across the street, sure that the round had to have come from that direction. He slowly stood, his head rising above the azaleas. He heard a crunch behind him, but before he could react, something crashed into the side of his face. His head whipped to the side, and he fell back against the building. A fist drew back again and slammed into him. This time he rolled his head with the punch, dropped, and barreled into Willie with all his weight.

Will took an elbow to the back of his skull that dazed him. He fell forward on his hands and knees, but pure adrenaline kept him alert. There were now multiple people firing at once. Will fought to get free of Willie's grasp. He had to get away. He needed to find Cayden and get him away from there. Will pulled free and hauled his arm back, nailing Willie in the throat. The man crumpled, falling to the ground.

Will took two steps toward the street before he saw a flash of something in his peripheral vision. He turned toward it a second before Derek, Savanah's husband, clocked him on the jaw.

"Grab his hands," Derek said, and Wade joined them.

Will was rushed through the side door of city hall and thrown to the floor. Buzz was on top of him in seconds, shaking him and screaming at the top of his lungs.

"I'm going to kill you! I'm going to gut that boy of yours. You took my son from me, and I'm going to make you pay. I'm going to skin your son alive right in front of you. You hear me,

Will Fontenot? I'm going to make you wish you'd never been born."

Will's head bounced off the floor repeatedly as he shook him. He could smell the stench of Blanchard's breath and feel its warmth on his cheek. At that moment, Will thought he was going to die. But if Buzz didn't kill him, he'd never let him get anywhere near his son.

The glass broke near the front of the building, startling Buzz. He stopped his assault on Will long enough for him to shift his weight. He arched and attempted to throw him off, but Buzz held onto his shoulders. A barrage of rounds struck the facade.

"Go!" Buzz told Derek and Wade. Secure the building. No one gets in."

As they ran toward the front of city hall, Buzz stood, hauling Will with him. Will repositioned himself and struck out with his foot, kicking at Buzz's knee. He dropped but pulled Will down with him. They rolled, each struggling to be the one that came out on top. Will landed a blow to Buzz's midsection and found himself on top. He reached back to deliver a blow to the man's face, but someone caught his hand from behind. He was yanked back and found himself on his back with Valson Blanchard's boot seated on his chest.

"Lucky for you, old man, that I showed up when I did," Valson said, as Derek and Wade applied flex cuffs to Will's wrists.

He was shoved into an office chair and wheeled into the council chambers. As soon as the swing doors opened, Will gasped. The smell was appalling. He couldn't believe he hadn't noticed it before now. The grotesque faces of the former city council members stared back at him from the seats on the dais. They'd killed them all and staged them there. All except the mayor. Had they refused to go along with Buzz taking over the town?

Will was pushed down the aisle toward the podium in front of the dais. What was the point of this? Will was having a hard time wrapping his head around such insanity. He tried to read the madman's face, but he was expressionless. If he was revolted by the scene before them, he wasn't showing it.

"What's going on here?" Will asked him.

"Shut up!" Buzz yelled. "You don't get to speak."

"What have you done here? This is madness," Will said.

Buzz rushed from behind him, spun the chair around, and got in his face. "You see what I'm going to do to your boy and the bitch with him. And whoever else is out there shooting at my men."

"He's just a kid," Will spat. "He's thirteen years old. He's never hurt anyone in his life."

"You think I give a flying flip how old your spawn is? They killed my boy. You people barged into my town, and now they're out there running around shooting people. We *will* find them and when we do, I'm going to make them an example for everyone to see." He leaned back. In his eyes was the look of pure insanity.

Whether it was the years of drugs or he'd been born mentally ill didn't matter at this point. There'd be no stopping him, no reasoning with him. Will prayed that Monte and Walker would just take Cayden and Isabella and get far away from Vincent.

"Find them," Buzz barked as he stomped back up the aisle toward the door.

As soon as he was out of earshot, Will tried to reason with Derek. They'd never been close but Will had always tried to remain civil and friendly to the man when he was still with Savanah. Whatever he was, he was still her children's father.

"Derek, you have to help me. You can't let that animal near my son."

"Why should I help you, Will?" He pointed to the dais. "That's what helping you will get my family and me." He leaned in. "Including your sister and her kids."

Those words were like daggers in his heart. The thought that they'd go after Savanah and the kids too chilled him to the bone. He tried to stand, but Derek pushed him back down. "There has to be something we can do?"

"If there was, don't you think the town would have done it already."

"How many of them are there? There can't be more of them than the people in this town. We can fight them together."

"After witnessing this," Derek nodded toward the dais, "the town is too scared to come out of the church basement."

TWENTY-EIGHT

Savanah

Blake looked like he was going to throw up. "You're sure they weren't some of ours?" he asked, his face in his hands.

Jason nodded. "We're sure. I don't know who they were, but definitely not US Military."

Luca twisted his hipster Viking braid around and around his finger. His fidgeting made Savanah's anxiety even worse. "How confident can you be that they were military at all?"

"They were all dressed alike and heavily armed. They looked to have some type of specialized communication equipment with their own satellite dish and everything," Jason said.

"Still, how can you be certain they weren't ours?" Luca asked.

"Well... they were all Asian and weren't speaking English."

Savanah rested her head on her knees. She'd been nauseated ever since Jason had first told her about the "scouts," as he called them. She couldn't imagine a foreign enemy on American soil. The United States had the best military on the planet. How could this happen? How could any of this have happened?

"I'm ninety-nine percent certain they were part of a foreign military force. Pete thinks that they are the ones responsible for the lights and everything not working. The question for us is, what can we do to protect ourselves?"

"What can we do? We're no match for an army," Jane said, reaching out and taking Luca's hand.

"For now, we should prepare. We should make sure we have water and food stored in various locations, not just here but somewhere else if we have to flee in a hurry. Also, we should expand our perimeter, so we have advance notice if we get troops in the area."

"We can hide until they pass. Surely we wouldn't be their target," Luca said.

Jason raised one eyebrow. "That's one option. I do think we should find a place for the children and those who can't fight." Savanah fought the urge to look at Mr. and Mrs. Bertrand. They'd been quiet through the whole discussion.

"In World War II, the Nazis went house to house," Mrs. B said.

"We have the false room," Savanah said. "Where we have all the food stored now, it's a hidden room. If you close the door, it just looks like a shelf inside the smaller pantry."

She and the children had hidden in there before. She'd told them it was a hurricane drill, but she'd been avoiding Wade, one of Mayor Thibodeaux's scumbags.

"We'll move what we can into there and plan on the children remaining there," Jason said.

"We'll stay with them," Mrs. B said, looking at her husband.

"I can still shoot. I can't run much, but I've got a damn good aim."

"Good," Jason said. "You'll be the last line of defense for the children then."

"We'd need to move my in-laws in there too. Herbert might complain, but he can't see worth a shit. He'd only be in the way."

"Herbert ain't never been a good shot. He couldn't hit the broad side of the barn if he was standing right in front of it."

"So, I'll prepare them for that possibility and arrange a way to move them over here quickly," Blake said.

"What about the animals?" Jane asked.

"We could have a few cages ready for some of the hens, but the room won't hold much more than that," Savanah said.

Jane frowned. It would be devastating if anything happened to the livestock and other animals they relied on for food. But there was nowhere to move them to that would be safe from an invading army.

"We need to beef up our perimeter defenses and add some early warning systems," Blake said.

"How? Look around. We're spread out with open fields between the homes. What kind of defenses can we possibly install to stop an army?" Luca asked.

Blake jabbed a thumb over his shoulder toward Savanah's driveway. "Buried spike strips for a start. There are many more things like that we can do for anyone on foot. They'd need to get out of their vehicles to search houses, right?"

"What about the early warning system?"

"I was thinking we should have a talk with the folks over near Choupique and see if we can work together for a common defense. Anyone coming from the south would pass through there first. They would be considered our outer security zone. We would ask them to send someone to provide us with advance notice at the first sign of an invading force. In exchange, we could be their fallback position."

"I have a cousin down that way. He has a big family. I bet they'd go around and get support for something like that. He served in the navy too. He might have some ideas," Mrs. B said.

Blake looked at Luca. "We need someone to ride over there and have a talk with them."

Luca raised his eyebrows.

"Can you ride a horse?" Blake asked him.

Luca cocked his head to one side and his eyes narrowed questioningly. "Yeah."

"You can ride down there then."

"How far away is it?"

"Eight miles," Mrs. B said. "I can write you a note to give to Walter."

"We need to establish an outpost at that Y-intersection two miles from here. They'd have to pass that way if they came by vehicle."

Savanah sighed heavily. "This is all getting so complicated. We just don't have enough people for this."

"We have Pete and his family, along with Rod. I think we should go back and talk to the rest of the neighbors who haven't fled yet and fill them in. They may be more willing to take part now, maybe guard an outpost," Jason said.

"While Luca runs down to Choupique, I'll work on burying our pre-emergency caches."

"Our what?" Jason asked.

"Pre-emergency caches—or essential supplies, like ammo and extra weapons, along with food and water in case we get pinned down or surrounded."

"Sounds good," he said. Savanah detected some skepticism in his voice.

They were in over their heads. They weren't trained fighters. None of them, besides Blake, had any tactical training or experience. They were farmers and homesteaders. Give her a goat with a sore hoof—no problem. An aggressive buck or ornery rooster—she knew how to handle that—but trained fighters with military-grade weapons, how could they possibly hope to win against those odds. Their only chance was to stop them before they reached the farms.

"We could take out that bridge over Gray Gully," Savanah said. "They could drive through the field, but not in a heavy truck, tanks, or anything. They'd get stuck for sure."

"How are we going to take out a bridge?" Luca asked.

Savanah lifted one shoulder.

"We may not be able to blow it up, but we could block it. It would slow them down," Mr. B said. "There are enough old tractors around that we could pull over there and pile up."

"If we had time, that might be worth doing," Jason said. "I just don't think that we do."

The wheels in Savanah's brain were spinning, trying to think of an effective way to keep a military force from entering their area. There weren't that many roads leading to Sugar Cove. The unincorporated area southeast of Vincent was home to maybe seventy people—most were related somehow. There had been an influx of new people in the last few years as the older generation moved into town or passed and left their farms to relatives—some of whom chose to sell—like the Guidrys who'd sold over a hundred acres to the developer of Sugar Hill.

She thought about the wall around their community. It was scalable, but it would slow someone down. She wished they had time to build something similar, but that could take weeks, if not months. The best they could do was the defensive measures she and Jason had employed to keep people from coming down her driveway.

"I can get the kids working on more spike strips," Savanah said.

Mr. B smiled. "I got some ideas for booby traps and punji pits."

Mrs. B cocked her head slightly and looked down her nose at him.

"I've watched Rambo dozens of times," he said.

"You're Rambo now?" she asked.

"If I were twenty years younger. I can build a fire with sticks."

Mrs. B chuckled and touched his arm. "And matches."

Savanah envied their loving relationship. No matter what was ahead of them, they'd had a long and remarkable life together with many beautiful memories. What would her children remember about the pre-apocalypse days? Derek—and Wade?

She shoved the thoughts of them aside and turned her attention to Blake and Jason. She studied their faces. They'd do what they could to protect the community and prepare them for what may be coming. It was a relief to have some type of plan, even though Savanah knew they were no match for a well-armed adversary. Before doing anything, she was going to repack her children's bug-out bags. As much as she wanted to fight and save the farm, it wasn't worth the risk of losing her children. If the enemy got close, they'd bug out—she just wasn't sure to where yet.

Savanah followed Jason into the house. He looked exhausted after being up for over twenty-four hours. His five o'clock shadow had grown into something closer to a beard. He could also use a shower or a stronger deodorant. She pulled her T-shirt up to her nose—they all could. She was amazed at the relief she felt having him back home. Home? A little more than a week ago, he'd lived in town and came out two or three times a week to help out around the farm. It wasn't that she'd never thought about a relationship with Jason. It was more that she'd thought about it and dismissed it —not really because of anything about him personally. It was his family. She'd made that mistake before and didn't want to repeat it. What about now? What had changed?

"Why don't you get a few hours of shut-eye before you run off again?" Savanah said as he peeled out of his sweaty shirt and threw it onto the stack of laundry piling up in the mudroom. He turned, flashing her his six-pack abs. Savanah had to look away. She didn't want the distraction. Not right now. She needed to tell him about talking to his brother and she wasn't looking forward to it. He would be pissed for sure, but he needed to know that his father may send his goons out looking for him. That could end badly.

"I just need to grab a bite to eat and maybe a cup of coffee, then I'll help you get things moved into the safe room for the kids and the Bertrands."

She'd hoped to have more time—that maybe he'd take it better after a nap—but it appeared that wasn't going to happen.

Savanah placed the steaming cup of coffee down next to Jason's plate and took a seat across from him. She waited until his mouth was full of Mrs. B's sourdough bread before blurting out that she'd been to talk to Valson.

"You what!" Jason spat, bread and spittle flying across the table. His face reddened.

Savanah tensed. "You were missing." Her voice was high. "I thought he might have done something to you."

"And you thought you'd just walk down there and ask him. Savanah...!" Veins popped out in his neck.

"I know. I know. It gets worse," She scrunched her face. "He was going into town to tell your dad." She leaned back in her seat and tried to make herself smaller.

Jason closed his eyes and huffed then shook his head and opened his eyes. After he drew in a deep breath and let it out, he said, "I appreciate that you were concerned for me. I do. And I'm glad that you didn't get hurt and leave your kids orphans."

Ouch! That hurt.

She didn't appreciate it. Was he calling her an unfit mother? She heard Derek's voice in her head.

No! They're nothing alike.

Jason looked after her kids in ways their biological father never had. She knew if something happened to her that he'd lay down his life for them. It was one reason she was falling for him—that, and he looked damn handsome when he was mad.

"I'm very sorry. I shouldn't have done that, I know. I can go back and let Valson know that you've returned and tell him to call off the dogs."

"No!" Jason barked. He paused and then held up a hand. "No. I'll do it. I don't want you anywhere near those animals."

She had complicated things, and now Jason had to fix it. In the mood he was in and as tired as he was, things could get ugly quickly. Regret stabbed at her heart.

He pushed away from the table, grabbed his rifle and the small backpack he'd taken to carrying everywhere, and started for the door. "I'll be back in thirty minutes. If for some reason I'm not, don't come looking for me, Savanah. Stay here and make things safe for the kids." He put his hand on the doorknob. "But I'll be back. Don't worry."

She'd worry—of course, she would. If something happened to him at Sugar Hill, she'd never forgive herself. In hindsight, she didn't know what she'd been thinking of going there. Jason had been right. She'd need to be more careful—her children's lives depended upon it.

Blake and Mr. B helped Savanah, Kendra, and Keegan roll barbed wire out on the ground along the fence line in a crisscross or lattice pattern where it intersected less than an average human step. It was tacked up with stakes at various heights from ankle to knee level in the tall grass and the undergrowth that ran along the canal at the back of the property.

"We'll leave this area here open," Mr. B said.

Savanah stared at the path that led to the canal. "Why? Don't we want to stop them from getting close to the house?"

"We want them to use the path. Think of it like a funnel. It's better than them spreading out. It will make them easier to hit."

"Counterattack kill zones," Blake said.

Savanah looked to see if the kids had heard them talking like that. They appeared to be deep in some conversation about what kind of food they'd miss as they tied the bells along the fence line that separated their property from the Bertrands'. She couldn't believe this was her life now. She was talking kill zones and setting booby traps with her neighbors instead of seeing them at the farmer's market or chasing her pigs across their pastures.

After seeing Luca off as he headed to Choupique to deliver the letter and ask them to join forces, Jane helped them in putting up defenses. She was young and strong and a great asset with the animals. They were coming together as a cohesive group. But would it be enough? She prayed it would. She so did not want to have to leave her home.

TWENTY-NINE

Cayden

DAY EIGHT

Isabella sounded pissed, but he had to try to reach the church. Cayden feared time was running out for his dad, and he knew there were people in this town that would help him if they knew. They'd all talked so highly about his dad every time they came to visit. Mr. Broussard at the bakery and Earl at the auto repair shop had boasted about him. Surely they'd help.

Cayden ran down the alley and jumped Mrs. Johnson's fence. He ran across her lawn and down the block toward the church. He stopped at the side of the building where he'd seen Earl. Colorful fragments of the once beautiful stained glass littered the ground beneath the windows. Cayden stepped behind the shrubbery and stood on his tiptoes, trying to peer inside. He just wasn't tall enough.

"Earl," he whispered.

Cayden listened but heard only silence.

"Earl, it's Cayden Fontenot," he said, just a little louder. He edged to the corner of the stone facade building and looked for any of the dudes that had chased them. The street in front of the church was empty.

Cayden stared back at the broken windows along that side of

the church. It was unlikely that anyone would have remained in those rooms, given that people were shooting into them. They would have moved into the basement of the building.

He pressed himself against the wall and took several deep breaths before bolting toward the door to the parish library. He yanked on the handle, but it was locked. Likely all the doors were locked. He just had to find a way inside. Cayden ran back to the broken windows and crept behind the bushes at the base of the building. The rectangular window leading to the mechanical room was just above ground level. Was it big enough for him to crawl through? He had to try. Pulling the pistol from the nice leather holster Alan had given him, he turned the weapon around and used the pistol's grip to break the window.

Cayden dropped to the ground and cleared away the broken shards that remained in the window's frame before crawling head-first through the opening and dropping onto a stack of cardboard boxes. He rolled and hit the concrete floor with a thud, cracking his right elbow in the fall. He cursed loudly, and his left hand flew up to cover his mouth. He was sure that if anyone were down there, they would have heard him and likely thought he was one of the bad guys.

He sprang to his feet and rushed to the closed door. His heart thudded wildly in his chest as he eased it open and listened. He waited a few seconds before opening it fully and stepping into the hall. Cayden thought he heard hushed voices but couldn't tell where they were coming from so decided to risk it and called out.

"Hello!" He moved toward the end of the corridor. "Hello! I'm Cayden Fontenot. I need help."

He heard voices again. They were louder this time. Cayden moved toward the stairs and stopped. "Earl! It's Cayden. I saw you in the window. I know you're here. I just need to talk to you." He placed his right foot on the first tread and waited for a reply. The door at the top of the stairs opened, and Mr. Broussard's face appeared.

The town residents who'd fled to the church had barricaded themselves in the annex of classrooms. They had boarded up the windows. Candles lit the room where desks had been pushed against the walls, and mats from the nursery had been placed on the floor for sleeping.

"How did you get here?" Mr. Broussard asked.

"In an old truck," Cayden said. "How many of you are staying here?" He didn't have time to tell them about their journey to get there. He needed to get them out there to help his dad.

"Thirty or so."

"My dad needs help. He was injured when we crashed our truck, but people started shooting, and me and the people I was with had to run away and leave him."

Mr. Broussard reached for Cayden's arm. "Oh my, were you shot?"

"No. I bumped it when I climbed in the window here." Cayden pulled back. "Mr. Broussard, I need to speak to everyone and get their help to save my dad."

Mr. Broussard's expression changed to a look of pity. Cayden had always hated that look. He'd gotten it a lot since his mom died. It was not helpful—at all.

"I don't know how much help any of us will be. Most of us are old or disabled."

Despair crept up Cayden's spine. Had Monte been right? Was he wasting time he didn't have by coming here expecting the town to go to his dad's defense?

"Cayden?" Earl's voice boomed in the corridor outside.

"Earl!" Cayden rushed over to him. "Earl, please help me. Please help my dad."

Cayden stared back at the residents of Vincent who'd sought sanctuary in the church. Mr. Broussard had been right. Most were elderly, but not all. Earl wasn't that old, maybe a little older than his dad, but he was healthy. Mr. Johnson had gone to school with his dad, so he could certainly fight back. There were two boys around his age and a couple of young families.

"What you need to do, young man, is to get out of here and go to your Aunt Savanah's. There's no way to fight those hoodlums that have taken over city hall," Mr. Bergeron said. Cayden could see why the old bank manager would feel that way. Those hoodlums, as he called them, were young and strong.

"He's right, Cayden. Your dad would want you to run and get away from here," Mrs. Robertson said, placing a wrinkled hand on his.

"Where is the rest of the town?" Cayden asked. "Vincent had at least four thousand residents. Where were they all hiding?"

"Some joined up with those Blanchard boys after a few days. Most fled during the shootout with the mayor's men. There are some holed up in the casino." Earl pointed a thumb over his shoulder, indicating east.

"The casino?"

"It's new. It used to be a bar. Anyway, Guidry and some of the RV park folks made a stand out there and even put up a roadblock to keep the Blanchards out. We've heard them in a few skirmishes in the last few days, so there must still be some of them out there," Earl said.

"They have guns?" Cayden asked.

"Yeah, that's probably why Blanchard hasn't wiped them out already. They have to be getting low on food though. The casino didn't have a restaurant or anything. They had plenty of beer and pretzels, but not much else."

Cayden tapped his fingers on his legs, thinking and trying to come up with a new plan. He had to decide if he should go and get

Isabella and the guys or go out to the casino alone. That question was answered before he could ask where exactly it was located.

"Cayden Fontenot!" Isabella sounded pissed.

Cayden shot to his feet. At least she hadn't used his middle name like his mom used to do. He thought for a second. He wasn't sure she knew his middle name. He decided he'd keep it that way.

"Isabella. You found us."

She ran over and grabbed him by both shoulders.

"You scared the living hell out of us. You can't run off like that. How are we going to go after your dad if we are chasing you around town?"

Yep, she's pissed.

As far as he could tell, their plan was to hide in Bobby Johnson's boat repair shop until the bad dudes found them. Someone had to do something. He'd done what his dad would have done, and he didn't regret it. At least it got the grown-ups out of hiding.

"This is Earl, and he's Bobby Johnson. That was his boat shop we ran into."

"You broke into my shop?" Bobby asked, stepping forward.

"No," Isabella said. "We were being chased, and we didn't break anything."

"Nice shop," Monte said. "Beautiful job on that Bayliner, man." He extended his hand. "I'm Monte."

Walker hung back near the doorway with his hand on his holster. "That guy there is a Texas Ranger. I forgot his name. I call him Walker—you know, like *Walker, Texas Ranger*—the show."

The corners of Bobby's mouth turned up, and he walked over to greet the lawman. As they engaged in a conversation about the show and what it was like being a "real" ranger, Cayden filled Monte and Isabella in on what he'd learned about the folks at the casino.

"I think we should join forces with them and go for my dad."

"First, we need to find out who has him and where, Cayden," Monte said. "With you guys fairly secure here, I can do some reconnaissance. Then, once we know something, I'll go over to the casino and round up fighters."

"You don't know them. You're an outsider. They may just shoot first," Cayden said.

"I may not be from this town, but I'm from Calcasieu Parish. I may know some of them. Hell, I may even be related."

"I think that's the best option, Cayden. Your dad would not want you going out there. He'd want you in here and safe."

"We're in here, Isabella. How safe is it now?"

Their presence put those that had sought sanctuary there in danger. If the Blanchards discovered they were there, they'd shoot their way inside. People would die. Maybe it was a bad idea, after all.

"We can't stay here. We put all these people at risk."

Isabella's head rotated, taking in the room. A pained look spread across her face.

She nodded. "You're right." Isabella turned and walked back to where Monte was filling Walker in on his plan. Cayden followed her.

"We should go. Now! We're going to get these people killed," she whispered.

Monte looked up and then to a group of preschool-aged children playing on the floor.

"Shit!"

"I guess we're all going to the casino then," Walker said.

"First, let me go see if I can find out where Will is," Monte said. "I'll be gone like ten, fifteen minutes tops."

"If they got him, he's at city hall," Earl said. "Buzz hasn't left there since he took control of the town. That's where they'd take Will. I'd bet anything on it."

"Can you draw me a map to city hall?" Monte said.

"I can show you," Cayden said.

"No! Your dad would skin me alive if I let you do that."

"I'll go," Earl said. He smiled down at Cayden and mussed his hair. Why did grown-ups do that? He was thirteen, not five.

Waiting for Earl and Monte to return was excruciating. Cayden passed the time like his mom used to when his dad still raced motorbikes and was late getting home. Fear crept in. Fear that they wouldn't be able to get his dad back or that he had died from his injuries in the wreck. The thought of being an orphan was too much for him.

When he heard the squeak of the door to the basement, Cayden shot down the corridor.

"Did you find him? Is he all right? Is he alive?"

Isabella approached him from behind and placed a hand on his back.

"We found him. He's alive. He's at city hall, just like Earl said he'd be," Monte said.

"Let's get the people from the casino and go get him," Cayden said, brushing past him.

"You sure that's a good idea? How do we know that they aren't just as bad—or worse?" Isabella asked.

"They're good people," Earl said. "But be careful and announce yourselves."

Cayden led them down alleys, across several unfenced yards, and down along the Vincent Canal that ran south and eventually connected to the Intercoastal Waterway, a man-made canal that allowed ocean-going vessels to sail between New Orleans and Houston without going into the unprotected water of the Gulf of Mexico.

"The casino should be through those trees and across the road.

That's where the bar was." Cayden smiled as he recalled a story his mom used to tell about his dad trying to impress her, trying to dance the jitterbug while he was drunk off his butt. She'd driven him home and spent half the night talking to Mawmaw Fontenot.

Cayden had planned to work their way around and approach the casino from the back, but they didn't make it that far.

"Cayden? Is that you?" a female voice called from a concealed position in the dense underbrush.

"Yeah," he said tentatively.

"What the hell are you doing out here running around like this, Ti-den. Don't you know you gonna get yourself killed," the woman said in a southwest Louisiana accent Cayden thought he recognized.

"Gabby?" It had to be her. His dad's cousin was the only one that called him by his Cajun nickname.

Gabriella Fontenot emerged from the underbrush, a twelve-gauge shotgun in her hands.

"She's my dad's cousin. They stopped speaking a while back. I don't know why," Cayden whispered.

Monte stood and stepped out from the cover of the trees. "Family's family." He let his rifle dangle on its sling and raised his hands in the air. "I'm sorry, but we don't have time for small talk. We came over from Houston with the boy and his daddy. We ran into trouble when we drove into town, and Will didn't get away."

"Oh shit!" Gabby said, approaching them.

Isabella stepped into view. "We came for help to get him back."

"Please, Gabby," Cayden added in his most pleading voice.

"Well, hell, let's go tell your uncles," Gabby said, shaking her head and holding her arms open for a hug.

THIRTY

Isabella

DAY EIGHT

The casino smelled awful. She covered her face with her shirt. It probably didn't look polite but she couldn't help herself. Between the body odor, cigarette smoke, and feces smell coming from a bathroom somewhere, it was sickening. She didn't know how anyone could breathe in there. It was dark and hot. Any second she was going to barf, she could feel it at the back of her throat.

"Listen up!" Gabby yelled.

Isabella could hear people stirring, and then a flashlight flicked on. People were everywhere. On top of blackjack tables, on benches, sleeping in booths, and on the floor.

"What the hell, Gabby? My shift just ended. I need shut-eye," a male voice said from somewhere in the back of the room.

"Get up, all of you. Those bastard Blanchards have my cousin, Will. His boy here came for our help, and we're going to go get him."

Isabella smiled. She liked this woman. She reminded her of Will—but maybe a little bossier.

There were mumbles and groans, but no one objected. More flashlights flicked on, illuminating the space. It was a mess. Trash and booze bottles were everywhere. Isabella cringed and pulled her shirt tighter against her face. "I think I'll wait for you outside."

"I'll join you," Walker said.

"Coming, Cayden?" Isabella called as she exited.

"I'll get 'em going. We'll be out in just a second," Gabby said.

Isabella, Cayden, Walker, and Monte waited by an RV parked near the road. That's when Isabella noticed a row of motorcycles and all-terrain vehicles lined up at the side of the building. At the very back of the property beyond the parking lot, a big guy sat on a side-by-side with his feet up, and a rifle across his lap. He didn't look that tough to her. If the group in town had been afraid to attack them, maybe going to get Will wouldn't be as difficult as she'd thought. She was more concerned about hitching themselves to the group inside at that moment. And then the door opened and out stepped four guys who looked like they were dressed for war. They wore camouflage print from head to toe, body armor, multiple weapons strapped to their bodies, and had military type rifles.

"That's what I'm talking about," Monte said, an ear-to-ear grin spreading across his stubbled face.

A gargantuan man with two sleeves of tattoos leaned over the hood of one of the cars parked in front of the casino. Laid out before him was a large piece of butcher paper that someone had drawn a map of the city on, including the buildings near where they'd crashed the truck.

"What's the plan, Tank?" a tall, lanky man asked.

Cayden leaned in and whispered. "He's my dad's cousin, too."

"Vinnie, you'll get up on the roof of the bank. You'll have a clear line of sight to the front door of city hall." He looked up and nodded to a tall, stocky man with a bald head who looked like Vin Diesel. "You and Troy are going to go into the shoe store. Those side windows there and there," he pointed to the drawing. "You'll have sight of the side doors." He pointed to a tall, lanky man whose hair reminded Isabella of Kramer from the sitcom *Seinfeld*. "You're with me at the back."

The way they were calmly planning out storming city hall, Isabella wondered why they had not done so up until then. The giant man made it sound as easy as a trip to the grocery store. Why wouldn't they have liberated the town?

"Buzz is mine. No one touches him but me. Got it?" he said.

"Valson is there with him," the lanky man said.

"Even better."

"Tank, he's going to know something is up. He's not going to believe that I just happened to go into town hours after he takes my cousin," Gabby said.

"He'll think that Cayden there came to fetch you, and you came running," Tank said. "It doesn't matter if he believes it. We want him to send his guys out. We'll pick 'em off, and there'll be less mess inside."

They had the plan worked out in less than ten minutes. Isabella glanced over at Monte and Walker. They'd been quietly observing the planning. There didn't seem to be a role for them.

"You four are going to escort Gabby to where you crashed your truck and—"

"Cayden? You want to put him in the line of fire?" Isabella's voice cracked. She couldn't believe her ears. Who would put a kid in danger like that? Weren't they supposed to be family?

"You're the bait to get 'em out of the building. They'll be so interested in you that they won't notice me and my boys sneaking up on them. They're cocky. They'll all run out, and we'll mow 'em down. While Vinnie, Troy, and the others are picking them off, me and Rick will slip in the back, take Buzz, and bring Will out."

Isabella spun toward Walker. He was law enforcement. He had training. "Walker?"

Walker was quiet a moment and then stepped closer to the

vehicle. He ran his finger along the crudely drawn street where they'd be acting as a decoy. "What's the range?"

"Over a thousand yards," Tank said.

"They got anything effective at that range?"

"We're not going to let them get a shot off."

"And you think they'll even see us that far away?" Isabella said.

"Their lookouts will."

"And they won't shoot us?"

"They're kids. They don't have guns."

Isabella could not believe that she was going along with such a hair-brained idea or that Monte and Walker had agreed to play decoys. Cayden didn't seem nearly as nervous as she was.

Will was going to be furious that she'd allowed Cayden to be involved in this.

But at least he'd be alive to be furious.

"Don't look toward city hall. Just act like we are going to get the truck," Gabby said as they walked past Brassourds' Bakery.

Fifty feet ahead was the truck parked at an odd angle with its rear end smashed into the side of a tow truck.

"Earl's going to be pissed," Gabby said. "That's his pawpaw's old wrecker."

"He knows," Monte said. "I had to restrain him from going after them when he saw it."

"Why haven't you all done something about them before now?" Isabella asked.

"Why risk it? They weren't any real threat to us. The elders seemed okay with staying at the church, and Blanchard was leaving folks alone after he had his rampage against the town council. Everyone else cleared out. Wasn't worth the trouble."

"What about the food at the grocery store?" Monte asked.

"Mayor Thibodeaux and his boys cleared that out by the second day. I don't know what they did with it. Buzz has had his boy, Valson, running all over the parish to keep them fed."

"What do you mean, running all over the parish?" Monte said.

"They're raiding the countryside," Gabby said.

Isabella's stomach tightened as they drew near to the truck. From that point in the road, she couldn't see city hall. She hoped that meant that no one from there could see them either.

The report of a rifle broke the silence. Isabella grabbed Cayden around the neck and pulled him to the ground behind the wrecker. The glass shattered. One of the tires blew. Tank had been wrong. Someone was shooting directly at them.

THIRTY-ONE

Will

DAY EIGHT

Will heard the shot, so did Derek and Wade. They both ran to the window. "What is it? Is it Cayden and the others I arrived with?" Will tried to stand or move, but all it did was cause the cuffs to dig deeper into his flesh.

"I can't see anything," Wade said. Derek moved in behind him to look for himself.

A round struck Wade in the head, and he slumped onto the floor. Derek jumped back away from the window and stared down at Wade for a long moment before realizing what had happened. As he turned and started for the door, Will struggled against his restraints, trying to free himself, but the flex cuffs held firm. He leaned forward and let himself fall. He rolled in time to see the light as the door opened a crack. The next thing he knew, the door was flung back and two men raced into the room. Wade's hands flew into the air as he scrambled backward.

The larger of the two men stepped into view.

"Tank?"

He squeezed off two shots, and Wade dropped to the floor.

"Tank? How did you—"

"Your kid," Tank answered before Will could finish his question.

"Cayden? He's all right. He's safe?"

"He's waiting for you outside, so let's go."

Tank nodded his head toward Will and the second man came into sight.

"Troy?"

"Hey, Will. Good to see you made it home."

To say that Will was shocked to see his cousins was an understatement. "I thought you were both still out on the west coast. You said you'd never come back here."

"We came back for Sissy's funeral," Troy said as he slid a long-bladed knife under the flex cuffs.

"I'm so sorry. I hadn't heard that your sister passed," Will said.

He lamented that the family had been so fragmented. They'd once been close. He'd played with all his cousins like brothers and sisters. That was before the falling out between his dad and theirs. It was just another thing his dad had taken from Will and Savanah. His grandfather had tried everything to get his boys to repair their relationship but the rift was just too deep.

Tank extended a hand and pulled Will to his feet.

"I'm sorry about your wife. We sent flowers," Tank said.

"Thank you." Will didn't know what else to say. He hadn't seen him since his grandfather's funeral, and they'd barely spoken then.

Troy reached back and slung his rifle over his head. "Here. You still know how to use one, don't you?"

Will nodded. "Thank you, guys, for coming for me."

"We're still family," Troy said as he pulled a pistol from a side holster.

"Okay, then. Let's go do this thing," Tank said, making a chopping motion with his hand.

Will gritted his teeth as he tightened the strap on his rifle sling.

Sweat dripped from his face as Tank pointed toward the door. Troy was smiling like he was enjoying himself.

Tank stopped and peered around the door frame before stepping into the hall. Will went after him, followed by Troy. At the end of the corridor, Tank stopped, held up a fist, and flattened himself against the wall. He leaned forward and peered around the corner to his right. He crouched and traversed the hall, pointing the rifle to his right as he ran. When Tank reached the other side, he motioned for Will and Troy to proceed, then darted toward a door at the end of the hall. He kicked the door, and it flung open. Gunfire rang out. Will was aware of Troy moving parallel to him on his left in a crouch, his rifle at the ready-fire position. Will hugged the wall of the building as he inched forward toward the door. He made eye contact with Tank, who had made it into the council chamber. Will followed him through the doorway. It was dark, the only light shining in from behind him.

A man popped up from behind the dais. Will ran forward while putting the HoloSight's red, floating reticle on the center of the man's face and squeezed the trigger. He watched as the man fell forward. Troy looked behind him, then back at Will—the smile gone from his face. Will sensed movement to his left. In a tenth of a second, he recognized Tank had stepped around him.

"Run, Will," he yelled, pointing to a set of double doors thirty feet away.

Tank stepped forward and began returning fire as Will sprinted across the room, slamming his shoulder against the door as he dodged bullets. Rounds peppered the door and wall around him. He kept his eyes on the light coming through the next set of double doors. Troy was right behind him.

"Where's Tank?"

"He's coming," Troy said, pushing through the doors.

Troy froze in the doorway. Will slid to a stop behind him, crouched, and pressed himself against the wall, ready for incoming rounds. "Hands up, Troy." It was Valson. Will glanced back over his shoulder, looking for Tank. He was still engaged with whoever had been firing upon them in the council chamber. Will leaned to his left slightly to see where Valson was standing as Troy slowly lowered his pistol to the ground. "Hey, Valson. We just came to get Will. There's no need for any of this."

Will caught sight of Valson through the small rectangular window. He raised his rifle and found him in his sights. Will heard footfalls and assumed them to be from Tank. He was just about to squeeze the trigger to drop Valson when a round whizzed by his head. He spun and brought up his rifle to fire. Buzz sprinted toward him, his face contorted in some psychotic rage. Before Will could fire, he hit him with the full force of his weight, sending them both toppling to the floor. They rolled and clawed, both trying to gain control of the rifle that had skidded across the floor. Buzz grabbed for it, and Will slammed his elbow down hard into the middle of the man's back, stopping him from reaching it. Buzz jerked back and clocked Will on the jaw with his elbow, causing Will to bite his tongue. He was momentarily stunned by the pain. It was enough for Buzz to roll, knocking Will off his back.

Will was vaguely aware of Troy and Valson, struggling just outside the doorway. Buzz rose to his knees and looked back toward Will. Their eyes met. For a moment, all the hate and rage contorting the man's face faded, and then he twisted his body to face Will who watched as he raised a rifle, pointing it directly at him. His life didn't flash before his eyes. Images of Cayden did. Rage boiled in his gut. A bullet whizzed past Will's left ear and slammed into the man, striking him in the face just above the bridge of the nose. A look of surprise showed in his eyes, and then he fell slowly forward. Will was frozen, watching as Buzz's face hit the floor. A hand on his shoulder jolted him from his trance.

"We have to move," Tank said, yanking Will to his feet.

Tank rolled Buzz over with the toe of his boot, bent, and retrieved Will's rifle. He handed it to him and moved toward the door. Will wiped the blood from the grip as he fell in behind Tank.

"Where's Troy and Valson?" Will asked.

"I don't know," Tank said.

"They were just there." Will pointed.

Tank stepped through the doorway, and Will followed him. "Will, move left," Tank yelled over a cacophony of rifle fire. Will dove behind the shrubbery by the walkway as bullets ripped up dirt ten feet from him. He'd lost sight of Tank. He was on his own. He crawled toward the end of the building and spotted Tank crossing the street and disappearing between two buildings. Will rose into a crouch and ran toward where he'd last seen Tank, his shoulder hugging the wall as he made his way to the back of the buildings. As Will crouched behind an air-conditioning unit, breathing in gasps, successive bursts of gunfire drowned out all other noise. He didn't hear Troy come up behind him. A second later, Tank stepped out from the back of where the florist shop's walk-in freezer jutted into the alley and gestured for them to follow him. Will followed and Troy followed closely, frequently looking behind them.

"Where are we going?" Will asked. "Where's Cayden and my friends?"

Tank didn't answer.

"Valson got away," Troy said when they stopped at the end of the alley.

"Shit, Troy. I had to drop Buzz. We've got nothing now."

"We'll figure something out," Troy said.

"We have to find Valson," Tank said.

"Why?" Will asked.

"It's personal. Has nothing to do with you," Tank replied.

Tank crouched low and checked the ammunition in his rifle. He dropped the magazine and replaced it with a fresh one before standing. "Your son and friends should be at the church. I suggest you get to them and get the hell out of here." He stepped onto the sidewalk and then looked back. "You could tell the people holed up there that they might want to take this opportunity to unass the AO."

"Why, Tank? What's going on?" Will asked.

"Just get the hell out, Will." Tank took off. Will stepped out to see where he was headed, but he'd disappeared around the corner.

"Troy!" Will called to his back as Troy ran after Tank.

"If Valson reaches King's grocery store before we do, the streets will be flooded with shooters. That's where his crew has been staying. Buzz promised to keep them out of the town if we left him alone," Troy said as he ran.

Will turned to his left and ran toward the church. He prayed he made it there and could get everyone out of town before World War III started.

Will turned the corner and came face to face with a military Humvee. It was parked in the middle of Main Street. The driver spotted him. Will's eyes traveled up to the turret. That was who he was concerned about. The gunner had the .50 cal pointed right at him. Will froze. The back passenger door opened and Walker got out.

"Walker?"

He smiled and stepped aside. Will saw the top of his son's head as he exited the Humvee and his heart leaped in his chest. "Cayden!" Will ran toward his son and threw his arms around him. Tears streamed down his face as he kissed him on the top of the head and repeated his name. "I love you, son."

"I love you, too, Dad. I can't breathe though." Will loosened his grip and stepped back to look at him. He checked his arms and legs for signs of injury.

"I'm fine," Cayden said. "How's your head?"

Will raised his hand and touched the back of his head. It was a little sticky and hurt some, but he'd live. "Fine."

"You probably need a stitch or two," Isabella said as she walked up behind them. "I can see that gash from here."

"It'll wait. We have to go. Troy said there's like an army of Blanchard's men heading this way right now."

Isabella smiled.

"What? I'm serious. We have to go now. These are sick and dangerous people."

She pointed inside the Humvee. "We have our very own army."

THIRTY-TWO

Will

DAY EIGHT

"Where'd they come from?" Will asked as Walker headed across the street toward an oncoming military transport truck.

"Fort Polk," the driver called back.

The army base was over seventy miles away. They couldn't have just been driving around the area. There had to be a reason for them being in Vincent. "So, what are you doing down here?"

"Chinese scouts," Cayden said as he climbed into Will's lap.

Will looked around the gunner's legs toward Isabella.

"They received a report of Chinese scouts in the area, so they came down to check it out," Isabella said matter-of-factly.

"Here? In Vincent?"

"East of here," the soldier said. "We came through to check with the authorities here to see if they'd seen anyone they didn't know around the area." The soldier put the Humvee into gear and pulled in behind a military transport truck filled with soldiers— along with Walker and Monte.

"What about the issue here? My family members are—"

"Being taken care of as we speak," the soldier said.

The convoy slowly moved through town and headed southeast toward Sugar Cove and the farm where he'd spent most of his childhood. Everything felt different. Somehow, Will knew that nothing would ever be like it had been.

The homes along that stretch of the road looked deserted as well. Will was beginning to worry about what they might find when they reached the farm. Dread filled him as they approached the final turn. Finally, the convoy turned south and stopped at an intersection within a mile of Savanah's.

Will had his hand on the door to exit when the driver stopped him.

"Hey, wait. You all seem like good people. Isabella said that your sister has kids. I think you deserve to know what's going on."

"We know. We were in Houston. We fought insurgents at Ellington Field Joint Reserve Base."

The soldier's eyebrows raised. "But obviously, you don't know about the trouble along the coast near Cameron."

"We heard something about that," Isabella said.

"I think you folks should be prepared to leave the area."

"Leave?" Isabella asked.

"You should think about heading north to Shreveport, or maybe even Texarkana. They are setting up a refugee facility there."

"Are you anticipating being overrun? Aren't you doing anything to stop them from landing along the coast?"

"I'm afraid they've already begun coming ashore. We're moving all our assets down there to confront them, but you could very well find yourselves behind enemy lines soon."

Isabella gasped. "Gawd."

"I just thought you deserved to know. My commander didn't want us telling folks yet. He doesn't want the roads clogged with refugees as we move units from Shreveport and points north of us down south."

Will swallowed hard. It was a lot to take in. Just when he thought he'd reached home and things would improve, the rug had been pulled out from under him.

"Thank you for alerting us. I hope you guys can stop them

before they get this far," Will said as he opened the door and Cayden stood. Will climbed from the vehicle and stood back as it pulled away. He stared at it until it disappeared from view and then turned to Isabella and Cayden.

"You lost?" Walker said as he seemingly appeared from nowhere. Will hadn't even noticed he'd exited the military truck.

"You decide not to head down with Monte?"

"I thought I'd stick around here for a bit if you think your sister wouldn't mind one more."

When Will didn't respond, Walker took that as she would object.

"I could go back to town. There's probably an empty house or two now…"

"No. She won't mind. I was just wondering how I was going to tell her the bad news."

Will and Isabella filled Walker in on what the soldier had told them as they made their way toward the farm.

Will stopped at the intersection where they were to turn west to the farm. Cayden stopped beside him a second later.

"What's with the roadblock?" Isabella asked.

"I don't know. Maybe they've seen trouble," Will said.

It wasn't the homecoming Will had hoped for. It had been silly for him to think life there at Savanah's would be the same as before. He'd been fooling himself to believe that people wouldn't want what she and the kids had there on the homestead. One thing was for sure. She didn't put up all those cars and trucks across the road by herself.

"Pete Ashby probably put those there," Cayden said. He pointed to a newer model Ford F-350 Super Duty truck. "That's his."

"How do you know?"

"He posted about it on Instagram."

Of course, he did. It was another reason he didn't like social media. Will never understood why people felt the need to post every aspect of their lives for virtual strangers to know.

"What do we do now?" Isabella said, wiping sweat from her forehead with the back of her hand.

Will studied the roadblock looking for a way around it. They'd done a pretty good job situating the vehicles so that no one could drive through, but he was looking for an opening to walk through. Deep ditches lined both sides of the road. Even the best four-wheel-drive vehicle would be unable to drive around it without getting stuck, and they'd ensured that anyone experienced with mud bogging couldn't make it by pushing small cars into the ditches, nose-first.

They could cross the pasture, but as wet as it looked, they risked getting stuck knee-deep in the boggy field. It would be a risk, and they could get shot out in the open like that and have nowhere to hide. The residents of Sugar Cove Road didn't want visitors and might mistake them for whoever they were trying so hard to keep out.

"What are you thinking?" Isabella asked.

Will chewed on his bottom lip as he tried to think of something positive to tell her. His eyes went from the field to the road and back. Isabella could barely walk, let alone run if need be. "Maybe," he said and stopped. "I don't see as we have a choice but to go down the middle and weave between the cars."

Will snugged his rifle to his shoulder and headed that way. "We need to be ready to leave in a hurry. I don't like hanging out here in the open too long."

As Will slowly approached the barricade, Cayden asked, "Dad, you think Aunt Savanah and them are okay?"

He hoped so. He told himself that the roadblock was a good

sign. They were proactive and prepared to defend their community. That the barricade was still intact likely meant they'd been successful. "I'm sure they're fine. Someone was thinking ahead. It doesn't hurt to be proactive."

Will stopped where the trees that lined the road ended and surveyed the field ahead before taking a step toward the first vehicle. He heard the crack of the rifle a second before recognizing it. As he dove to the ground behind Pete's truck, he heard a scream. Isabella dropped next to him, bringing her rifle up.

"Who screamed?" Will asked, hearing someone yell his name. It startled him. He slowly moved to the middle of the right side of the road and got to one knee. He peered around the bumper in the direction of the voice then got to his feet but remained concealed behind the truck, unsure who'd fired the shot at him.

"It's a kid, Will," Walker said, peering through his rifle scope.

"Uncle Will," Karson yelled as he ran toward him.

"Karson?"

"Don't shoot him. That's my nephew," Will said as he stood and rushed to the edge of the roadway.

"Uncle Will, are you all right? Are you shot?"

"No, I'm fine," Will said as he stepped out into the open. There was only a foot or so between the front of the truck and the drop-off to the ditch. His foot slid, and he had to grab hold of the brush guard on the bumper.

"Did you shoot at me?" Will asked.

"No. That was Luca."

"Where is Luca now?"

"Behind that tractor over there," Karson said, pointing over his shoulder.

"Is he likely to open fire at me again?"

It would really suck to come all this way only to die half a mile from his destination.

"No. I told him you were my uncle."

"Karson!" Cayden yelled.

"Hey, Cayden. It's so good to see you guys."

Karson filled them in on the trouble they'd had with the Blanchards and news of the Chinese military in the area. Will was relieved he wouldn't have to be the one to break that news, but from the sounds of it, they had every intention of staying put on the farm. He would have to see how his sister would react when she heard the dire warning of the soldier.

"But everyone is all right?" Will asked his nephew.

"Mom, brother, and sisters are, but some of our neighbors got killed." A sad expression filled his face.

Will placed a hand on Karson's shoulder. His nephew was much too young for this. "What are you doing out here?"

"Guarding the road. The others are having a meeting."

"And your mother let you come out here without her?" That didn't sound at all like his sister. She was very protective of her children.

"She doesn't know. You won't tell her, will you? I'll get in so much trouble."

"I…" Will started. Karson looked upset, but that wasn't something he could keep from his sister. "If you promise me you will never, ever, come out here by yourself again, I won't say anything this time."

"I'm not alone. Luca is with me,"

"Who's Luca?" Will asked. He'd been gone a while. He used to know all the neighbors, but not anymore.

"Luca is a neighbor. He and his wife, Jane, have been staying with us. I gave them my room."

He looked so proud of himself. Savanah must have trusted the guy to allow him to stay in her home around her children, but why had he brought a ten-year-old boy out to guard a roadblock?

"You want to meet him?" Karson asked, grabbing Will's hand, and turning him around to face the tree line.

"Sure. After that, let's get you home before your mother realizes you are gone."

THIRTY-THREE

Will

DAY EIGHT

Karson led them across the field toward an old barn. A young man stepped away from a tractor and waved. "Sorry, I didn't know who you were," he said.

Will gave him a double-take. He didn't look like the farming type. Will imagined he was a relative of some of the old-timers around these parts.

"So, are we to the point where we shoot anyone we don't know?" Isabella said sarcastically.

"Yes," he said flatly.

After what they'd been through themselves on the journey there, Will could understand the man's stance on the topic.

"Have you had to shoot many strangers?" Will asked.

"A few," Luca said. Karson stepped over next to the man. He looked so grown up standing there with his rifle in his hands.

What had he seen? He thought of all Cayden had witnessed. Will's gaze dropped to Karson. "And your mom and siblings are all right?" Will asked again.

"Yeah. They're all fine. Mom, Jason, and some of the neighbors are having a meeting to decide what to do about the Chinese."

"Who?"

"Jason Blanchard. He helps us on the farm," Karson said.

"Blanchard?" Will's voice pitched higher than he'd intended.

"What is..." He stopped himself. The answers he needed should come from his sister, not her son.

"Why don't we get you home before your mom comes looking for you." Will dropped his head and eyed Luca.

"I didn't know he'd followed me until after you arrived," Luca said.

Will looked down his nose at his nephew. "You can't do that again, Karson."

Karson hung his head. "I'm sorry. I just wanted to help guard everyone. I know how to shoot." He held up his rifle.

"I know, but it's too dangerous. You have to leave that stuff to the grown-ups, okay, buddy?"

"I'm tired of everyone treating me like a little kid," Karson whined.

"I know how you feel," Cayden agreed.

"Don't worry. You'll both be growing up sooner than you think," Will said. "Now, let's get you home."

"You coming, Luca?" Karson asked.

"No. I'll stay here to keep an eye on the road."

Will waited until Karson was out of hearing range and then approached Luca. "I don't know what's been going on out here, but we just had some major issues coming through town. You might need more than one person standing guard out here."

"The Blanchards?" Luca said. "We know they took over the town. We haven't had any issue with them yet."

Will looked to the ground and shook his head. "Well, you might now. We kind of stirred things up, and some of the Blanchards left mad."

"Really? Oh shit. I bet they'll try to join up with the rest of them over at Sugar Hill."

"Sugar Hill?"

"The gated community at the end of our road," Luca said, pointing over his shoulder.

"I haven't been home in a while. I didn't know there was a subdivision back that way. And there are Blanchards living in there?" Will couldn't picture any of Buzz's kin being welcome in any neighborhood, let alone an exclusive community.

"They moved in after the lights went out. They've been terrorizing the farms out here."

"And my sister is organizing a response or something?" It would be just like her. She took after their grandmother in stepping up when the community needed her. She was always on some committee meeting at the church.

"She and Jason have pulled together some of the neighbors," Luca said.

Jason? Why would he be working against his relatives? Something wasn't right here and he needed to get to the farm and find out what the hell was going on.

"I'll talk to them about putting an extra guard out here. You good for a bit?" Will asked.

"Yeah. My shift isn't over for three more hours."

Will nodded and then set off across the field to join Isabella and the others.

The first thing Will noticed to be different about the farm was his grandfather's old tractor parked against the gate.

"I'll have to lead you up to the house," Karson said, climbing over the gate.

Will glanced back at Isabella. "She can't climb over the gate. I'll have to lift her over," he said, though he wasn't sure if he could lift her with his ribs busted up like they were.

"I'll catch her," Cayden said.

"I can climb over. My leg is not that bad. Just help me lift it," Isabella said, hiking her good leg up on the pipe gate.

Cayden took hold of her pant leg and placed it next to the other leg and Walker raised his hands to steady her while Will jumped over the gate. Isabella leaned forward as Walker pushed her from behind, helping her throw her leg over the top bar. Will's hands were on her waist, lowering her to the ground when he heard his sister's voice behind him.

"Need a hand?"

His heart leaped, and he turned, placing Isabella on the ground next to him. Savanah's beautiful smile told him he was home. He couldn't recall the last time he'd experienced that feeling. It was as if suddenly everything was right in the world. The energy seeped back into his body.

"Hey there, sister."

Cayden took hold of Isabella as Will threw his arms around his sister, picking her up and spinning her around. He chuckled. "Have you gained weight?" Which earned him a punch in the arm.

"You look like something the dog dug up," Savanah said as Will placed her back on the ground.

"You know what, little sis, I feel like something the dog dug up."

The stabbing pain in his ribs and abdomen from all the lifting caused Will to bend over slightly.

"You okay?"

"Fine. Just a little sore from the journey," he said, rubbing his rib cage.

Savanah tugged on the bottom of his shirt. "Let me see."

Will's head pivoted to Isabella, and his face turned red.

Savanah followed his gaze. "Fine, but I'm going to take a look when we get up to the house."

"This is Isabella. We met after the EMP," Will said.

"The what?" Savanah asked.

"I'll tell you later." It was too complicated to explain out there on the road. His sister really should be sitting down for that type of information.

"Dad pulled Isabella from her burning car," Cayden said, beaming with pride.

"Yes, he did. He saved my life that day—and practically every day since," Isabella said.

"Yeah, that was badass what you did with that steel pipe," Cayden said.

Will wanted to scold him for the language, but he was so taken aback by his praise that he was speechless.

Heat surged beneath Will's cheeks. "You both saved us a few times as well."

Savanah stepped between them and held out her hand. "I'm Will's sister, Savanah. I'm very pleased to meet you."

"I'm so glad to meet you as well. I've heard so many wonderful things about you and your children."

"I'm Ed Sudeski," Walker said, stepping over and extending a hand to Savanah. "But everyone calls me Walker."

"Nice to meet you, Walker. Welcome!" Savanah said, waving her hand toward the homestead.

"Where's the kids?" Will asked.

Savanah looked back over her shoulder. "Doing chores. Karson was supposed to be looking for one of the pigs. They get out practically every day."

Will wasn't going to tell on Karson. They'd just keep that their secret.

Jason appeared beside the tractor.

Will gave him a curt nod and tried not to let his displeasure show on his face.

Jason nodded back.

"You remember, Jason, right?" Savanah asked.

"I do," Will said. "How's it going?" It seemed wrong to be standing at the end of the drive exchanging pleasantries with a

Blanchard after what they'd just been through. What Will wanted to ask him was what the hell he was doing there?

Jason walked over and stood beside Savanah.

"You remember my brother, Will?" Savanah asked him.

The corners of his mouth slowly curled up, but his smile was strained.

Will extended his hand as if his father and brother hadn't just tried to murder him. His brows snapped together as he watched Jason Blanchard put an arm around his sister's waist. Isabella smiled at Will like it was all completely normal. She didn't know him as Will did, or she wouldn't have.

"Karson, honey, you're needed in the pigs' pen," Savanah said, giving him that "mom" look. "Now, let's get you three up to the house and get you fed and cleaned up. You look like you've been through hell."

"That's an understatement," Will and Isabella said simultaneously. They exchanged glances as Will held his arm out to assist Isabella down the drive.

"Wait!" Savanah said. "You'll need to follow me. There are a few surprises buried along the way."

"It sounds like you guys haven't been having a day at the beach yourselves," Will said.

"Not really. I'll tell you all about it over some sweet tea."

"You have ice?" Cayden said.

"No, but I have honey."

As they rounded a bend in the driveway, Will spotted people in the backyard under the big oak tree. "Who are they?"

"A few of the neighbors. We were just discussing forming a neighborhood watch," Savanah said, her eyes bouncing between Will and Cayden.

"Karson said you'd been having trouble with some folks," Cayden said.

Jason avoided Will's gaze and walked off toward the barn as they approached the house.

"Why don't you guys go on in and get cleaned up. I'll be inside in a minute," Savanah said, stepping toward the path leading to the backyard.

"Cayden and Isabella, why don't you two go on in. I'd like to find out what's going on around here before I get too settled," Will said.

Savanah's expression changed to one of sadness. "All right," she said. "Let me introduce you to everyone, and we'll fill you in."

"As much as I'd love to wash up, I want to hear what's happening too," Isabella said.

Cayden smiled. "I'm going to go find Kendra. Boy, is she going to be surprised to see me."

Will watched him run off toward the barn. It warmed his heart to see his son so happy to be there. He knew it would be good for him to be around family and they could finally get some rest. They so desperately needed it after all they'd been through.

After all the introductions had been made, Will studied the group. They looked nothing like the people they'd seen the last few days. They lacked the shell-shocked expressions and haggard appearances. Rob, Pete, August, and Mr. Bertrand he knew. It was Jane and Blake he was unfamiliar with. Without even being told, he'd already guessed that Jane was with Luca, the guy from the roadblock. They both had the appearance of hipsters. They'd likely moved out there to grow organics or something. Blake didn't look like he had much farm experience either. It was probably his hands —too soft looking.

None of them looked like they'd slept much though. Dark circles ringed their eyes, but they were generally clean and uninjured. That fact alone made Will feel better about the situation. They hadn't seen battle yet. Definitely not like he and Isabella had.

He wondered why the Blanchards had left them alone and then remembered Jason. He was dying to ask, but he waited.

"Where'd Jason head off to now?" Pete Ashby asked.

"He went to check on the kids," Savanah said. "He'll join us in a minute."

"He's still upset about his brother?" Blake asked.

Savanah nodded.

"That's understandable," Pete said.

Blake gave Pete a look Will couldn't read. Did they know about the incident in town already?

"So, what now? Jason's brother is gone, and Pete says the cousins moved back into town," Mr. Bertrand said.

Will was taking it all in, trying his best to piece together what had occurred there. If Jason's cousins had fled to Vincent, they weren't there now. Tank, Troy, and the military had cleared the town.

"I say we should reach out to the residents of Sugar Hill and let them know that we don't blame them," Jane said. "We should see if we can work together—"

"Work together? Those kids would have killed my wife and me. They did kill people. Work together—with killers?" Mr. Bertrand was outraged.

"So what's your suggestion? Are we to treat them all as enemies?" Jane asked. "We have to all live together."

"Why? We can never trust them. They just need to be driven from the area," Mr. Bertrand said.

"And how do you propose we are to do that? They have children. Small children. Do you really want them to be homeless?" Jane asked.

No one answered her. Will had no idea what the residents of Sugar Hill had done, but it appeared that their presence could pose a threat to his family.

"I feel like we should continue to be vigilant as if they were a threat, but take no further offensive measure unless they act aggressively," Savanah said.

Everyone grew quiet.

Will studied their faces. Were they trying to convince themselves that the plan would work?

A moment later, Savanah stood and pushed her chair away from the table. "I hope you will all agree because the alternative is war."

Will didn't have enough information to know whether that was even a possibility, but from their hesitation, obviously, the others did.

"How many people are we talking about?" Will asked.

"Fifty or so," Savanah said.

"When did this subdivision go up?"

"A couple of years ago. Some developers bought the farm and started advertising to rich folks in Lake Charles. I never dreamed that many families would want to live out here. There are plenty of golf courses in the city. The forty-minute a day commute would have been enough to deter me," Savanah said.

"It was the price," Pete said. "After that ole boy's wife sued him for divorce, he had to lower the price on the lots to buy her out of his business."

"That's why they filled up so fast after sitting empty so long," Savanah said, returning to her seat.

"And Jason's family is involved, how?"

"They took over and were forcing the teens and young adults to steal for them."

"And they're not there anymore?"

"Someone from town said that Valson and his right-hand man had been killed. The rest fled," Blake said.

News *had* traveled fast.

Will knew that wasn't going to be the end of the story. If there were any Blanchards left alive, they would want revenge. He stiffened. He needed to tell them what the soldier had told him. "I just got here, and I have no idea what this group has done, but I'd say if you can avoid a battle with them, you should try." Will rubbed his hand over his abdomen. He'd seen enough fighting to last him a lifetime. Besides, they needed to reserve any ammunition they might still have for if the Chinese showed up.

"Do we put it to a vote or what?" Blake asked.

"All in favor of just keeping an eye on Sugar Hill for now and maintaining the roadblocks, raise your hand," Pete said.

One by one, everyone raised a hand. Savanah smiled and turned toward the house.

"I'm going to spend some time with my brother and nephew, and then I'll take my turn at the road."

"I'll go fill Luca in on the plan," Jane said.

"Let's get you guys inside to clean up. Mrs. B will have dinner ready soon," Savanah said.

"Wait," Isabella said. She turned to Will. "You should tell them."

"Tell us what?" Blake asked.

Will eased back into his chair and looked up at his sister. "You're going to want to sit down."

They took it much better than Will anticipated. He had imagined crying and freaking out.

"After Will's cousin used Monte, Cayden, and me as bait to draw them out, all hell broke loose. Earl, the tow truck guy, showed up and got us out of there. We were running for our lives when I heard the military coming. Remember that sound, Will? Remember that day on the bridge when we met Lieutenant Sharp?" Isabella said.

Will nodded. It was hard to forget the sound of miles of military trucks.

"I ran out in front of them and flagged them down. They said they'd help."

"What was the military doing in Vincent?" Savanah asked.

"Looking for Chinese scouts."

"We're aware their scouts have been in the area. I just didn't want to scare you your first day home."

"You know, and you aren't packing up?" Will asked.

"We have things in place. We have an agreement with the folks down near Choupique. If they see them, they'll send word. We'll have a little time to prepare. If it looks like there are more of the enemy than we can handle, we'll bug out."

"Savanah, they could drop bombs on us here if they wanted."

"We'll learn if there are significant forces in southwest Louisiana. Mr. B's nephew has been running up and down the canal, letting us know their movements. So far, there have only been a few landing along the coast, and they are more interested in heading west than messing with us. Don't worry, brother. We're planning to be very cautious."

"The waterways could be very useful. You all know them. They don't," Walker said.

"That is one of our advantages. We have a few," Savanah said.

She took Will's hand. "Now, let's get you guys inside, fed, and cleaned up. You stink."

Will laughed. "Gee, thanks."

The house looked the same as the last time he'd been home, even though Savanah had lived there the last four years. Their grandmother's afghan still draped the back of the dark brown sofa, and grandpa's recliner was there next to it. The place had a different smell, though. Grandma was always cooking but now the home smelled like the herbal soaps his sister made. He liked it.

"Isabella, you can have my room, and Will, we'll have to put you and Cayden out here in the living room on the air mattress."

"No, I can't take your room," Isabella said.

"I insist. It's just until we can figure something out."

"Where are you and the kids going to sleep?" Will said.

"Upstairs in the attic."

"No way. It's hotter than Hades up there. You'd cook."

Savanah appeared to think it over. "We could sleep in the outdoor kitchen. It would be like camping. The kids will love it."

"Why don't you and the kids sleep in here on the mattress, and Cayden and I will sleep out there. It will be much cooler anyway." Will had been looking forward to sleeping in a comfortable bed, but he wasn't about to let his sister and her kids sleep on the ground at their own place.

"We could bring the camper over. It sleeps six," Mrs. B said.

"You have a camper?" Savanah asked.

"We do. We haven't used it in years. It's parked in the shed by the barn. It might need airing out, but it would be more comfortable than sleeping on the ground outside."

"Bless you, Mrs. B," Savanah said. "I'll see if Jason will take the tractor and pull it over."

"I can go with him," Walker offered.

Will reached for her hand as she headed toward the door. "I can go. I wanted to have a conversation with Jason, anyway."

Savanah put her hands on her hips. "You aren't going to go all big brother on him, are you?"

Will cocked his head to the side and smiled. "Would I do that?"

Will heard the children's laughter and stopped outside the barn. He closed his eyes and drew in a deep breath. It was so good to be home again. He and Cayden weren't alone anymore. It would be challenging, but he knew that all the adults gathered on the farm would do whatever it took to protect those kids. From one of the bedroom windows, Will heard Savanah and Isabella giggling like schoolgirls. It was strange. Despite the apocalypse that they found themselves in, he was happier and more complete than he had been in the last two years. Whatever they faced from there on out, he knew they'd take on as a family. There wasn't anything on earth more important than family.

His conversation with Jason had been brief. It was evident to Will that Jason was grieving. He knew what that was like and didn't want to be the source of any additional pain. He'd taken Karson and Cayden to pick up the Bertrands' camper and left Jason to work things out in the barn.

Will slung his arms over the top of the gate overlooking the pond and stared out at the farm that had sustained his family for years. It would be tragic to have to leave there now. Savanah appeared to have the start of a strong community, and they could have a comfortable life there.

"Penny for your thoughts," Isabella said, walking up behind him.

Will chuckled and turned to face her. "I don't think money is worth much anymore."

"Are you glad to be home?"

"I'm glad to be with my family." He reached over and took her hand. "I'm grateful that we all made it here alive."

"Me too," Isabella said as he pulled her close and wrapped his arms around her waist.

"One thing that I've learned on this journey is to be grateful for what I have. The world may have gone to shit, but I have my son, we all made it safely here..." he paused and lifted her chin. "And a relationship with you, if you'll have me."

Isabella raised herself on her tiptoes and kissed him. "I'm all yours, Will Fontenot."

∿

Thank you for purchasing No Turning Back, book three in the Fall of Houston series. **The story continues in book four, No Surrender.**

Have you read my Days of Want series? If not, please check out the sample chapters for Turbulent, book one in the series or visit Amazon.com and order your copy today.

If you enjoyed No Turning Back, I'd like to hear from you and hope that you could take a moment and post an honest review on Amazon. Your support and feedback will help this author improve for future projects. Without the support of readers like yourself, self-publishing would not be possible.

Don't forget to sign up for my spam-free newsletter at tlpayne.com to be the first to know of new releases, giveaways and special offers.

No Turning Back has gone through several layers of editing. If you found a typographical, grammatical, or other error which impacted your enjoyment of the book, I offer my apologies and ask that you let me know so I can fix it for future readers. To do so, email me at contact@tlpayne.com. In appreciation, I would like to offer you a free copy of my next book.

Sample Chapters

Chicago O'Hare International Airport
Chicago, Illinois
Day of Event

Terminal Three of Chicago's O'Hare International Airport was filled with pissed-off passengers. After a four-hour delay, Maddison Langston was feeling cranky herself. Her flight from San Diego had arrived at eleven that morning. By three that afternoon, her connecting flight was still not boarding, even though the plane was at the gate.

When the lights in the terminal cut out and the flight departure screen went blank, Maddie sighed.

Looks like my flight will be delayed. Again.

Sitting in the dim light, Maddie pulled her cell phone from the Silent Pocket Faraday backpack Uncle Ryan had given her. Although she had promised him that she'd keep her phone in the bag while she was in the airport, she was having social media withdrawal. She was not as concerned about a thief scanning her RFID chips as he was.

She pulled the charging cord from the pack and started to plug it into an outlet before realizing that it wouldn't charge with the power off. Maddie tapped a social media app on her phone, but it wouldn't load. Her phone didn't have a signal. After shutting it down and restarting it half a dozen times, it still wouldn't connect to her wireless service provider.

To pass the time, she listened to songs from her music library. She usually listened to her favorite music using streaming services. Luckily, she had a few games on her phone.

Maddie looked up to see an angry man in a sport coat and trousers with one knee on the American Airlines service counter. The terrified woman behind the desk had her back pressed against the wall as far from the out-of-control passenger as possible.

Maddie pulled the earbuds from her ears.

Two men had gripped the arms of the angry man, who was yelling obscenities at the woman, as the woman yelled for security.

"Why can't you tell us what the hell is going on? My flight was supposed to leave three hours ago. Now the lights are out, and it is freaking hot as hell in here," another passenger yelled at the petite woman.

"I do not have anything to tell you. I am in the dark too," she said.

"Oh, is that your attempt to lighten the mood? De-stress the situation? Did they teach you that in customer service school?" the man mocked.

"My cell phone isn't working. I need to use a phone. I have to call my husband. He'll be expecting us to arrive in Nashville any minute," a woman called out.

A tall man in a sports jersey and jeans stepped forward. He towered over the other passengers. Holding an arm up, the man said, "Listen up, folks. All this yelling and getting aggressive with customer service isn't going to get us answers that the woman clearly doesn't have."

"Well, someone sure as hell better start explaining pretty damn fast," the man in the sport coat barked, shaking his arms loose from his captors.

"Look around you. It is a chaotic mess in here. It's not just American Airlines' flights that are delayed. No planes have taken off or landed here in over an hour. The power is out to the airport, and something has disrupted the phones, including cell phones."

Just then, an explosion rattled the windows. The ear-piercing sound of metal on concrete was followed by the cockpit of a jet skidding down the runway. It hadn't occurred to Maddie that planes might collide mid-air without access to tower control for guidance. People rushed from the shopping area of the terminal, dragging their wheeled bags behind them, and huddled near the window to stare at the burning wreckage of the plane on the tarmac.

Maddie slowly rose to her feet. Grabbing her backpack from its position beside her, she flipped it over her shoulder and reached for the extended handle on her suitcase. The terminal was in darkness, lit only by the windows where a surreal show of flames and black smoke was casting long shadows toward the center of the concourse.

As Maddie stared out the window with her mouth open wide at the flaming, smoking, twisted mass, a second Boeing 737 dropped from the sky in pieces, scattering onto the runway and bursting into flames. The lights were out, there was no cell service, and planes were colliding in the sky above them.

Maddie came to a startling realization. It had happened. The EMP—the electromagnetic pulse—her dad and Uncle Ryan talked about had really happened. Her hand shot up to cover her mouth. Maddie's feet would not move, even though her brain said run.

She couldn't catch her breath. While her fellow travelers stood with eyes peeled to the horrid sight and their mouths wide in shock and terror, Maddie ran.

Her bag's wheels skipped off the floor of the concourse as Maddie bolted toward a family restroom. Her backpack smacked the wall as she spun around to turn the lock. Maddie dropped her pack and suitcase by the door and slid to the cold tile floor. Hugging her knees to her chest, she sobbed, rocking side to side. Mixed with the crushing fear was a pang of guilt. She had mocked her dad for his paranoia. A wave of grief threatened to crash over her without mercy. As she cried, the years of repressed grief burst to the surface as she recalled the training and warnings her father had tried to communicate to her over the years.

Maddie hadn't cried this much since the accident. The day her dad died. The day her world changed forever.

As the tears flowed in torrents, Maddie rested her head on her arms. She was startled by loud banging behind her. She jumped to her feet and spun to face the door, her heart pounding against her chest. In the blackness, she couldn't see her hand in front of her face. Maddie pulled her phone from her back pocket and activated its flashlight feature. Holding it over her head, she turned and looked around the small room.

I can't stay in here forever.

How long before a plane came crashing through the terminal? How many were up there circling the airport? How many had diverted from their flight paths to land after they lost their navigation system and contact with the control tower? Pilots would only have line-of-sight to avoid a mid-air collision. How soon would it be before they ran out of fuel? Maddie's thoughts raced.

She had to get some place safe right now. That was what her dad always told her. The longer she hesitated, the more dangerous it would be.

Maddie stood and blew her nose. She bent over to reach for her pack.

She froze.

Maddie's heart dropped. She was stranded in one of the country's busiest airports in the middle of one of the most populated cities. And she had never felt more alone.

Maddie turned and put her back to the door. She slid once more to the floor, curling her arms over her head.

Dad was right.

Her friends had called her father, Greg Langston, a doomsday prepper—a title that brought Maddie embarrassment. Before he died, her father had taught her and her brother, Zach, survival skills and how to prepare for disasters. She never took it as seriously as she should have.

"What do I do, Daddy? What do I do?" she cried.

Her mind raced, searching for answers. Images of her rolling her eyes as her dad lectured her and Zach on what to do in a world-ending scenario brought a new round of guilt and shame.

"You were right, Daddy. I am so sorry I mocked you. I didn't listen to you, and now the shit has hit the fan, and I don't know what to do."

She curled into a fetal position. Time seemed to stand still in the tiny, cold room. She stared at the shadow cast by her cell phone. Her mind went blank. She slid into a familiar numbness. Sleep had been her comfort, her only solace in the days and weeks after her dad died. She wanted to go there. She let her breathing slow.

She was shaken back to reality by the sound of the growing chaos outside the bathroom.

Maddie heard her dad's voice in her head.

"Maddison Grace Langston, pay attention. Someday, you might find yourself alone when the shit hits the fan and you will need to know how to survive and get home."

She sat up, brushing loose strands of hair from her face.

The get-home bag her dad had given her containing all the essentials to survive on the road was in her dorm room in Ohio. It would do her no good now. But she had the everyday-carry items with her. Uncle Ryan had picked up where her dad left off in making sure carrying her EDC was a habit. Maddie looked down at the plain, waterproof backpack on the floor next to her. There were times in the last few years when she had resented Ryan for trying to take her dad's place. At that moment, she was grateful he had.

Maddie got to her feet and walked over to the sink. She looked in the mirror. Mascara streaked her face, and her hazel eyes were bloodshot. She ran her hand through her long, blonde hair, pulling it into a messy bun on top of her head and securing it with the hair tie from her wrist. She stared at herself in the mirror.

"You've got this, Maddie. You can do it."

She pointed to the mirror with her index finger.

You have to.

Unzipping her carry-on bag, Maddie was relieved that she had brought her hydration pack on the trip. Knowing she'd need to run every day to maintain her current level of endurance, she had thrown it in her bag. Pulling the vest pack from her suitcase and emptying all the pockets and pouches, she quickly inventoried its contents. With the Jelly Belly Sport Beans, sports gels, and energy bars, she had about ten thousand calories with her. Her hydration bladder and water flasks held at least two liters of water. She added the weight up in her head. She'd be carrying around ten pounds.

When running a marathon or endurance race, she didn't take the hydration bladder or as many energy gels. There was an aid station along the route, and her crew would take position between stations in case she needed a quick pick-me-up. But Maddie had carried that much weight when she did backcountry and trail runs, so she knew she could.

In a Ziploc bag were two headlamps, extra batteries, a compass, and a multifunction mini tool—all requirements from her last race. From her every-day carry pack, she removed the emergency bivvy bag, her Sawyer MINI water filter, and a LifeStraw personal water filter. Maddie shoved them into the kangaroo pouch of her vest pack, along with a Ziploc bag of socks and thermals. The last thing in was a weatherproof jacket.

Maddie undressed and pulled on her running tights. After putting on a tank top, she put on a fresh pair of socks and slid on her running shoes. She wished she hadn't chosen to bring the red ones. They would stand out too much, but there was nothing she could do about that now.

Gathering up the water flasks and bladder, Maddie filled them in the sink. She pushed the bladder into the pouch and placed it in the hydration vest pack.

Placing her arms through the arm holes of the vest, she adjusted the straps across her chest. Her runner's pack was a vest-style. It wrapped around her, fitting snugly against her body. She tugged on the cords. It felt secure. After placing the soft flasks in the front pockets, she strapped one squeeze flask to her wrist. Lastly, she pulled on her dad's Marine Corps Marathon head-band and adjusted it to cover her ears.

She looked down at the half-empty suitcase and her clothes strewn about the floor. She picked them up and threw them into the bag. Maddie didn't consider herself overly materialistic, but her suitcase contained some of her favorite clothes. It pained her to just leave them there.

This is crazy. How am I going to run all the way to St. Louis?

From her Silent Pocket Faraday backpack, Maddie retrieved her earbuds, car keys, and a pack of gum. As she placed them in the right-side pocket, her hands shook so badly that she dropped her car keys on the floor. She was alone in Chicago and the end of civilization as she knew it had occurred—just as her dad had predicted. She was scared shitless and was not afraid to admit it. Maddie shook her head, attempting to fight back the tears that threatened to spill down her face.

Harden up, Maddie.

No one was coming to save her. If she was going to make it, she'd have to protect herself. She couldn't afford to let self-doubt and indecision keep her prisoner in the airport.

St. Louis was about three hundred miles away. The previous week, she had run the New Hampshire 100-mile endurance race in twenty-six hours. So, with needing recovery time between runs, it would take at least a week or more to get home.

How long will it take if I have to avoid dangerous people?

She wanted nothing more than to sit back down on the cold tile floor, curl into a ball, and stay there until her mom came to her rescue.

Mom is not coming, Maddie. Mom is stranded in California.

She had gone with her mother to San Diego. They had brought her grandmother home from the hospital. Her mother wanted Grand to enjoy her last days at home in her own bed surrounded by the things she loved, including her one-eyed dog, Jack. The sudden realization that her mom might not be able to make it back home to Missouri shook her to her core. She had been so focused on herself that she hadn't even thought about where her mom and brother were. When she had last received a text message from Zach, he had been coming back from his school field trip to Washington, D.C.

Maddie placed her hands over her face and rubbed her forehead.

Where did he say they had stopped?

Maddie retrieved her cell phone from the floor beside her suitcase, opened her messages app, and clicked on the last message from Zach. He had been in Marshall, Illinois, right before the lights went out.

Maybe the lights aren't out there?

Although she was unsure where Marshall, Illinois, was, she doubted it was anywhere near Chicago. His bus had been heading southwest back to St. Louis.

He will be all right. There were six teachers on the trip. They'll get him home.

She checked for cell service one last time before putting her phone in the front pouch of her vest. The light from the phone shined through the mesh fabric. She patted her pockets, adjusted her straps, and pulled the cords tight.

Time to get going.

Maddie slowly unlocked and cracked opened the door. The scene out in the corridor was even more chaotic than before. She could hear raised voices and crying.

How long was I in there?

She checked her watch. It was four o'clock. She had at least two hours before it would be dark. Walking down the terminal toward the main hall, she could see that most of the activity centered on the restaurant area of the concourse. People were fighting over what was left of the food.

She needed a map. She had seen a place that sold books and newspapers when she'd gotten coffee earlier.

They should have maps. There are tourists here, right?

Maddie raced around a corner and saw a floor to ceiling mural of the city of Chicago. It wouldn't replace a paper map that she could take with her, but it would give her a direction to head out in at least. Not knowing the scale of the map, she made a fist and stuck up her thumb, using it as a ruler to calculate distance.

"Which way are you heading?" a man asked.

The voice startled her, causing her to jump. She twirled around to find a man in his mid-thirties. Beside the man stood a woman, maybe a little younger than him, and a girl of about ten years old.

"Um— I— South," Maddie stammered.

She chastised herself. She had just given out critical information to a stranger. She could hear her father scold her.

OPSEC, Maddie, her dad would say.

Operational security meant keeping your big trap shut about what you have and where you plan to go. She was sucking at this already. She looked at her feet.

"Your dad serve?" the man asked, pointing to Maddie's Marine Corps buff.

"He did. Did you?" she asked, pointing to the U.S. Army National Guard Minute Man logo on his hat.

"I did."

"Two tours in Iraq and four in Afghanistan," the woman added.

"Yeah, my dad spent a lot of time in those places too."

"Is he with you?" the man asked.

Maddie looked away and swallowed hard, resolved to fight back the tears. She'd give anything to have her dad with her right now.

"I'm Rob Andrews, by the way, and this is my wife April and our daughter Emma."

Emma gave a timid wave as April stepped forward and extended her hand. Maddie shook it and said, "I'm Maddie Langston."

"Look, it is getting bad in here. It's going to get worse in the city very soon. We're not going to wait around for the lights to come back on. We're getting out of here, and it looks like you have the same idea," Rob said.

"Um... Yeah. I mean, I was thinking about it. With the airplanes crashing, I was trying to decide how to leave to avoid the runways. I need to head toward Interstate 55, but that is southwest, and it looks like most of the runways are in that direction."

"You could go due south and then cut over, say, around here." Rob pointed to 143rd Street on the map mural.

"I wish I had a map to take with me, in case I have to adjust course quickly."

"I have a map. We're heading south too. We live about fifty miles from here. You're welcome to join us until you need to head west."

"I don't know if I should."

"You shouldn't be out on the streets alone. It's not safe on a regular day, but now with the power being out..."

Maddie was leery of leaving the airport with strangers, but he was right. It wasn't safe to go alone. Safety in numbers, as her dad would say.

She looked the man over. He had been in the military like her dad. He had his wife and daughter with him.

It should be all right, right?
"Okay. When do you want to leave?"

CHAPTER TWO

San Diego, California
Day of Event

Beth's drive back to her mother's house after dropping off her eighteen-year-old daughter at the San Diego airport was difficult. The doctor had put her mother on hospice care just days before. She hadn't had time to adjust to the news that her mother would not recover from cancer this time.

Beth's mother, Florence, had beaten breast cancer twice. The third time, it was in her bones. Her mother was sixty-eight and had led a full, vibrant, active life before this most recent diagnosis.

The traffic was heavy—heavier than Beth remembered from when she had lived there before marrying her first husband, Greg Langston. But that was ages ago. She had lived all over since then, settling in Missouri. When Greg left the Marines and took the job in St. Louis, Beth had been thrilled.

For the first time in their marriage, they had been able to settle in the place of their choosing. To be honest, though, St. Louis hadn't been her first choice. She could think of much nicer places to live, but Greg had received a great job offer from a military defense contractor. The job allowed him to be home with Beth and their children, Maddie and Zach.

Beth pulled the car into the third bay of her parents' three-car garage. She unloaded the groceries and placed them on the marble countertop.

"Beth, is that you?"

"Yes, Mom, it's me. Can I bring you some juice? I stopped at

Panera Bread and bought you some of the chicken and wild rice soup you like."

"Maybe later, dear. I…"

She was getting weaker and sleeping longer. Beth wasn't sure if it was because of the cancer or the pain meds. She was incoherent a lot when she was awake. Beth had moved the dining table and china cabinet out of the dining room to set her mother's hospital bed up there. Her stepfather, Frank, was set up in the den, where he spent most of his time. He had suffered a stroke the year before, leaving his left arm paralyzed.

Beth finished putting the groceries away and went into the den to check on Frank.

"Frank, can I get you some soup or a sandwich?"

He didn't answer, so she said it louder. The television was blaring, so she had to yell to be heard over the commentator's gloomy newscast.

"Frank," she yelled.

"What? Why are you yelling at me?" Frank asked, glowering over his shoulder.

He turned back to stare at the television before she could finish her sentence. She rolled her eyes and went back to the kitchen.

"I'll just make him a tray, and if he's hungry, he'll eat it," she said out loud, exasperated.

"What did you say?" Frank called from the den.

Beth shook her head and pulled a bowl from the cabinet next to the sink. She made Frank a tray and set it on the coffee table in front of him.

"You're blocking the television," Frank barked, craning his neck around her.

China's president, Xi Jinping, is said to have facilitated the talks between North Korean leader Kim Jong Un and the United States. U.S. State Department spokesman, Robin Payton, said Monday that the president had rejected calls from China, Russia, and North Korea to lift sanctions imposed on the isolated state. The U.S. remains committed to only doing so when Pyongyang makes further progress toward denuclearization on the Korean Peninsula. Further talks between Chairman Kim and President Rhynard have yet to be scheduled.

"You can't trust those damn commie North Koreans. Are they nuts or something? What the hell are we talking to them for anyway," Frank yelled at the television.

Beth had never been so tired of listening to the news in her life.

Why in the world did they invent twenty-four-hour news stations, anyway? All they do is repeat the same bad news over and over.

Sandy, the hospice nurse, arrived shortly after one o'clock that afternoon. She took Florence's vitals and adjusted her morphine pump.

"She is sleeping most of the time now. Is it from the meds?" Beth asked as she walked Sandy to her car.

"Her urine output has decreased again. I increased her fluids, but I think her kidneys are shutting down."

The nurse put a hand on Beth's shoulder. Her eyes were full of sympathy.

"It is just a matter of days now—maybe three or four. If you have family to call in, I'd say now would be the time. She'll likely slip into a coma in a day or two."

Beth inhaled and held it. She had known those words were coming. She had felt it in her heart, and she'd thought she was prepared for it. Beth thanked Sandy and walked back into the house. All she wanted to do was go upstairs to her room, crawl into bed, and pull up the covers. That was what she had done after her husband, Greg had died. She had shut down. Sleep was her only comfort. She didn't have the luxury of retreat today, however. She had ill parents and a lazy, one-eyed dog to care for.

Jack slept in the bed with Beth's mother. He rarely left her side. She stroked the dog's head as she stared down at her mom. He lifted his head, shifted position, then put his head on Florence's leg. Feeling sorry for her mother's furry child, she decided she'd reheat the chicken and rice she had made him the day before.

"Jack, you want some lunch?"

Jack's paws hit the wood floor, and a flash of white fur streaked by her feet. Jack loved food.

"What are we going to do with you, little guy?"

She hated the thought of taking him to an animal rescue, but her husband, Jason, would never allow her to bring him home with her. They already had a dog he didn't like.

As Beth followed Jack into the kitchen, an ear-piercing emergency alert tone came from Frank's television. Beth's first thought was the alert was for a wildfire. They hadn't had rain in a while. Beth placed the kitchen towel she held in her hand onto the counter and walked into the den just as the emergency alert message began to scroll across the screen.

We interrupt our programming. This is a national emergency. The Department of Homeland Security has issued a national emergency alert. Residents are asked to shelter in place until further notice. Stay tuned to this channel for updates. This is not a test.

Beth heard the alert tone on her cell phone and ran to the kitchen to retrieve it.

Presidential Alert
  THIS IS NOT A TEST. This is a national emergency. Shelter in place until further notice.

"What the hell?" Frank said.

Beth clicked the news app on her phone to check for news about the emergency alert but found none. She opened the Facebook app and scrolled through the messages. She stared down at her phone as her news feed refreshed. A story from a San Diego station informed the city that the nation had been attacked. Beth dropped to her knees, her cell phone skidding across the floor. Crawling over to pick it back up, she leaned against the kitchen cabinets and read the article.

San Diego Daily News has been informed that at approximately twenty-three minutes past three this afternoon, a nuclear device exploded in the atmosphere above the United States. Information is still coming in regarding the extent of the damage this detonation has caused and the areas affected. But right now, we know that communications with most of the nation have been interrupted. An official with the governor's office has told Daily News that they have no information regarding further attacks. A state of emergency has been declared, and residents have been ordered to shelter in place until further notice. We expect a formal statement from the governor later today. Stay tuned for further details.

Beth kept scrolling through her news feed, hoping for more news. She tapped on contacts, selected Maddie's cell number, and pressed the call button. The call failed, so she couldn't even leave a voicemail. She opened her message app and typed a message to Maddie and Zach, then tapped the send button. She waited. A moment later, a message appeared telling her that delivery had failed.

Beth buried her head in her hands. Being cut off from her children during a national emergency was beyond any heartache she had ever experienced. Rocking back and forth, she tried to control her panic. She repeatedly tapped the message's send button, hoping desperately that it would go through.

Placing her hands on the counter, Beth pulled herself to her feet. She ran her hands through her hair. Her mind wanted to go numb, but she couldn't give in to that. Walking over to the sink, she washed her face and dried off with a kitchen towel. She heard a news anchor discussing the shelter in place order and headed back to the den.

Frank was unusually quiet as he and Beth sat staring at the television screen. All anyone could say was that no one knew what the damage was throughout the rest of the country. All planes had been grounded, and a state-wide curfew had been ordered. No one was allowed out of their homes except essential personnel.

It was hours before news reports came in about the blackout caused by the EMP. A so-called expert explained the effects of an EMP detonated at a three-hundred-mile altitude. As far as they had determined, the unaffected areas include parts of California, Oregon, Washington, and Alaska. Beth didn't need to listen to the rest. She understood the effects of an EMP. Her deceased husband, Greg had studied it as one of the possible scenarios he foresaw happening.

She was cut off from her children and her current husband, Jason. She was two thousand miles away, and there was nothing she could do to protect them. Worse yet, they were both away from home and separated from each other. Zach would have his teachers for help and support, but Maddie was stranded in an airport in a large, densely-populated city.

Beth paced the room. No matter how hard she tried, she couldn't think of a single thing she could do to help her children or even try to get to them. The roads were shut down. The authorities weren't allowing anyone to travel. Walking two thousand miles without any gear was impossible.

"Beth? Where are you, Beth?"

"I'm right here, Mom. I'm coming."

No matter how desperately she wanted to get home to her children, she knew she could not leave her dying mother, and it would be foolish to go alone anyway. She wouldn't make it out of California, let alone across four states of chaos and devastation.

Even though every cell in her body wanted to get to her children, she'd have to stay there and care for her parents.

If you've enjoyed this sample of Turbulent: Days of Want Series, Book One, visit Amazon.com and order your copy today.

Also by T. L. Payne

Fall of Houston Series

No Way Out

No Other Choice

No Turning Back

No Surrender (Per-order Now!)

No Man's Land (Coming Soon!)

The Days of Want Series

Turbulent

Hunted

Turmoil

Uprising

Upheaval

Mayhem

Defiance (Coming Summer 2021!)

The Gateway to Chaos Series

Seeking Safety

Seeking Refuge

Seeking Justice

Seeking Hope

Seeking Sanctuary (Coming Soon!)

About the Author

T. L. Payne is the author of the bestselling Days of Want, Gateway to Chaos, and Fall of Houston series. T. L. lives and writes in the Mark Twain National Forest of region of Missouri. T. L. enjoys many outdoor activities including kayaking, rockhounding, metal detecting, and fishing the many rivers of the area.

Don't forget to sign up for T. L.'s spam-free newsletter at www.tlpayne.com to be the first to know of new releases, give-aways and special offers.

T. L. loves to hear from readers. You may email T. L. at contact@tlpayne.com or join the Facebook reader group at https://www.facebook.com/groups/tlpaynereadergroup

Made in United States
Troutdale, OR
10/03/2024

23403529R00159